A Cold Retreat

A COLD RETREAT

To Lindsay
All the best
Jim

JIM ODY

Jim Ody

Copyright © 2018 by Jim Ody
All rights reserved. No part of this publication may be reproduced, distributed or transmitted in any form or by any means, without prior written permission.
Crazy Ink
www.crazyink.org
Publisher's Note: This is a work of fiction. Names, characters, places, and incidents are a product of the author's imagination. Locales and public names are sometimes used for atmospheric purposes. Any resemblance to actual people, living or dead, or to businesses, companies, events, institutions, or locales is completely coincidental.
Content edit: Rita Delude
Proof edit: Samantha Talarico
Cover: RJWright Design and Crazy Ink
A Cold Retreat/ Jim Ody. -- 1st ed.

A Cold Retreat

Jim Ody

Part 1

A Cold Retreat

Prologue

The air was musty and masked the smell of death. A hundred years of memories had been boxed up within these attic walls, but none more emotional and sad as the scene before me.

Her skin was cold and clammy to the touch. I tried in hope for a pulse again, but it was obvious from the amount of blood pooled underneath her that this body was lifeless.

"Is she going to be alright?" a scared voice from behind me said in hope. We both knew that everything was far from alright. My initial response would be impotent words that could not convey the harsh reality of this situation. The heart and soul of this human being was no more. The macabre situation cast inappropriate thoughts in my mind—references to Monty Python and a Norwegian Blue parrot. I kept these to myself. This was my way of dealing with shock. The mind is a very strange thing, more complex than any man could ever imagine, and we are guilty of using only a fraction of its capabilities. She, of course, had ceased to use anything ever again.

Jim Ody

I took a deep breath and thought about the best course of action in this situation. I pulled out my mobile phone, pressing and sliding my fingers over the screen to activate it into action. A face with a smile looked back at me from my phone before I turned it into a keypad.

There was no signal. Of course there was no signal. It was just one thing after another.

I just couldn't believe it. An hour ago, we had been sitting around drinking and laughing. We had been making plans for the future and sharing secrets, and now…?

"What happened…?" the scared voice said again, except there was something else that had crept into their speech: an underlining question of accusation aimed at me.

"What do you mean?" I said, turning around and wiping the blood from my right hand onto my trousers. There is always someone who thinks they know better. I should never have picked up the knife.

"You found her, yeah? I was… I thought that maybe…you know, you knew something?"

My stomach was turning in knots, and my blood pressure was increasing. There was anger building up. A stranger is lying dead and bleeding on the attic floor, and I am the one whom the fingers have

A Cold Retreat

suddenly pointed to. No doubt some elaborate motive will be spun into action like some *Jonathan Creek* reveal. Perhaps I had used complex physics in my great feat of killing a woman that I had been nowhere near. Maybe I increased the temperature, igniting something from a chemical reaction that I had miraculously devised. How about a tilting of the room, or mirrors, flashing lights with magnets…?

"I heard a scream," I started and then corrected myself. "I heard *her* scream, so I came up here…"

"To the attic?"

"Yes. That's where the sound appeared to come from." My response was close to having come through gritted teeth.

The questions were now becoming a tad more rapid. I was beginning to feel that I was on trial.

"When did you know that there was an attic here?" Again, the voice had more bite.

"I didn't know. I heard a scream, *her scream,* from here and found the door. I tried the door handle and came up the stairs. If you had heard her scream, what would you have done?"

The eyes looking back at me narrowed and nervously looked down at my right hand. I held the knife tightly—small droplets of blood still fell slowly from it. I don't know what made me pick it up. It just felt like the right thing to do. I'm beginning to think that I may've gotten that wrong.

"I really don't know what you are insinuating," I said, looking around the poorly lit room. Although I did. There were two dirty windows trying to let in light, but they looked like they hadn't been opened in centuries, and there was one door to enter or exit.

Many pairs of eyes looked at me, all judging and all accusing me of something that I was pretty sure I had nothing to do with. I heard someone coming up the attic staircase and instantly dropped the knife with a clatter.

All eyes turned away from me toward the approaching footsteps.

A policeman was the last person I expected to see.

"Please step away from the body," he said. "Now who wants to tell me what has been going on here first?"

We all looked at each other, most of us strangers before tonight, now bonded together through tragedy. It was really hard to know exactly where to start, but I had a feeling that sooner or later, I would be in handcuffs…

A Cold Retreat

Chapter 1

Penny

Disney had unknowingly constructed the preconceived ideas of love and romance in my mind from an early age. I had always wanted long, flowing hair that cascaded down my back over a beautifully cut dress with a lithe body underneath. With little to no effort, my Prince Charming would appear in my life to whisk me off to a castle to live happily ever after. It seemed so simple and so obvious.

Okay, so there were the odd obstacles that I fully expected to be thrown into my path like: having to get home by midnight, not pricking my finger, or being hunted down by witches, so as I grew older, somehow the utopian dream died a little each day, and the barriers and bad luck increased until any dreams that I once had no longer bore any resemblance to those original fantasies. Did I really expect a band of men who were short in stature to sing around me whilst the wildlife came closer to be loved and adored without fear of being harmed? Or perhaps the crockery would suddenly come to life and sing and dance around the kitchen, and without question I would accept this as normality?

My life, however, had been filled more with poisoned apples, friends who closely resembled the ugly step-sisters, and lonesome hours of solitude locked in my tower-esque bedroom gazing out a window at the mundane surroundings. The views were less about white horses with carriages, rolling walled gardens of roses, and princes falling over themselves to slay dragons and liberate me from my prison. They more commonly involved a 1981 Ford Capri on bricks riddled with rust, a small front garden with grass taller than a toddler, and dog shit like mole hills, whilst the local lads stood about with baggy hoodies and shouted up to me periodically with a romantic, "Show us yer tits!"

As I grew older, the princess fantasies had faded as the harshness of reality bullied its way into my world, stealing the tiara from my head, slashing away my long hair, and ripping my dress to shreds before storming off with any remaining hopes and dreams. The squeaky-clean Disney portrayal of life gave way to teen comedies, which showed a watered-down version of bullying and social-awkwardness before the huge warm hug of a happy ending. But gradually, we come to understand that,

A Cold Retreat

whilst this might play out for one lucky girl at school, the rest of us are not even the extras in her movie. We star in our own unadulterated version where friends bully friends, manipulation is part of a hidden curriculum, and a day without tears is considered a success.

This may be something that played out around houses in individual lives all over the country or even the world, but at that time, I felt that I was the only one. I fell deeply into a depressive state from which I would find it hard to ever shake free.

Teenage years and adulthood should bring forth other challenges, hopes, and dreams that are as equally exciting and scary. However, I never really got over the loss of those princess fantasies. I felt cheated by a world that denied this. And later on, I would have more than just my innocence stolen away from me.

Here I sat staring at a wall that offered me no sympathy—just a blank, open canvass like the screen from a projector, flashing the montage of a twisted history that wrestles between pictures of abuse and lost love, the lines between blurred.

Sometimes I wanted to go back to being that naïve little girl with the inane smile planted on her face, the one with big bold dreams full of bright lights, magic, and glitter. I wanted to shout at her and tell her to look around the world. *How many princesses do you know, you stupid bitch?* I wanted to scream, but this just brought a lump to my throat and welled up my eyes with tears of sadness. I mourned the death of that little girl. An invisible tombstone marked the end of Life had robbed me of those seemingly endless dreams. The men that I had met took out the bright cartoon colours of my world and dampened them to a duller palette. The beautiful songs sung with a smile and danced along with on light dainty feet had been replaced by the adrenaline-pumped beats of dance music played out in clubs where men were given a free rein to grope you at will.

So now I thought back over them—the cancerous cells that the men had implanted into my heart, my head, my self-esteem, and my whole sense of worth—how they had made me feel then and how they made me feel now. Maybe Kate was right. I was abused. I was raped. I was cheated on. I was led to believe that I was special.

If only I could get my own back. If I could make them pay.

Would I hurt them? Would I murder them?

I definitely couldn't say that I wouldn't, given half a chance.

Chapter 2

Travis - 2004

I was bored with life and craved excitement. Even my breathing was so inanely rhythmic that I felt the need to do something to jolt it into action. I held my breath for as long as I could just to feel that rush when I finally exhaled. I enjoyed the adrenaline rapidly flowing through my veins and sought out different ways to trigger it.

The problem was that, for what it was worth, I had pretty much done it all. As we all know, things are never as exciting the second or third time, so now I was left wondering just where I should go next—without breaking the law, of course.

The final drops of the last rain shower ceased overhead, and the sun forced its way out from behind the clouds, which to me were not the fluffy and cuddly dense masses favoured by many, but forces of power suppressing the goodness of sunlight. You never see the clouds hanging back behind the sun, do you? No, they appear en masse marching together, thick and dark, preparing to bring forth flashes of their doom onto the land, sending the sun packing, with its rays hidden away. Of course, I was not one of those stupid spiritual hippies, and I therefore knew that the sun is millions of miles above the clouds, which have the vulnerability of being within touching distance of us with a little help from a plane. I was thinking this as I was then overcome with a sense of power and excitement toward the day ahead. The power of Mother Nature will do that. I was quite capable of glossing over clouds and sunlight, for they are predictable, and predictability was not something that could ever be associated with me.

I quickened my pace as I strode down a pavement that, like society, showed many cracks, with the purpose of a businessman with an unrelenting disregard for tardiness. I liked to give the impression of an important English gentleman wearing a smart navy single-breasted Ralph Lauren suit and well-polished loafers; my hair was near-on perfect, and my strong chin was shaved and moisturised, so it had a healthy, youthful glow. I could have quite possibly been on my way to a deal-clinching meeting on this Monday morning, but you have no idea whether or not that is true.

The mundane reality of it all hit home again. My mood, which was known to yo-yo, plummeted once

A Cold Retreat

more as I passed the familiar faces of people that I barely knew, but saw daily. The weekend-warrior guy with his heavy-metal hairdo, black jeans, Doc Martens, and corporate white collar shirt and tie, who has his head buried in some Terry Pratchett or Tom Holt book, nearly bumped in to me once again. His glance was apologetic, but I suspected that I held no fascination to him over the world of humorous fantasy novels. Then there was the guy and girl on their way to college with matching backpacks, who held hands and smiled a lot but didn't say anything to each other—apart from last Tuesday when there was a definite tension in the air. He was too good for her, and they both know it. It was only a matter of months before he realised it and more than likely banged her more attractive friend. Then there was the woman who smiled at me with a slight twitch in a flirtatious way, and I wondered about the two of us in another life, one where we were a couple and the probabilities were in favour of us no longer speaking after a month, and she would therefore be left to flirt with other handsome businessmen on their way to work. I could tell that she wondered about me by the way she made sure that she caught my eye each time we passed. She was married to a rich guy; I could tell this because she had the platinum engagement ring with a larger wedding band around it. It had been bought for show, not affection. She, of course, had married for money and not love, and so she was now longing for a relationship, however fleeting, with the likes of yours truly, a guy that she should stay well away from, but of course this is what would attract her even more. She was hungry for me to say something; it was there in her eyes—begging me. There was a mild satisfaction on my part at my ability to control a woman I'd never even uttered a word to before. Just one word and she would do almost anything that I asked…

I headed up to the Fletcher Building in Swindon's town centre, which was one of those large and ghastly city eye-sores, towering above the town with prominence and false authority, all the things I loathed and loved all at the same time. I was renting an office on the fourteenth floor, which of course was quite aptly the thirteenth floor, however if it wasn't called that then the superstitious little corporate folk wouldn't shit in their shorts at the thought, and would quite happily work there.

I grabbed my coffee from the last Starbucks before the building, smiling and flirting ever so slightly with a girl in her late teens—the way I did every morning. I enjoyed it even though I had no

A Cold Retreat

real intention of taking things any further than she might think. I was not flattered, as this was an emotion that derived from an unexpected slice of delusion, and on the contrary, I would have been more disappointed if she had showed no interest in me whatsoever. I took a lot of time making sure that I was nothing if not charming, and dare I say appealing, to the fairer sex. I suspect that this might well appear a little bit egotistical and cock sure, but then you have not walked in my shoes.

"Have a great da-aaaay!" She smiled, drawing out the sentence, and deliberately brushed the back of my hand as it took hold of the cup in its recycled sleeve. I knew that she would fantasise about me later.

"You have a beautiful smile," I told her, as a fact rather than with feeling. She liked that, as she held my gaze, but she was lost for words save for an uncontrolled giggle.

Her ring-finger was naked, but she had a cheap silver ring on the forefinger of her right hand. Her name was Penny, and she has worn a total of sixteen different tops in the past few weeks, my favourite being the small tight white t-shirt that told me her left nipple was pierced. Today she was wearing a pinstriped black-on-white shirt from Topshop with four buttons open, giving me more than a healthy glimpse of a pink lacy bra, and the tops of breasts that some men would say were too small, but I thought looked just fine. These were all details that I took in like a photographic snapshot in seconds, but they remained with me, locked up within the rooms of my mind forever. It is a fallacy that people have bad memories, as the problem is in fact the location of where these memories are stored in our brains, and not the actual memories themselves that are hidden. We remember everything, even the things that we wish we would forget.

She knew I'd glanced at her breasts; it was written deep inside her brown eyes. I could tell by the way there was a playful grin on her lips as she tickled her throat—a throat that now had a ruddy rose rash that had appeared thanks to her increased self-consciousness—and then touched her fringe before turning to the next customer in need of their caffeine boost of the day. She had to take a second to compose herself before igniting a false smile that was a million miles away from the one she saved for me. *A Penny for your thoughts, my dear*, I mused. *Maybe I will see you later...*

It was less than six minutes before I had walked through my office door, closed it behind me, and sat back in my large fake-leather chair with my coffee.

A Cold Retreat

I sniffed it, taking in the full dark, strong roasted aroma that danced around my senses, leaving me slightly dizzy before I satisfied my insatiable need for it and took a small but hugely satisfying sip.

I had a customer's portfolio to finish before I submitted it for review. If they didn't like it, then I might just drag them out of their beds at night and beat them in the back of a Transit van until they were crying uncontrollably... Haha, I was of course joking. It would be a Mercedes Vito van; Transits were so common.

I fucking hated having to work to somebody else's satisfaction. If you asked what it is I do, I wouldn't tell you, but believe me when I say I was great at it. The top dog, and the king of the castle, but to you fucking people it may seem like I was just tugging the line or dancing to someone else's beat.

I felt my head get light, even though the sides of my skull were pounding and there were small red beads cascading down my vision from stress.

Okay, you've got me. I hated this work. I should have been some manager sitting up in his own office, lying back in a proper leather chair, scratching his balls and screwing his secretary. But instead of that, I worked for myself, and each time I stopped to scratch my balls, I knew that I had less time to finish that damn proposal. I had no secretary…and perhaps that was what I hated the most about my little situation.

It would take a while to calm myself down, which was a real fucking shame. It was at this point that my mobile rang, and I realised that it was my girlfriend, Chanelle.

"Hi, Travis," she said in those high-pitched tones that made her sound about ten years younger than she was and that I likened to freshly manicured nails being raked down a slate blackboard slowly.

"Chanelle," I replied—and you'll note that my tone was very level and deliberately without feeling. It is amazing to me how people can want to believe something so badly that they don't see what is plainly there in front of them. My feelings for her decreased each time we had sex—or rather, after we had sex. It would be fair to say that during the aforementioned naked activity they increased slightly.

"Meet me for lunch, yeah? About 12?" She was almost giggling this out in her bubbly and overly affectionate way. Her voice and her brain, I believed, were similarly stunted and stuck at about seventeen years old. I fucking hated how immature she was. Some guys would love it, but I felt like I was her carer some days. Or worse: her father.

A Cold Retreat

"I would rather beat myself with a dead badger," I began, to which she giggled. I conceded. "12 would be agreeable," I said and put the phone down. She found this amusing. However, the truth was that I couldn't stand to hear her whiney voice anymore. Everything about her made me want to do very bad things. I thought of an old song. "Is this love?" Seal once asked, so let me take this opportunity to respond to that. No it fucking wasn't.

I was this side of telling the client to go ahead and perform something quite unsavoury with himself when I thought better of it, knuckled down, and produced some of the best work that I had ever done. Naturally.

I was thinking about heading back to Starbucks later. Penny finished at three.

Chapter 3

Penny - 2004

I spent a lot of time in my bedroom with headphones on listening to Emo bands. I suppose I was a cliché of today's youth. I made no apologies for that, it was just those things that made me happy.

Sometimes I flicked through the pictures in my photo album of when we went on holiday last as a family. Everything seemed great. It was amazing what a little time, and the rose-tinted glasses of sun-soaked pictures, could do for you.

We always smile for the camera but less for ourselves.

The holiday had been good. Mum and Dad had only argued a couple of times, and I think that had something to do with a topless woman one day, and another in a skimpy dress the next. My dad had a weakness for barely clothed women. It was like he was okay when they were dressed normally in dismal Swindon, but somewhere even slightly exotic (and most places outside of Swindon appear

A Cold Retreat

this way), when faced with a woman lacking in clothes, he became this weirdo that even he warned me about.

My dad had started to go away on business trips, which in turn became pleasure trips, up until Mum found naked pictures of women on his PC. They had started to row loudly, which saw me retreat to my room and escape to the songs of Fall Out Boy and My Chemical Romance. I had jumped straight onto the musical bandwagon and had even bought a Nirvana t-shirt (the one with the smiley face on) like it was the Emo-uniform to a movement that I had suddenly enrolled in.

I think that was one of the reasons why I got my nipple pierced: to get back at Dad. And Mum came with me only because she also knew that he would hate it. We had made sure that it was a female piercer. I had never had a boy touch my bare boobs before and was scared that a man I didn't know would do it. The girl was really good, all smiley, and talked me through the procedure, giving me the opportunity to back out, before letting me take a deep breath and going for it. Yes, it had hurt, but almost instantly, most of the pain went.

Two weeks ago I turned eighteen, and I was trying to come out of my shell a bit more. Last week, I went to a nightclub for the first time and felt petrified. It was like I was some sort of prostitute, with men staring at me and making excuses to brush up against me. My friends had loved the attention though. Kate went off with some guy who looked about forty, and Shelly had sat on one of the sofas with a drunk guy who had his hand up her skirt—right in plain view of everyone, and she hadn't even seemed to mind!

A couple of months ago, I started working in one of the many Starbucks around town, and I found that it was helping me to become a little more easy going. It was a much nicer environment. I still had guys (and girls) flirting with me, but there was no expectation attached to it. They were not coming to a coffee shop for the sole purpose of having sex. No, they came for their cappuccino or flat white and gave me a little smile, and that was it. I could handle that.

Today I saw this guy whom I guess you'd call a regular. I called him Dieter. He was tall and dark, and of course, he was handsome. He was well-groomed like a model or a celebrity who was expecting to be photographed. He might have been famous, I didn't know. He was back in today ordering his usual black filter coffee, and there was something about the way he acted that put me at ease while making me embarrassed too! I read the

A Cold Retreat

odd romance novels (okay, I would admit it—and what girl didn't?), and he was what I pictured the main love-interests to look like. He had a strong jaw-line and black hair that could be slightly floppy on top if it wasn't combed back and then shaved almost to the skin underneath like he had just come from the barber's.

"Hi, how are you?" I asked him. I didn't mean to, it just sort of came out.

He almost looked a little taken back but regained his composure when replying, "I'm very good. You have such a beautiful smile." Of course, this only made me smile wider.

"I bet you say that to everyone," I added, feeling my face heat up.

"Only when it's true... Look, maybe we could meet up sometime, or do you have a boyfriend?"

"No... I mean...yes, we could meet up, and er, no, I don't have a boyfriend!" I felt a little giddy. I knew that I needed to rein things in, as I was probably coming across like an over-excited school girl, which couldn't be an attractive trait.

"Okay, then. Perhaps I'll see you at the end of your shift, unless you have other plans?"

"Yes, er, no, to plans. Yes, maybe see you later. I finish at three." He grabbed his cup, winked, and walked away.

OMG! What if he did meet me? What if he wanted to kiss me? Or have sex? My mind was racing a million miles an hour for the next few hours. Would he meet me? Who knew?

I went back to work, but found myself looking around in the hope that he might come back.

Chapter 4

Travis - 2004

I had learnt a long time ago the power of keeping your emotions in check. Overt emotional outbursts suggested a lack of self-control, and that was not something that I cared to portray. Inside though, I was incredibly excited. Such a little thing could mean such a great deal, and this was a great deal. Signed and delivered, the contract weighed next to nothing but financially meant a hell of a lot to me. The ramifications could be endless, and that really was what this was all about. I once again felt like the king of the hill.

I picked up my phone because I needed to speak to someone. Unfortunately, the only person that I had to speak to was Chanelle, but "needs must" and all that.

"Hey, baby!" she squealed even though I had only seen her less than an hour ago when we had met for lunch. I had eaten a steak sandwich with thick, fat chips covered in truffle-oil and a lettuce leaf that appeared to mock me into leaving it. She had nibbled on a salad with an oil-based vinaigrette that would supposedly not put an ounce of fat on her body. She had sipped water with a slice of lemon wedged onto the lip. I can only assume that this act was one to fool the senses into thinking that the body was absorbing something slightly more flavoursome than the basic tap water that we knew it to be. The zest fragrance also helped to kid our senses whilst making the extra price appear more acceptable. Perhaps one day I would tell her that sex with a fat girl was definitely more comfortable.

"Hey, how's things?" I always ask her this. I cared not what her answer was, as it was purely rhetorical. I was not enquiring as to her well-being, but merely establishing contact and attempting to gain permission to say what I rang up to say.

"Good, you?" Now, she *did* want to know how I was, and what I'd been doing, and whether I had been thinking of her, and whether I had thought about what we should do tonight…and so on. I ignored this, as I always did, and got down to it.

"I got that big contract back today, and they have not only agreed to everything, but have signed it!" I heard a loud screeching sound, which I knew to be her expression of happiness. She was always loud. At first when we were intimate, her squeals had been quite an ego boost, but holidays, sleepovers,

A Cold Retreat

and the odd quickies had become embarrassing, with me having to almost smother her with anything I could find within reach.

"We must celebrate!" To others, this would mean a meal out at a moderately expensive restaurant, but to her, this meant a weekend in Paris or a trip to Vienna. I made an acceptable noise, but I was having second thoughts about the whole of this relationship-thing between us. She didn't have an engagement ring for a reason, even if she had dropped a thousand hints. The thought of being with her until the day I died almost brought on cold sweats.

"Let's go out tonight for a meal and then drink wine until we cannot stand up!" I suggested instead. I felt like going out and pretending that the cash I was going to make from a new contract, I already had. That was the true point of earning a lot of money: not just spending it, but showing other people that you were flippant and carefree in your spending.

"Can't," she said. "I'm off to Bath with the girls, silly. D'you forget again?" I hadn't forgotten, as I clearly hadn't been listening any of the times that she had told me. She was still speaking, but I was picturing her growing older and wrinkling up whilst her voice remained like Barbara Windsor if she came from the home counties.

"That's tonight? I thought it was at the weekend?"

"No! Do you not listen to me?" As usual, her voice had an edge, and her mood was descending into something ugly.

"Have fun," I said half-heartedly. "I'll celebrate myself."

"Don't be such a fucking child!" she spat, and I was left with the dialling tone. *Bitch.* She had such an ability to piss on my parade. All I wanted was *some recognition,* but that was too much for her.

I grabbed my jacket and left the office—one of the perks of being my own boss. *Well done, Travis! Take the afternoon off, son!*

I sat down on the bench and looked down at my phone like I was waiting for an important phone call. An Asian girl glanced over to me, the sides of her mouth twitching, unsure whether or not to smile. Perhaps she knew that I would happily take her back to my flat and fuck her senseless. Even the chubby mother pushing her child suddenly held some attraction to me. She wasn't unattractive, and with the kid in another room and her looking up at me, she would certainly begin to be more appealing.

A Cold Retreat

But then I saw her: the girl from the coffee shop. She was glancing at her own phone and putting the thin straps of her bag onto her shoulder.

I got up and casually walked over. She looked up, smiled, and stopped.

"Anyone important?" I said to her.

She went red and replied: "My mum. She won't be home until late, so I have to get my own tea." She flipped closed the phone and slid it into her bag.

I nodded, accepting this as an answer. "Are you busy now?" I asked. She looked a little unsure at first, no doubt weighing things up in her mind. They did this: the quick risk appraisal. *Is he going to kill me? Is he too handsome to care?*

"I guess I'm free for a while."

So we walked around the shops for a bit laughing and joking. It felt good to be doing something a little naughty. It felt comfortable to be with someone new that might disappear from my life straightaway. It was slightly off of the cuff, and each glance at her skinny body made me ache for her.

"Come with me," I said after an hour. "Why don't I cook you something back at my flat?"

"Okay," she replied in a small nervous voice, and we walked back to my flat. She grew quieter the further away from town we got, but I think that some of this was the excitement and anticipation of what might happen. I was new to her, and she didn't seem like the type of girl who did this sort of thing normally.

"You want a drink?" I said as we went through the front door.

"I guess," she said, a little unsure, probably thinking that this would only put off the inevitable a little longer. I took her into the kitchen and poured her a generous glass of vodka. Girls like vodka. They say it is aphrodisiac water from the gods.

"You're very pretty," I said. This was, of course, the classic first line to foreplay. It makes the woman blush, feel that they are perhaps not good enough, and often lends itself nicely to contact. A brush of the cheek. A touch of the hair.

"Thank you," she replied. I took her glass from her hand and placed it on the side table. Classic move number two.

Our eyes met, and slowly we connected to kiss. Like an animal, you have to move slowly and carefully so as not to scare them off. This is very important, and if done right, will save you a lot of time and frustration. Most men I knew would then be pulled into this long-winded charade of moving slowly, step-by-step between kissing, hands moving, and clothing removal, which could take upwards of an hour. Not me. After the initial kiss, I showed them who was boss.

"Was that okay?" I asked when we had finally stopped kissing. Of course, what I was actually saying was, *Are you going to let me go further?* She looked a little dreamy and shocked at how lucky she was. She nodded. We held hands and, without a word, walked into my bedroom.

"Take off your clothes," I said calmly and firmly. She stopped for a second, taking in the words that I had said and, then like a tease, took them off almost in slow motion, down to her underwear.

She was self-conscious. They usually were. Her arms tried to cover herself, but the peek-a-boo routine only made it more sexy.

"And the rest," I said, and slightly reluctantly, she did. I think she had longed for my hands to be on her long before now, ravishing her and taking her to places that she had not been before.

It was like Christmas. My present unwrapping itself. She stood there, and I took in her fresh naked body, aware that she wanted me to touch her.

I bent and kissed her lips slowly. I heard her moan as my arm glided down the contours of her back. I turned her around and kissed her neck;

feeling her back arch, I knew what she wanted. I undid my trousers, fumbling a little with excitement, but not enough that she would notice. I bent her over and thrust myself inside her. She cried out in pleasure. This was what she had fantasised about all those times she had served me in the coffee shop. It came down to this: her bent over, gripping the bed sheets, her face in the pillow as I thrust harder, feeling her hip bones on one hand and her clavicle with the other. I felt on top of the world. This was the proper way to celebrate the contract.

And then it was over.

She was lying down out of breath, her head still buried into the pillow, as I slipped out. I could only imagine the massive grin on her face and what else she wanted to do to me. We had now become part of each other's history, a connection forever.

I walked around the bed and bent and kissed her from her neck and down her back a number of times. She turned to face me, and I helped her to sit up. She seemed overwhelmed by the whole experience. I pulled her head into my belly and traced circles around her back. I could feel her nipple ring on my thigh.

"Kiss me," I said, beginning to get hard again. She looked up at me and then realised what I meant.

A Cold Retreat

I was engulfed by the heat of her mouth, feeling even better than before. I heard the door to the flat open.

Chanelle had surprised me after all.

"Quick, the wardrobe!" I hissed, pulling her by the arm and almost shoving her in. I quickly grabbed her clothes and chucked them in on her.

As quietly as possible, I got under the covers just as the bedroom door opened. Part of me wanted to get caught.

"Trav? Look, I'm sorry."

I smiled. Sometimes life deals you a wonderful hand. "I know," I said, pulling back the covers.

She grinned and took off her clothes to join me.

Chapter 5

Penny - 2004

I was daydreaming as I left work. I had the next day off, so was toying with going to the cinema tomorrow or seeing my friend Kate. I was texting her when I almost walked past him.

"Hi Penny," he said. This caught me off guard, as I hadn't realised that he even knew my name.

"Hi," I said. I couldn't believe that he was here waiting for me outside of my work. He smiled, and I suddenly felt a little giddy.

"Are you off somewhere now? Or do you fancy going for a walk? Maybe have some dinner with me?"

"Really?" I said. I nearly rolled my eyes. I could not believe that I was sounding so much like a little girl. I had to be more like Kate. She would act like it wasn't a big thing. Guys loved that. Vulnerable and nervous was off-putting. They wanted a challenge, right?

I then added. "I guess I have an hour or so."

A Cold Retreat

"Well let's make this a lot of fun!" he said with a twinkle in his eye.

But it wasn't that much fun. I mean, I enjoyed being seen with him, and we shared a couple of stolen glances as we walked around the shops, but it seemed that his heart wasn't quite in it. He kept looking around and glancing at his watch.

"Why don't I cook you something back at my flat?" He then suggested, and I was slightly taken back. This sudden meeting was turning into an actual date. My heart was beating hard, and I tried to compose myself when I replied, "Okay then."

His flat wasn't that far out of town. As we walked, I was unsure as to whether this was such a good idea. I didn't really know him, did I? I had such an electric feeling pulsating through me, but also a tentative worry that this might end up being a *Crimewatch* reconstruction in the future.

He pushed open the door and led me into the kitchen. I was impressed at how spotless the place was. I suddenly felt very grown up. Maybe he would be my boyfriend and this kitchen would suddenly feel as familiar as my family kitchen at home.

"D'ya want a drink?" he said.

"I'm okay," I replied, and I saw how his face dropped in disappointment. I quickly added, "What are you having?"

"Wine or vodka?"

I took a deep breath. I didn't really drink. It wasn't a conscious decision, just not something I had ever gotten into. I was only just legal, and my parents were not the sort to have it around the house. I didn't want to disappoint him, so replied, "I'll have whatever you're having."

He put down the wine, pulled out a pair of tumblers, and poured the vodka neatly into each. He downed his straightaway. I tried doing the same, and I felt the fiery after-burn of the spirit in my throat and insides. I coughed hard, which only made him laugh. He rubbed my back and then poured me some more.

"You'll be okay," he said with little or no feeling, but then after I took another swig, he came in close, and before I knew it we were kissing.

It felt really good. I could've stayed like that for ages, but he pulled away. He looked at me with eyes that looked like he might want to devour me and grabbed my arm a little hard. I felt slightly shocked, but went along with him. He was almost pulling me as we got to his bedroom.

A Cold Retreat

Then he was on me, kissing me hard. It was still nice, but the gentleness had slipped into something that I suppose was passion. He was gripping me tightly and moving from my lips to my neck. I felt slightly panicked, as I was no longer in control, but it did feel good. I had only had the odd quick kiss before today, and those were with boys of my own age, clumsy and sloppy, and it had always been easy to call a halt and walk away. I was completely out of my depth. There was that underlying sense of excitement that danger brings, but I also felt on the edge of panic too.

When he stopped, I felt relieved, but then he said in a commanding voice, "Take your clothes off."

I looked at him and hesitated. I was sure that, earlier, this had been what I had wanted, but I had thought that the scene would be much different. I wanted candles and cuddles, which may or may not lead to roaming hands and the loosening of clothing. To have someone suddenly demand that you jump past this left me feeling cheated. His face was serious when he added, "Now."

I fumbled with buttons, zips, and clasps. I had never been seen fully naked by a man before, and I was suddenly self-conscious. I stopped at my underwear, hoping that this was as far as he wanted me to go.

"And the rest," he said. When I slipped off my underwear, I naturally hugged myself.

"You're very beautiful," he said, his voice now softening. I had a lump in my throat and could only nod. He kissed me gently whilst his arms snaked around me, his fingers sliding over my skin. I eased slightly, but as I did, he turned me around. I tensed and felt his hand suddenly between my legs. I gasped out of shock. It wasn't that it hurt, but I was just not used to it. I wasn't sure that I wanted it. I tried to relax and enjoy the moment, and had it remained like that, then I might have even still enjoyed myself.

As one hand grabbed my breast, he was suddenly there directly behind me. I heard the fumbling of his trousers, and then I felt his manhood poke me in a failed thrust. Then he pushed again and again. I gritted my teeth as, on the third time, I felt him painfully enter me.

I fell forward onto the bed, my head in the pillow. I began to sob. I hadn't expected the day to end like this. I had flirted with him, and he had misread the signs. I was here now having sex for the first time with a guy, and I didn't even know his name.

It was over pretty quickly, I suppose, although I had no other experience to go by. He pulled out and

A Cold Retreat

tapped me a couple of times on my backside. I couldn't look at him. I stayed face-down, hoping that it was all a dream, but then he was pulling me, helping me to sit up. I turned, and he kissed me on the forehead like a father might do to his daughter. That didn't make things any better. I was lost for a minute, trying to look happy but numb inside. And then, with him still standing up, his manhood was there in my face growing hard again, and he was guiding my face towards it. I was once again not in control and scared of what might happen if I didn't comply. I didn't know what I was doing. I just opened my mouth and hoped for it to be over.

It carried on for about thirty seconds until suddenly he pulled out of my mouth. I thought that he was going to spare me the finale, but then I heard something. He was then hissing at me to get into the cupboard. In a whirlwind of utter panic, I found myself crouched up into a ball with my clothes on top of me and a sour taste in my mouth. I was sore and aching, with only the tickle of tears down my cheek doing their best to gently offset the discomfort.

Another woman burst through the door, speaking in a squeaky voice that sounded like a child or the woman Alabama from the *True Romance* movie. Through a crack in the door I saw her standing there, slowly removing her clothing. I wiped another tear away. I felt violated physically and mentally. If I ever thought that I had meant anything to him—and I was still hanging on to this thin thread of hope—then to see him now having sex with a very attractive woman told me that I was a fool. He didn't have her bent over. He was sitting up with her on his lap, and they kissed tenderly. I didn't know what I was, other than nothing. I wanted to burst out and demand an explanation, but to what end? What if she didn't care? At first, I struggled to remain quiet and could hear my own breathing, but then the woman was squealing in delight, which only made me feel even worse.

It was a long time before they finished, and only when she had wiggled her way out to the bathroom did he summon me out. I had my shirt and knickers on when I was ushered out of his flat. A neighbour caught me pulling on my trousers, still holding my pink bra, as he fussed about with his phone doing all that he could to get an eyeful.

I ran out of the building before slowing down to a walk, and I cried all the way home. I handed my notice in the next day, never to work in Starbucks again.

A Cold Retreat

Chapter 6

1999

It was a hot day in May, and she was on the school field on her lunch break. She had been walking with her friends to where some of the older lads were playing football. They had been singing Blink 182 as they walked. It was not their usual music, but everyone seemed to be playing them on their Discman, and like most trends, it was easy to get caught up in it too.

The bottom of the school field was surrounded by fields, which was the main reason why everyone congregated down there. It was the furthest point away from the school, and teachers tended to turn a blind eye to what happened there so long as there were no reports of misbehaviour. This was also the easiest way to sneak out, should someone feel the need.

"We're heading back," her friend Sian said, following one of the lads who had just walked away from the football game. Sian had a huge crush on him. He didn't know she existed. He walked off

Jim Ody

unaware of Sian and her shy other friend Cally, who was wandering behind with her head down.

She was left on her own. She saw him suddenly look up at her. He was a year older and slightly taller than the other lads and, from what she could tell, was one of the best footballers there. Some of them ran around without doing much, getting almost overexcited when they got the ball, but he controlled the ball straight away and stroked passes seemingly at ease to wherever he wanted to. He would glide over the grass and pass the ball into the goal to score, while others lashed at it with all of their strength, getting nowhere near the jumpers that were being used as goal posts.

He walked over to her, smiling. He knew the effect that he had on girls. This one was no exception.

"You wanna go for a walk?" he asked, though this was really him requesting permission to do more than walk.

Her heart beat fast. She nodded, unable to form words in her mouth. She wanted him to hold her hand, but he turned, almost pushing her forward with a hand on her back.

She pushed her chest out as she walked. The school fashion meant that her tie was loose, but she had opened a couple of the buttons on her white blouse. She knew what she was doing. She just hoped that she was doing it right.

They pushed through the hole in the hedge to the hollowed-out bush. It was a known make-out area, so the rest of the lads would know what was happening—although with a football in close proximity, their focus would be elsewhere.

"Do you like me?" he said, and again there was no shyness. He was so confident that he almost seemed bored with it. He talked in riddles. What he was actually asking was: "Will you let me?"

She nodded. Kiss me, *she thought, staring at his lips.* Hold me.

He looked around at the flattened ground and pulled her down gently so they were sitting close together. Then he was on her, kissing her deeply with hands roaming all over her. She almost gasped, but his tongue was hungrily exploring her mouth. One hand had already undone a few more buttons on her blouse, and he then freed the top of one of her breasts. It was being squashed up by the underwire from her bra until he released his mouth and dived straight to her nipple.

She felt out of breath. This was nothing like what she had ever experienced. It was exciting, and she liked it, but it also felt a little like opening a present that you had wanted almost forever and feeling a little disappointed. He was sloppy, pawing at her with no finesse. This was not about her. She could be anyone.

He was feeling pretty good. Part of him wanted to still be playing football with his mates, but this was just as good for now. He couldn't believe that she had let him get as far as he had already. But if she told him to stop, he probably would. There were other girls, but he had not had her before. There was something about her that was a mix of innocence, but that had such slutty potential. He could tell that she wanted to be liked, maybe even loved.

Why not keep trying his luck? If she didn't ask him to stop, then she was up for it, right?

She was rubbing his back as he was nibbling her nipple. She thought that this might be arousing. She had read that this was often the case, but this was more annoying than anything else.

Then his hand was on her thigh and sliding up under her skirt. Her heart was pounding now. Finally, his touch was gentle there, and the feel of his hands slowly rising up the inside of her thigh did make her slightly aroused, but she found it hard to relax. The hard ground, the lack of privacy, this being her first time, and his forcefulness were all working against her.

A Cold Retreat

He rubbed her gently through her knickers, not entirely sure he knew what he was doing, but it just had to be rhythmic pressure, right? He kept his mouth on her nipple even though he was bored with it now, but he thought that going back up to kissing might give her the opportunity to pull away. He didn't want to be looking at her either, just in case she had that weird look that he'd seen before—the one where they are deciding whether or not they want to be there. He had asked her though, hadn't he? She had come willingly and had not made any noise or movement to leave.

He slipped his fingers under the side of her knickers. He felt her tense suddenly, even gasp, but then she relaxed a little more.

It was nice at first, she thought, but then the gentle rubbing stopped as he tried to thrust his fingers inside of her. It was like he thought that it was some sort of challenge to see how many fingers he could push in at once. It hurt now and was uncomfortable. She squirmed and pulled his arm away.

"What?" he said, using this opportunity to start kissing her neck.

"It was hurting a little," she said and turned to him, searching for his lips to kiss.

"Maybe you're just not used to it."

She nodded as she felt him pulling at her bra and releasing her other breast.

The kissing was nice. He seemed less forceful this time and even grabbed her hand. It was nice to feel his touch. He pulled her hand towards him. She gulped as she felt the hardness that he had put in her hand.

"What's the time?" she said, suddenly pulling away. Glancing at her watch, she realised that lunch was over and she should be in Geography. She sat up quickly and began to sort her bra out.

"Sorry, but I'm going to be late."

He nodded and shrugged. She couldn't help but feel like she had blown it. But she also felt a twinge of relief.

"Maybe tomorrow we could carry on?" she said in a small voice bordering on desperate.

He smiled but only on one side of his mouth. "Maybe we could," he said. "Maybe we could."

She got up and walked out of the bush. She turned to look at him. "See you tomorrow?"

"Sure thing," he said, noticing how she beamed with a great big smile and then jogged off back to the school.

He looked over to where his mate was coming out of the bushes a little further down. "You dirty dog!" Barry shouted.

A Cold Retreat

He grinned at Barry. "Yep. I'm sure you can have a go when I'm done, mate."
"Nice one."

Chapter 7

Sasha – A month ago

I had been driving for a while, and I was tired. I just hoped that when I got there it would be worth it. I had applied for the job online, which was a bit of gamble. That was why I had enclosed a photograph—my ace in the pack, if you will.

Leonard had found me on Twitter. I had a few naked pictures of myself posted on my account. Well, I say *myself*, but what I really mean is that I found an account of someone in America with a similar body to mine, and I stole her photos. I would put them up, mixed with face shots of myself.

It was something that I had seen other people do, and the funny thing was, if you put a link to your Amazon Wish List, sometimes without even mentioning it, people would buy you things off of there and send them to you. Can you believe that? You know how some men are: sad and pathetic. All I had to do was answer a few messages and put on a new naked picture every few days. It didn't even have to be naked. Most of the time it was pure

A Cold Retreat

suggestion: a bit of thigh and a flash of underwear, *her* nipple on occasion, and once a week, a full flash of *her* breasts. Talk about money for old rope. It wasn't long before Leonard was messaging me, with saucy lines that were more innuendos than the explicit straightforward talk from others, like that sicko Bigman84 for instance, whom I could only assume was fourteen years old and had never touched a naked boob since being breast-fed as a baby. He would message me all sorts of things, but he did buy me Cher's greatest hits...

I am not going to lie, my life had been one big shitfest. For too long I'd been used and abused by men, so it felt good to be on the other side. I wasn't having sex with them—only in their sordid minds. I was in control here, giving them what they wanted on my terms. When I wanted and how I wanted. The truth of the matter was that I needed a proper job.

Okay, that was not the truth. I had something that I wanted to achieve. I thought that the Twitter-thing was enough, and at first it was, but I wanted to see it in their faces that I was in control. I wanted to see the fear and misunderstanding in their eyes, the way that I had previously, and finally put the past behind me.

Jim Ody

People think that the internet is an easy front—hiding behind an avatar that may or may not be you, inventing a back story and becoming someone else. This is all completely true, but you do not have to be an expert in cyber-crimes to dig a little and uncover the true identities of people. We know there is a popular show on MTV that does this with seemingly great ease. A few key strokes into a search engine has the true identity of the person there for the world to see. This is mainly because most people do not think to check, question, or dig into someone's true identity, but take it at face value. It is mostly fantasy based, which is to say that we know it will not become reality, and in fact, deep down, we don't want it to become reality; we are drawn to the *what if* and the *if only* mindsets, because these are our own personal desires that reality cannot live up to.

Case in point: I have so many movies to watch that I find myself constantly thinking of other movies when watching one, almost unable to enjoy it. I assume that another movie will be better, and feel disappointed that I have now chosen this one to waste my time over. However, back in the dark ages when you watched a movie on TV and sat through all of the adverts, and possibly even the news halfway through too, you never had this. The lack

A Cold Retreat

of variety only enhanced your desire of the limitations on offer. Society and advancements in technology have now made us impatient and unsatisfied. We always want more. We demand more. We now form loose relationships that can be built, and dropped easily without a strong bond or connection. We would rather have a handful of meaningless cyber-connections than the hard work and emotional strain of an *actual* relationship. How sad is that? About as sad as the fact that for me it is reality.

From my detective work I revealed that Leonard owns a B&B in north Wiltshire, but now required a Bookings Manager. It was unclear as to what had happened to the previous one, although more digging revealed that too. The title of the job was slightly misleading, as it actually meant: someone to clean, cook, and take care of the guests as well as answer the phone. My experience was non-existent, but my CV boasted a couple of similar fictional jobs, with references from old friends who would lie through their teeth if I asked them to.

I had sent my photo because I knew that Leonard was in love with me. I was pretty sure that the photo itself would get me the job. I only hoped that he wanted to turn his fantasy into reality, or else I would be back to the drawing board again.

Jim Ody

His email back had suggested that he was pleased that I had shown an interest, and he had invited me to come and meet him. He omitted the fact that, a few weeks back, he had sent me what was known in sordid circles as a Dick-Pic. It should be fairly self-explanatory as to what that might be a photograph of.

It had also occurred to me that I might be a lamb going into a wolf's lair. He was an older wolf, so really, how dangerous could it be? Of course, I already knew the answer to this. Very dangerous indeed.

My only hesitation had been whether or not I should stop the Twitter pictures or close my account. I had grown to enjoy the attention and, if I was honest, craved it. I wondered whether it was an addiction—the need to be desired.

My sat nav told me that the next left would take me to my destination. I turned in past the "Vacancies" sign as Alicia Keys was singing about an unfortunate girl that was on fire. The drive was lined with mature trees, and then gravel curved to the front of the grand house. It was a beautiful place.

My baby-blue Fiat 500 seemed out of place next to a BMW and an Audi. I got out, brushed down my pencil skirt, and hoped that the blouse said "sophistication" rather than "call girl." Sometimes that line could be a thin one, I mused.

I looked up at the two doors and took a deep breath. It was then that I noticed Leonard waiting for me. When he saw that he had been spotted, he grinned and came out with a bounce in his step, his arm already out searching for my skin to touch. His eyes were hungry and eating me up. I swear that he licked his lips before speaking.

"Sasha! How lovely to meet you. Do come in, won't you?" He was in his fifties, slightly older-looking than the pictures I had seen. He had on a V-neck jumper with an eagle logo, something that I had seen men wear in the eighties. His hair was grey, but he had a weathered, still-handsome look to him. I didn't fancy him, but I could imagine that if in twenty years' time I had a husband that looked like him, it wouldn't be the worst thing.

"Hi, Leonard," I said as he gripped me with his right hand. His left arm found the small of my back. He blushed at the contact and pulled away as if shocked.

"Follow me." He turned, and of course I followed, but not before looking up at an attic window where a scared face mouthed something. I was inside the house before I realised that it was, *Help me.*

Chapter 8

Dex - 2005

The double garage was situated slightly away from the house, but unfortunately it was still quite close to the next-door-neighbour. It was band practise, and the whole street knew it. The tall guy, Jez, plucked at the strings on his bass with his right hand whilst his left did its best to resemble something like an 'E' chord. It wasn't quite it, but the bouncy notes along with the sound of Jonesy on drums was okay and at least in time. Dex was on guitar, also chugging an interpretation of the 'E' chord, and Marco was standing at the microphone singing about girls and toilet humour, like a third-world poor-man's Blink 182. They all sported spiky hair or Mohawks, polo shirts and cargo-shorts, and skater branded trainers by *Vans* or *Macbeth*. They were all in their late twenties or early thirties, so they were never going to make it now, although this was mostly due to their lack of musical ability. There were a couple of semi-decent tracks, most notably, "I Wish I Had A Pillow Like Kim

A Cold Retreat

Kardashian," and "She Dumped Me For My Grandpa," but the chances of Simon Cowell picking them up was non-existent.

"C'mon, guys, we have to get our shit together on this," Marco said again, exasperated that he appeared to be the only one with any sort of musical talent, which was probably because this was indeed the case.

"Nothing wrong with my shit," Dex added. "It's Jez that keeps fuckin' shit up."

Jez had been day-dreaming up until his name was mentioned and looked hurt by the accusation. "Me? I'm like Billy Sheehan."

"Who?" Dex and Marco both said in unison.

"You know... *Jonesy*? Hey," Jez said, but Jonesy was lost in a world of smoke, puffing on something so big it looked like it had been born rather than rolled.

"Shit... what?" he muttered. His eyes had glazed over. A large spider ran across his shoulder without him even realising it.

"Billy Sheehan? Y'know him?"

Jonesy paused in contemplation, or—as he was when in this drug-fuelled state—like somebody was pissing about with his pause button. He would suddenly just freeze for a few seconds, silently. If you looked closely, you would see that he never blinked nor took a breath. Then he would suddenly snap back to life again, talking in a slow motion as if it were all quite normal.

"*Billy fuckin' Sheehan*. That blond-haired fucker from the poncey band Mr. Big. Played bass."

"They were not poncey," Jez said, clearly hurt. He looked down at his feet, which due to his tall height and loping ways had him bending over ever so slightly.

"Had that song 'To Be With You' back in the early 90s. Acoustic guitar and singing," Jonesy said with his slow delivery and his Ramones-style haircut. Marco then started to sing it almost perfectly.

"I remember," said Dex. "It was one of those songs that the drummer fucking hates. Like that Extreme song… What was it?"

"'More Than Words,'" Jez replied.

"Yeah, that's it," he continued. "You spend your life with the band touring around shitty little clubs, and then you make it big with a chart hit… The song that everyone knows you by is the song that you didn't play on. Then to add insult to injury, you have to sit there in the heavily played music video on MTV flicking through a magazine or smoking a cigarette whilst the rest of the band get the glory.

A Cold Retreat

It's the song that the women love and that all of the fans want to hear. Fuck MTV!"

"I'm not sure you can blame MTV for the success of the song or the fact that there are no drums in it, Dex."

"It was on heavy rotation. Back then, there were only a couple of music channels, so when they decided to play a song every hour, you can bet your arse it was going to be a hit. Remember Dial MTV?" They all nodded. "That show late afternoon, everyone rang in and voted on their favourite video, meaning that bands like Bon Jovi always seemed to be played…"

Jez jumped in. "The song 'Always' always seemed to be played as I recall."

Dex clicked his fingers at him. "My point exactly!"

"So what were we saying?" Marco then said.

"Dex said that I was shit at playing bass," Jez mumbled.

"It was a joke." Dex quickly said. Jez could be sensitive about his playing.

"Not that funny," he said, putting his bass away. "Not that funny at all."

"C'mon, big guy!" Marco said. "We've got a gig to play tonight."

"I know," Jez said over his shoulder. "I'll be there." With that he was gone.

"We still singing Mr. Big?" Jonesy then said.

"No, Jonesy. We've never played Mr. Big."

"Really? What about Extreme?"

"Practise is over, Jonesy. You can go home now."

"Sweet." He up and left with a joint that was so large sticking out of his mouth that it almost looked like he was following it. A thick line of smoke was left in his wake.

Dex played a couple more licks. "I think we're the band, mate. Those two are holding us back." Marco nodded but felt that Dex and him sounded better, and whereas they attracted girls, Jonesy only attracted dealers and prostitutes, and Jez—God knows what Jez attracted…

It was going to be a long night.

Chapter 9

Penny - 2005

Kate was a wonderful friend and had tried to explain to me that basically all men are bastards. They felt it was their God-given right to impose themselves on unsuspecting women and make them feel cheap and nasty in order to get their own way.

"You know that he raped you, right?" she said after I told her what had happened with the guy from Starbucks.

"I never said no, Kate," I said, holding my coffee. It wasn't from Starbucks. I couldn't even walk into any of their shops anymore.

"That's not the point, love," she said. "He forced you to do something against your will. Twice!"

I was confused by it all. Maybe I had seen too many films and read too many books with courtroom scenes. It was easy to build a case for both sides. Had I wanted to have sex with him? Yes, at first, I had. But then I had felt uncomfortable. Had I told him that I was uncomfortable? *No, I didn't.* Had I at any point asked him not to do what he was doing? *No, I didn't.*

I sat in silence mulling this over. The more I thought about it, the more I felt that I was overreacting due to my inexperience. I was eighteen, and most girls my age had already had sex with at least one other person. Of course, twenty years ago this wouldn't have been the case, but things moved quickly nowadays. I had always been shy, so had the fact that this was not with a boyfriend or someone that I knew, been clouding my judgement at looking for signs? I had been drinking and kissing him back. I had let him lead me to his bedroom and had taken off my clothes when he asked me to.

When a man took you towards his bedroom, what would you think he was going to do? Show me the view from his window? I didn't want to admit it, but from the very first steps, I had known that the likelihood was that we would have sex, and I had been pretty much okay with that. Or so I thought.

"I'm sorry, what was that?" I said, realising that Kate was talking to me. She had concern in her eyes, and I wished that I could speak to my mother about this.

"Did he mention sex?" she said. I noticed how she had taken on a more conservative look

A Cold Retreat

nowadays. Before, she would wear skimpy and tight clothes, showing off her breasts that had developed a year before most of the other girls that I knew and had been a means of her getting whatever she had wanted from boys and men alike ever since. Now she wore a shirt buttoned all the way up. *Her new boyfriend's influence?* I wondered.

"No, but I guess that he implied it."

"If I wanted to buy your house, I would ask you outright. I would gain your approval that this was what you wanted. I would then get a contract drawn up, a survey carried out, and so on. I wouldn't imply that I wanted to buy it and then move in." I loved Kate, but sometimes she was just so frustrating.

"He started to kiss me and took me to his bedroom."

"So what? I look in the car showrooms each day I pass them, but it doesn't mean that I have any intention of buying a car from them."

"He asked me to take off my clothes."

"I think you said that he demanded that you take off your clothes, right?" Sometimes it felt like nothing good came out of our conversations when she was like this. I know that she had my best interests at heart, but it felt like she was being so self-righteous. It made me want to ask her about the college lecturer she had given a blowjob to for better grades—or the drunk bloke that she had sex with in an alleyway even though he had just pissed himself beforehand. There were so many stories that I could bring up, but I didn't, because I was her friend. But, it seemed like this *one* mistake she was all over, half-accusing me of being irresponsible like I was her daughter, or like the other half wanted to bring criminal charges towards the guy and Starbucks.

I put my hand through my hair, something I always did when I was getting stressed. I was feeling a bit cross and upset with the situation.

"Look, I just want to forget it, Kate."

"I know you do, love. I know you do… It's just that you can't always let these men get away with this… What if he does this again? And he will, mark my words. That's what predators do."

"But what if he didn't realise?"

Kate held up her hand to stop me. "Pen, he took you back to his house, plied you with liquor, made you strip, raped you from behind, and made you suck him before stuffing you into a wardrobe and fucking another woman in front of you! You cannot tell me that he is not to blame for how shit you are feeling!"

A Cold Retreat

Of course, she was right. To hear the grim details simplified into mocking bullet-points only made it worse.

***

It was six months before I started to go out again at night. I was too worried about what might happen. I was watching all of these stupid movies where the girl gets the guy, and then I was going up to bed and reading throwaway chick lit, but when it came to making a move for a man, I was just plain scared.

Now freshly single again, Kate had an invite to a party in an old warehouse. It wasn't like the stories that I'd heard from the 90s when this would turn out to be an illegal rave set up on a generator with happy, hardcore music thumping out some God-awful techno-jungle-rave shit, whilst everyone was getting off-of-their-tits on acid and speed, wearing baggy clothes, peace-signs, pork-pie hats, glowsticks, gloves, and breathing masks. No, this was a local pop/punk band that she knew of and a host of fans who would more than likely just jump up and down a lot and dress like skaters.

"It'll be fun," she said to me. "Let's just go and get hammered!"

"Okay," I said. "Let's do it."

And so we did. And that was the problem.

Chapter 10

Dex – 2005

We had bust our arses to get to the warehouse on time. My van was new, which is to say that I had only had it for a week or so, but it was a classic VW Campervan from the 60s. It looked great, but was incredibly unreliable.

"You realise that a new vehicle is meant to be better than your old one," Marco muttered from the back. He hated being late anywhere, especially for a gig. He was convinced that even in his thirties he was still on the edge of making it big.

"It just needs a tune-up," I said.

"You want a Transit," Jez added. "Most reliable van on the planet."

Aerosmith was pumping out "Ragdoll" when we finally got there, and Marco was singing along, doing his best Steven Tyler impression.

"Hey, Jonesy! We're here!" Jez shouted to the back where Jonesy was asleep. Even with the shouting, Jonesy didn't stir.

A Cold Retreat

"What've I said about him smoking that shit before a gig?" Marco said, seething. He reached over and smacked Jonesy on the forehead with a big slap.

Jonesy blinked a couple of times and opened his eyes. "Where the fuck's the fire, mate?" he said in a slow, stoned reply.

"It will be here when I set you and your fucking drums alight!" Marco spat and then shook his head in disbelief.

"Jonesy, mate, you can't be getting wasted before a gig. That's uncool, mate," Jez said, trying for diplomacy.

"I needed something to calm my nerves... Stop the old... an-xi-ety... yeah?" He straightened his bandana. God knows why today of all days he had decided to wear a bandana for the first time. He looked like a hair metal band's roadie from the late 80s.

"What is that on your head?" Marco commented, looking out in the opposite direction like the answer might pass him by.

"Bandana," Jonesy replied.

"You look a little silly, mate!" Jez grinned.

"Says the fucking talk freak...with a nose that's trying to...like, eat the rest of his face...haha!" Jonesy laughed.

Jim Ody

"You are a mean little man," was all that Jez could say whilst slowly pawing at his own nose self-consciously.

We got the instruments out of the van and set up within twenty minutes. The guitars and bass just had to be plugged into the amps, so once the power source had been identified, it was a relatively quick process. The microphone set up too was simple enough, they were plugged in, stuck on a stand, and off you go. However, the drums always took forever, and Jonesy was particular about where his drums went. Except tonight he was too wasted to remember how he wanted them, so they had to keep being changed.

It was time to look for a new drummer.

An hour later, we were doing exactly that. Jonesy had completely fucked up the set, first by falling off of his stool, then by dropping his sticks a number of times, before the end of his bass-drum pedal flew off and put a hole in the bass-head. With that, he stopped playing, got up, and walked off. We had no choice but to play that Mr. Big song followed by "More Than Words." The crowd loved it, but Marco was fucking furious.

"I liked it," this girl said to me an hour after the gig. I had been drinking beer after beer with a couple of whisky chasers, and she was a little drunk

A Cold Retreat

too. She was cute and a little shy. I had spotted her and her friend at the bar, at the opposite end of where the DJ had now set up and was playing some music that sounded computer generated and lyricless, or more to the point, pointless.

"We weren't meant to finish with those songs," I had said in response.

"Well they had a tune and words like beautiful poetry…unlike this." She held up her hands in a way that suggested it was the repetitive dance music bleeding from the speakers.

"Lucky for us, I guess." I was playing it cool—or at least it felt like I was playing it cool. More than likely, I was slurring like a complete drunken fool and dribbling on the bar.

We talked for a while and then went for a walk. I wanted to speak to her in a voice that wasn't shouting. I guess I also had some romantic notion of kissing her in the moonlight. Marco would have taken the piss if he had heard me talking like that, but that's the truth.

"I'm going to get some air," I said to her. "Are you coming?" She looked a little uneasy, and for a second, I thought that I had misread the situation and completely blown it. She looked away, and I think I saw her make eye contact with another girl before she turned back.

"Okay," she said.

It is amazing how hot it is in the warehouse, although with that number of people jumping around, and the mild summer evening, it probably made more sense when you thought about it. The air outside was nice, and as we walked down to a stream that cut around the back of the warehouse, we looked around us to see the fields ahead. There were the twinkling lights of Swindon in the distance, and behind us next to the warehouse were a couple of smaller abandoned buildings on this forgotten industrial estate.

Here before us was a little bit of beauty, something of the forgotten that we had found. The moon was not as bright as I would've liked it, but it danced off of the water nevertheless.

I looked deeply into her eyes and, whilst nervous, followed through with a kiss. I felt her inhale before our lips met, and then we stood, our arms slipping around each other, pulling each other closer like romantic boa-constrictors.

"This is nice," I said as we came up for air, and I immediately felt stupid for saying it. She smiled a little and touched her face emphasising that she was blushing, had it not been so dark. I guess that it had been okay to say.

A Cold Retreat

We kissed again, and after a while, my hand slipped under her t-shirt, making its way up onto the material of her bra. There was an intimacy that was a little psychological; all I could feel was thick, padded material, when really, I wanted to be touching a naked nipple.

She placed her hand under my t-shirt but then removed it, seemingly unsure of things.

"Maybe we should stop," I said, pulling away. She nodded and turned back to the warehouse. I stifled a yawn. We had been out to the small hours last night, and I was really feeling it now.

"Look, I'm going to head back to my van. We're sleeping in it tonight, but how about I give you my phone number and we can go out again… If you'd like, that is?"

She nodded, and we swapped numbers. "You want to meet tomorrow?" she said.

"Of course. Look, our van is the orange-and-white VW Campervan. You know, just in case you wondered!"

She grinned at what I was saying, but gave no indication that the details mattered. We kissed again and then said goodbye. There were times that I wished I was a little more like Marco, or even Jez for that matter. The two of them could easily talk to women in their own special ways. Marco had a confidence that bordered on him being manipulative, listening carefully and knowing how to twist things in order for him to get what he wanted, whereas Jez had this ballsy naivety, which meant he said what he wanted without an ability to get embarrassed. He was like a small child who had suddenly grown very big. And I was the dumb bloke from a rom-com that you want to cheer on but you wish he'd get a bloody backbone!

I felt like I was skipping back to the van. There was no one else there, which was not surprising. Jonesy was gone completely, Jez would be passed out somewhere, and Marco would more than likely have gotten lucky somewhere—and not just the once.

I pissed against the side of the van before stripping down to my underwear and getting into a sleeping bag. I slipped a couple of tablets into my mouth to stave off a hangover and closed my eyes. With Jonesy around, I usually needed to check the tablets before stuffing anything in my mouth, but I was suddenly tired and out cold.

When I opened my eyes, I was naked and cuddling an equally naked woman. I had no recollection of the night before after I had gotten into the van to sleep. I was still incredibly drowsy, so I closed my eyes and was gone again…

Chapter 11

Penny - 2005

"Steady, girl," Kate said. "You'll have them queuing up with that sexy outfit on!" It was pure sarcasm. Whilst she was happy to let her breasts almost fall out of her top, I didn't think that this was how I wanted to meet someone, so I had on a plain white t-shirt.

"I'm not wearing anything else," I said almost defiantly. I checked my watch again just as the doorbell rang telling us that our ride was here.

We opened the door to our friends, Sarah and Tim. Sarah grinned, decked out in an outfit that was probably a cross between mine and Kate's. Tim found it hard to look past Kate's chest. He once again thought that tonight his luck might be in. Who knows, maybe he was right.

A short drive out of the east of Swindon found us pulling up to the old industrial estate. There was a time when this place was busy with vans and lorries constantly coming and going, along with a number of shift workers clocking on and off from twelve-hour shifts. However, two of the large distribution companies had gone bust, and so a handful of the smaller units remained empty. There were cracks in the concrete where grass and weeds now grew, adding an air of neglect to the landscape. Even the "For Rent" signs looked forgotten.

There were a number of cars already parked, which made this area more populated tonight than it had been in almost ten years. There was talk of the land being made into another housing estate, with the adjacent green belt suddenly being built on. The London overspill had slowly trickled down the M4 and had massively increased the population of Swindon, seeing it gradually join up all of the small towns surrounding it.

We got some drinks in plastic beakers and watched the band play. They started off well. They were a strange band of aging punkers that appeared to think that they were a boy-band. This turned into an Oasis charade with attitude when the drummer up and walked off halfway through. The band appeared better without him, finishing with a couple of old classic acoustic numbers that I remembered my dad playing.

Kate had disappeared with a guy who sported a beard that had seen better days. When she was between partners, she had a tendency to want to try

A Cold Retreat

anything on offer, her theory being that one day she hoped to be with one man for the rest of her life and so didn't want to regret any opportunities lost. Personally, I thought this was just a recipe for disaster—or infection if nothing else. I think she genuinely believed that kissing a frog or cuddling up with a beast would unleash some handsome prince one day.

I sipped my drink at the bar as the DJ started to pound out music that was okay. I then realised that standing next to me was the guitarist. He looked better up close, with surfer-blond hair that was slightly shaggy like Kurt Cobain.

"Nice gig," I said when he caught my eye.

He nodded. "I guess these things happen."

"What? Playing good music?"

"No, we weren't meant to play those songs at the end," he said with real disappointment. Creative types can be so moody and serious sometimes.

"It worked out well though. Better than this music." He nodded to that.

"Can I get you a drink?" he then said, suddenly grinning at me. He had cute dimples when he smiled.

"Of course you can," I said. He had a way about him that made me feel at ease. I think it was that he tried to be confident, but you could tell that he didn't really believe in himself, and so it came off as sweet.

We chatted for a while, and at some point, he suggested us going outside. I couldn't help it. Suddenly, and without warning, I panicked and looked around the large warehouse, relieved to see Kate. She was making out with the beardy guy, but as if telepathically aware, she abruptly stopped and looked over. She gave me the thumbs up, which could've meant anything really, as we didn't have a set of coded hand signals that we worked to. She seemed to be encouraging me, so I turned and smiled to the worried face of the guitarist. I think his name was Dax or Dex, although I think of him as Kurt.

It was a warm night, and I wondered whether he would put his arm around me or make an excuse to touch me. I only hoped that he wouldn't demand I take off my clothes.

We walked down to a brook. He seemed taken by it, whereas I was surprised that there wasn't the usual discarded shopping trolley, tyre, or single item of footwear commonly found in the abandoned waterways of life throughout the world.

Something drew us together ever closer—a magnetic pull of attraction—and before I was able

A Cold Retreat

to overthink things and panic, we were kissing, and it felt just right.

At some point, our arms went around each other. I was relaxing and enjoying it when suddenly his hand was up my shirt and cupping my bra. I pulled away, and he removed his hand as if bitten by a snake.

"I'm sorry…" I started, but I had nothing to add to it. I wanted to carry on. I wanted to tell him in great detail what had happened to me, but knew that all it would achieve was to scare him away. I wanted his hand on my bra. I wanted his hands on my breasts, but we were here out in the middle of nowhere, and I couldn't even remember his name properly.

"It's okay," he said, but I could see his disappointment.

"It's just…" I again tried some lame justification.

"I'm sorry, I shouldn't have done that…"

I shook my head and said, "No, it's not that. I… Look, maybe we can go back in."

"I'm beat. We were out late last night, and that music sucks, so I'm going back to my campervan. We're sleeping here tonight."

"Oh, okay." I knew it. I had scared him away. He wanted to get away from me as quickly as possible.

"It's the white-and-orange VW van…" he was saying, but I just nodded. We swapped numbers and kissed again, but the moment had gone.

"You wanna hang out tomorrow?" he shouted to me as I walked away.

"That would be great," I said, feeling a little better about things.

I headed back in and got another drink—a double. Shit, I deserved it. Twenty minutes later, Kate saw me and walked over with her bearded companion in tow.

"Where's Kurt Cobain?" she said, referring to Dex (he'd confirmed that was his name).

"He's gone to sleep in his van."

"He didn't invite you?" she asked with an over-exaggerated, furrowed brow before making swift motions with her hips.

I shook my head. "Nah, I said I was coming back in here."

"Really?" She took a deep breath and then caught the eye of the barman. "Double rum."

"Coming up," he said, already grabbing a bottle and a shot glass to measure. It was a pop-up bar after all.

"And another double for her," she said, pointing to me.

"And a beer," Mr Beard said gruffly.

A Cold Retreat

"Penny, you've got to get back on that horse, girl. Ya know what I mean? You can't let that fucker win."

The doubles came again, and again…until everything seemed like a good idea, so off I went to find the VW Campervan.

I passed a Transit and a big white Mercedes van before I saw it. I smiled and walked up. I guess sometimes you just had to take the bull by the horns.

I slid back the door, and there he was, lying naked on his back. Another girl with braided hair was gyrating on top of him. He didn't even seem to notice me, but she just grinned. I turned around without closing the door and ran off.

Kate was suddenly there with me as I sobbed into her shoulder. The fact that I fucking hate men was all I could think of.

Jim Ody

Chapter 12

1999

It had been a few days now. Slowly she had been pushed to go further and further. Each time, she felt that she wasn't ready, but it was in some way like being on a slide: once you started, there was no way you could stop until it was over. What would he think of her if she did? She wondered a number of times.

Last night she had struggled to get to sleep. She cried into her pillow so that no one could hear her. This wasn't what was meant to happen, was it? She still thought back to the John Hughes movies, Molly Ringwald getting the unbelievably gorgeous guy in Sixteen Candles. *This was nothing like that. It was not* The Breakfast Club, Pretty In Pink, *or even* Maid In Manhattan. *This was growing up at a school in Wootton Bassett. There was no obligation for a happy ending.*

Yesterday it had gotten as far as a fumbled attempt at sex. He had pushed himself against her a number of times, but a mixture of him and her, the

A Cold Retreat

ground, and it beginning to rain, meant that things never fully got there. He had clearly been frustrated and had blamed her.

The flimsy house of cards that she had built in her head as a symbol of their relationship looked to be falling down around her. She wanted to please him so much. The misplaced affection that she craved was there—but at a price. It was like making a deal with the devil. You were never fully aware of the risks until it was too late.

She longed to be Samantha and him to be her Jake, again like in Sixteen Candles. *He was the almost unattainable guy that suddenly noticed her, but John Hughes had polished it up with romance and happy endings, never touching on pressures to go further than she felt comfortable to. Each meeting was slightly colder and less personable than the last, a straight to business account looking to start where the day before had finished.*

She knew deep down that, each time, a very small part of her was dying. A percentage of her being numbed to the point of paralysis, never to turn the feelings back on.

Today she reluctantly walked to the end of the field. She had secretly hoped for rain or that the lads would not be playing football today, but they always played no matter what else was happening in the world. Football and boys seem inseparable at times. This, she would learn, could also carry on into later life.

He was standing at the side, completely uninterested in the match. Looking back, perhaps this should have been a warning sign, but of course, her naïve mind conjured up visions of him longing to hold her, to kiss her deep and perhaps say, Why don't we just talk today? *to which she'd nod and smile and feel on top of the world.*

He could be bothered to walk a few steps towards her, almost grabbing her arm and nodding by way of a hello. *It was hardly the moves of romance that, as a child, she had dreamed of.*

"Y'alright?" he muttered to her when out of earshot of his mates.

She nodded and managed a "Yeah." It never occurred to her just how little they had spoken throughout all the times they had been together.

The bush no longer was exciting. It wasn't even familiar and boring; it was something else. It almost felt sinister.

He was prepared this time. He felt good that he had thought this through. He wasn't sure whether she would've turned up again today. You just never knew, did ya? Sometimes girls got spooked. He

A Cold Retreat

hadn't done anything wrong though, and it was obvious that she wanted him.

He got out some gel that he had found in his brother's room. He didn't want to ask his brother anything, so he had swiped it and hoped to return it tonight. It was some sort of lubricant. He went straight under her skirt and slipped down her underwear.

"It might feel a little cold," he said and felt her tense as he rubbed it in her.

It was all a little too much for her. She felt a tear in the corner of her eye and quickly wiped it, trying to disguise it with a sniff. He was too occupied with the condom that he was fiddling with like it was some new Rubik's *toy.*

He swore under his breath. These things were so frustrating. Each time he was in this position he had to piss about with these things just so they didn't get pregnant.

He slipped it on and then almost asked her whether she was ready. He couldn't do that; that would make him seem like he didn't know what he was doing, and that wasn't the case. He'd had sex with three other girls.

With a grunt, he thrust himself at the hips, unsure whether or not he was fully in. He carried on nevertheless, burying his head in her neck. He didn't want to kiss her or look at her. It would spoil his concentration.

She had prepared herself for him, but it was still painful. Once he was going into a rhythm, it still hurt, but nowhere near like that initial thrust. She closed her eyes and tried to calm her breathing.

It was over quite quickly. Her heart sank when she heard another voice. "Got another one, mate?" She opened her eyes to see his mate grinning and grabbing at another condom.

"Ya don't mind, do ya?" he said, getting up off of her. Surely they saw the horror on her face?

"What...?"

"I won't be long, I promise," his mate said with his back to her, already fumbling with his trousers.

"I dunno. I just..." she began.

"Ya don't have to," he began. "Maybe we could go out to the cinema or something?"

She found herself speechless and slowly moving her head—neither shaking it nor nodding—and then his mate was on her. A large hulking mass, he was suddenly inside her, and he was thrusting her hard. Too hard.

"Yah...yah..." she said loudly, trying to tell him that he was hurting her, but he took this as encouraging sounds and stuffed his fat tongue in

A Cold Retreat

her mouth, the taste of cigarettes and Monster Munch crisps making her almost gag.

And then it was over. His mate whooped and left her alone.

"Y'okay?" he said to her. She nodded, but it was all she could do not to cry.

"God, he's been onto me about you for ages. I think you've made his day."

She tried a weak smile, but it failed. The whole situation was far from something to be smiling about.

She got her things and left.

She never went back to the bush with anyone ever again. Part of her is still there trapped in the circumstance, crying and trying to get back home.

She was thirteen years old.

Chapter 13

Sasha – A month ago

The interview had gone well. I had sat in an untidy study decked out with books and taxidermy whilst Leonard asked me some generic questions that he appeared to be making up as he went along. He had nodded excitedly when I answered and had given me the impression that he was definitely going to give the job to me. Based on the way he had looked at me when asking how much I really wanted the job, I could tell that he had toyed with asking me to perform some act in order to guarantee my success. I got the impression that his restraint was a sign that he had been thinking more long term. He knew that, once I was his employee, he would hold the ever-so-important power over me.

His eyes had been bulging out when he'd looked at me like some slimy lizard. Frequently, his tongue had darted out to lick his lips, and he rung his hands when glancing at my breasts. I could only imagine why he kept shifting position in his seat. He was a sick man. I was the woman to stop him thinking these thoughts ever again.

Leonard had a history that I was well aware of. I had done the usual Google checks, followed by the standard Facebook stalking, but had found absolutely nothing about him. In this day and age, it was beginning to become rare for someone to have no online presence. Either they stayed completely away from the internet, preferring to correspond by telephone or letter—in which case, they might well be over the age of sixty, under the age of ten, or else living on the moon—or they sent emails at birthdays and Christmas, and banking still required them to go into whichever local branch had not already been closed down. Or they were deliberately hiding under another identity.

Leonard was not his real name. Stuart Fengion had been his real name up until he was arrested for sexual harassment, two charges of exposing himself, three of attempted rape, and two of rape in 2005. He spent four years inside before being released and changing his name. He took over the running of his parents' B&B when they both passed away within months of him being released. He was originally from Kent, so the Wiltshire locals were not aware of his offences when he refreshed The Oaktree Manor five years ago.

Jim Ody

I had been speaking to a Polish girl called Hania who had worked for him in this very position a few months ago, and she had been constantly harassed. Things had gotten so bad that one night she left and never returned.

So why put myself in this position, you may ask yourself? The answer was that I was no longer a victim. A victim is someone who has no power, and that power derives from the ability to call the shots, understanding the full picture, and being completely prepared for anything. Leonard would take his time in charming me, to get me comfortable before he unleashed the nasty side that I had heard all about.

Except I was not going to be the one to allow this to happen. I was going to turn the tables and show him exactly what it was like to be the victim. I knew his type. They were not much more than playground bullies. He had attempted, and on a number of occasions succeeded in, forcing himself onto women. These were women that hadn't expected him to attack them, so what chance would he have with me? I would be ready. He wouldn't know what'd hit him when I attacked.

I parked my car around the side of the house in the allotted staff-parking area. This amounted to a handful of spaces, which were for Leonard, a cook, and a spare couple for any contractors.

A Cold Retreat

I got out of my three-year-old Fiat and slammed the door shut. When I looked up at the house I saw the beauty of the place. The old stone of the house was marked with time and weather, but still looked as solid as it had been the day it was built. Behind it was an impressive walled garden around which I had been shown during my interview. This was originally a farm and farmhouse. The buildings had been knocked down, save for a large outbuilding, and the farmhouse had been extended.

I looked towards the front door and saw Leonard grinning at me. His arms were held open, which seemed extremely odd.

"Here we are then," he said, being the first to speak.

I smiled, unsure of how I should be feeling. "It's so nice to be here," I managed to say through a false smile.

"It's wonderful to have you." He looked me up and down. The excitement in his eyes reminded me of when my Fiat 500 had been delivered. For a second, I thought about the similarities. The initial excitement of picking and choosing a new car is a great feeling, but it is only when you see it in the flesh, and know that it is all yours to do whatever you please, that you truly understand that desire.

I was Leonard's new car.

I followed him into the house but suddenly had a flash of the previous time I had done this—the face at the window mouthing for help. I could not believe that I had pushed that from my mind. That was two weeks ago. I wondered, where was she now?

In the hall I recognised the large staircase in front of us, the lounge area to the left, the dining area and kitchens to the right, and the study down the hall where my interview had been conducted.

"Can I get you a tea?" he said. "Ease you in." His voice strained to remain level; he was suppressing the clear excitement as much as he could.

I nodded. "Yes, please." Any time sitting and talking to Leonard would enable me to understand him better and lay down my plans. You have to know your enemy before you can kill them.

He looked pleased with my answer and clicked his heels as he turned and headed off to the kitchen. I took a moment to look around the lounge. There was a picture above the fireplace of his family. You could make out Leonard with his parents and what must've been a younger brother. It was a posed affair, although clearly no one had been told to smile. It was unclear whether it was either a very good painting or a slightly poor photograph.

A Cold Retreat

Foreboding, it was surrounded by a large gold ornate frame that seemed overly fancy for the joyless family within.

A stag's head was staring back at me, but with nothing to say, I looked away. I remembered the other taxidermy in the study and wondered whether Leonard or the family had any real interest in hunting, or if these were just the ideal furnishings for what they considered to be a typical Wiltshire country house. Or was it here as a psychological threat, a warning of what could happen to anything living that crossed his path? I dismissed the last point almost as soon as I thought it.

A rattle of silver against china, along with the shuffling of feet, made me look up. Leonard came in with a large tray and placed it down on the table in front of me.

"Help yourself to milk and sugar," he said, gesturing towards both.

I took a seat near the drinks. "Thank you," I replied and added sugar and a splash of milk.

"This is going to be a lot of fun," he said. This, again, seemed an odd thing to say to a new employee, but it was not out of character from someone who had lustful intent.

"I'm sure," I said whilst thinking of something else to say. "Are there many guests here at the moment?"

"We have an old couple who come here each year: the Darby's. A sweet pair... And a woman on business. She'll be gone in the morning."

I nodded and drank more tea. The day was beginning to catch up with me. I had put a lot of time and planning into this, and now suddenly, sitting down with a drink, I felt the fatigue wash over me. Perhaps it was the relief of everything going to plan. Although there was still so much that had to be done—and of course more than a handful of risks.

"You look a little tired. How about, when you finish your tea, you go up to your room and relax. Dinner is served at 6 p.m."

I nodded. That suddenly seemed like a really good idea. There was no rush. Tonight at dinner I would be able to ask more questions and perhaps as soon as tomorrow I could start my plans.

It was less than ten minutes before I placed my bags in my room and sat down on the bed. It was strange to think that I had left a nice four-bedroom house to now live in one bedroom with an en-suite. I wondered just how long I would be here.

A Cold Retreat

The room was very nice. It was decked out with a bookcase holding a number of books from authors that were experts at their craft. There was a coffee machine, a small fridge, and some fresh flowers on the windowsill. I then had a sudden weak spell where I momentarily thought about abandoning my plan and just enjoying this for a few days, but then I had flashes of being held down, my face pressed into a pillow and rough hands hungrily grabbing me, and I easily shook away the nice thoughts. But for now, with heavy eyelids, I lay down and closed my eyes.

Chapter 14

Penny - 2010

There is something about your first real relationship that shapes all the rest thereafter. After that first time you lay your heart out on the line and bare your soul to essentially a stranger, everything from that point on changes in your life.

You could easily dismiss this as clichéd lyrics from a million songs that have graced the music charts either side of the Atlantic, these sentiments resonate with other memories good and bad. Each thought was another snapshot of laughter and emotion locked-away in my mind.

I later found out that my first crush, Dieter, was in fact named Travis. The problem with crushes and fantasies is that they can never quite live up to the perfection they have been built up to. I had wanted to be the kind of girl that a guy like Travis wanted to be with, but I just hadn't been ready. I had thought about this for a long time. He had treated me dismissively, like a groupie to a rock star. He had expected me to want to sleep with him without any of the wine and dine of a date beforehand. He had known at that moment outside of Starbucks, when I agreed to spend some time with him that it would end up purely as sex. There had been something predatory about it. I could see that now. Kate could see that, she had told me so. She had said to me, "Penny, you have to know straight away who in the relationship has the upper-hand. That is the person who will selfishly manipulate the other one to do exactly what they want!" She was right. I struggled to be the dominant person. I was sick of trying to please them. Even with this insight, I set out to be the one with control, but after one compromise too many, I realised that I had missed the opportunity to stamp any authority and conceded to pleasing them instead. I was then in the submissive position throughout.

I sometimes wondered whether I was better off living alone. I was hardly Bridget Jones, but relationships just never seemed to work out for me. Men on the whole treated me badly.

I had been in a relationship for six months a while back with a guy called Gareth who was extremely intense. He should not have been the next person that I slept with after being used as a human sex-doll, but hindsight is a wonderful thing. He worked in IT, and it was plainly obvious that he cared more about computers than he did me. I had met him online (of course) and he could be quite witty on the keyboard. We had met up at a pub, and he had spent twenty minutes discussing the wonders of the local ale with the barman when ordering our drinks. This and his deadpan humour had been oddly intriguing. He was straight out of a sketch show. Sometimes I would laugh out loud at him, only to realise from his perplexed face that he was serious and not trying to be funny. But he had seemed so harmless.

He liked his own space and would disappear off into a room to don his headphones and microphone to talk to fourteen-year-old boys whilst shooting them on *Call Of Duty*—or whatever shooting game was popular; they all look the same to me. I would curl up on the sofa with a book about the romance that was devoid from my life, whilst wondering again where I had gone wrong. Every now and then the silence was broken when my boyfriend swore at, and tried to kill, the children with whom he was playing. This was a good summary of our relationship and in a nutshell why it would never work.

Gareth had never exactly been attentive. He would come at me like a guy might an Airfix model. He was quick to get started, uninterested at

A Cold Retreat

doing it properly, and wanted to finish it just to be able to say that he had done it. But he had never forced me to do anything. He often got embarrassed when naked, and so I had been shown this vulnerable side to him. But ultimately, it was boring and not what I wanted.

I had broken up with him halfway through one of his silly little games. I just couldn't wait any longer. I was not sure whether what I had said to him hurt or he was embarrassed that his little boyfriends had heard over the microphone and had laughed hysterically at him. I heard him crying later on, and it was the most pitiful sound that I had ever heard in my life.

Next, I met Keith in my local pub. Kate and I had started to go there specifically to look for men; her idea, not mine. Keith was twenty years older than me, and when Kate had started to date a guy called Micky, I was left with Keith, who turned out to be Micky's uncle. He was kind and would let me talk shit about men for hours. On the third evening of me ranting about the evil males of the world, he told me that he'd take me out for dinner. And that's exactly what he did. But as the weeks went by, the gifts became more lavish. The pub night then ended up being just his house and no longer the pub first, and I had the candles that I had wanted and the massages…but he just wasn't the one. He looked after me in that typical fatherly way. He wanted a young model that he could do everything for, and again, he was ultimately the one in control. He didn't make me do anything that I didn't want to do, but he was the one with the suggestions and the one who had the last say in what we would do.

Kate was no better. She fell into relationships quickly and out of them even quicker. She enjoyed the chase. Although she would never admit it, she was addicted to those first few months of a relationship. Her excitement levels had to be up there in the red, and the minute that they dipped below the line, it was bye-bye. She had no type. She liked to go for men that she really shouldn't have gone for. She especially liked attractive married men. It wasn't enough that, at first, they appeared to be out of her league; they had to be either in a relationship or married to a skinny bimbo. She thought it was like a blindfold game of hook-a-duck—or hook-a-dick, if you ask me. Despite all of this, she was still quite happy to rough it every once in a while with men who looked like their home-plumbing was broken. She just liked to not be single.

"When are we going to find Prince Charming?" Kate said to me one evening over a glass of wine.

A Cold Retreat

"That's fairy tale, love. We live in times where all the princes were killed and only the village knobheads were left."

We sat in The Swiss Chalet pub, a place we frequented a lot. Kate liked it, as she always pulled at some point, although she quite fancied the barman. Rumour had it that he had a girlfriend who was at Uni somewhere, which attracted Kate to him even more. He was polite and friendly but never offered any indication that he was interested—not that it mattered to Kate.

"Maybe we should become lezzers?" She winked, and I nearly spat out my Bacardi and Coke.

"Nah, not for me," I said.

Kate tried to look hurt. She placed her glass down, and then with her hands, squashed her ample boobs together. "What's wrong with me?" she asked.

I shrugged. "Dunno. I'm just not attracted to women."

"That's because you've not found the right one yet."

"Maybe...or perhaps it's just not my thing?" I had never so much as had a slight crush on another woman, let alone thought about engaging in something a little more erotic. The logical side of me wondered if due to my underlying hatred of most men, and the lack of trust in finding a decent one, that it might be the right thing to try. But the heart wants only what it dares to desire.

"You know what?" I said, taking another sip and then looking across the bar. "I don't know which man I hate more."

Kate poured more wine from the bottle into her glass. This was how her evening went; she bought her drinks by the bottle and not the glass. "Let's see? Travis raped you, Dex cheated on you, Gareth ignored you, and Keith smothered you. Is that about right?"

"I dunno if those are completely accurate," I began, but even as I said it, I realized that there was always something in the way that Kate could summarise things that rung true. Travis had raped me on some level. I had not wanted to have sex with him at the point that we had sex. He had set out that day to have sex with me, and therefore it was premeditated. He had seen me look uncomfortable and had plied me with alcohol. He had demanded that I take off my clothes. But I had not uttered a word to him, no less the all-important words of *No, Stop,* and *I don't want to*. So was he just a boy being a boy?

"Hey, Penny!" I realised that Kate was clicking her fingers. "Whoa, we lost you there! C'mon, tell

A Cold Retreat

me, what's the verdict? Which one do you hate the most? Rapist, Cheater, Ignorer, or Smotherer?"

I took deep breath. "Maybe Dex…" I paused as Kate gave me a surprised look with raised eyebrows and an over-exaggerated, down-turned mouth.

"Really? Not the rapist? Interesting."

"It's just…" I began. Things were so confusing in my head: the wrongs and rights and the way that I should be feeling. "I really thought that Dex was my Prince Charming."

"And not the violator. So you dislike someone because of what could've been over someone who actually did something bad to you? Wasn't Travis your Prince Charming beforehand?"

"Only in the fantasy sense. Don't get me wrong, I cannot get over what happened with him, but I went straight from idolising him to hating him. That night with Dex… We connected, we had something…"

"He came onto you though?" Kate pressed.

I nodded. "But unlike with Travis, I felt like I could do whatever I wanted to do."

"As did he, as he fucked that other chick." The vision came flooding back. It was awful. After Travis, it was possible that Gareth and Keith were just types of men that I was trying out, types I didn't think that I wanted, and they had confirmed as much. I know that what hurt was the shattered fantasy. The million times that a potential relationship with Dex had played out, he had been donning the prince's outfit and gallantly riding on the back of a beautiful white mare, pulling me up and on to the back as we rode back to the castle. He would carry me up the spiral stairs into a wonderful tower and onto a large four-poster bed covered in rose petals. By the flicker of candlelight, we would make slow and meaningful love, my cries of pleasure ringing out below him. But of course, I had never had the chance to get this good stuff, nor did I get to be put off of by any of his bad habits—apart from the one annoying habit, which was fucking another woman…

"Hi," said a male voice, suddenly interrupting my thoughts. He stood smiling, a little rough around the edges like he might work outside, but he was in good shape. "Can I buy you ladies a drink?"

Kate looked at me and winked. "What, just the one for us to share?"

"I think I can stretch to one each."

Kate grinned. "That you can, lad. That you can!"

He trotted over to the bar and returned a little later on with a friend in tow.

Chapter 15

Ben - 2010

"Don't ever fuckin' call me again!" she said, swearing down the phone before cutting me off.

"You called me," I muttered to the handset. She was one crazy fucking bitch.

Her name was Bronwyn for fuck's sake. Who calls their daughter that? It sounded like she was from some middle-class family from Kent and not a rundown council estate in East Swindon.

I had known her since school, and we had had this on/off thing for as long as I could remember. We had dated other people, but somehow, we would end up back together whether for the night, for the week, or even for a year or so. It was like it was written in the fuckin' stars of that astrology crap or whatnot.

We knew that when things were good, then we were great. She was my best friend, and we had a right laugh and shit. But all too often, she got possessive. I get it, ya know? I understood that we were brilliant together like fifty percent of the time.

Bronwyn, though, she had it in her head that we should be together whatever happens. I sometimes thought that she pulled her hair back too tight in a ponytail and it did somethin' to her brain. She knew, deep down, that shouting at each other in public was not love. I'm not no fuckin' love doctor or nuthin', but screaming out in town at me when I mishear you should not result in bein' called a "Fuckin' wanker!"

Tonight's bomb exploded because she was going to a party and wanted me to go too. It was going to be full of women, but it was a fuckin' sit around and talk about shit and nails, or a "Load of old shallocks!" as I put it, which I thought was a fuckin' hoot, but apparently, I was not a sensitive man. *Well, fuck that. Go and find your George Clooney or Tom Hardy; I'm going down the boozer with Dave.*

The other thing is that sometimes I just didn't want to plan things. She'll want to come round and sort out dinner, and where we are going, and who we are going to see, and what time this, and what time that, and I will be like...whoa, whoa, whoa there, lass, either I missed our fuckin' wedding day, or I am still very much single. Dave, on the other hand, was a man of little words, and this suited me down to the ground.

A Cold Retreat

Earlier, when I was ignoring the phone call from Bronwyn whilst illegally downloading the Swindon Town match on the internet, I got a text from Dave:

Boozer tonight?

Short and sweet but none of those fuckin' shortcut-typing things that misses out letters. I couldn't read those, and I felt like I should be a code breaker just to understand what the fuck they were trying to say. It wasn't the fuckin' war; we were allowed to speak in English now—for fuck's sake!

I replied back with:

7pm

There was none of that *How are you* (or fuckin' *How R U*) crap. He didn't care, and neither did I. We were there as wingmen until the other one pulled, whilst we also drank a few pints in between, either in silence or discussing football, movies, and fit women.

It also meant that I got to watch the football without missing anything, order an Indian, and then shower. Experience told me that women didn't always like sweaty balls. One girl had, but she had been more than filthy herself…

I left my house at seven. The arranged time was a suggested time of meet. Dave and I were not on a fuckin' date, so it didn't matter. It was only a few minutes anyway, and I hated standing or sitting in the bar on my own, so I deliberately got there late.

The Swiss Chalet pub had a band on tonight, playing rock covers, and they were beginning to draw in quite a crowd. I saw Dave standing there like a Norman-Knobhead; he was halfway through his pint and talking to a guy with an impressive white beard.

"Wanker Dave!" I shouted as I walked up to him, which looked like it made him uncomfortable until he realised it was me. He had already bought me a pint, which was quite sweet, I suppose, although he did owe me to be fair.

After a while, I spotted two birds sitting in the alcove where the owner's family usually sat when they were around (tonight they were not). One had blonde hair and looked cute in a pixie sort of way, whereas the other one had large hair and even larger breasts bursting out of her top. Her clothes were a little too tight for her. Either she had suddenly put on weight, or she thought that these clothes were figure-hugging and sexy. I was not so sure. I looked at Dave and told him to put his balls away.

"Eh?"

"Eyeballs. You're staring."

"And that's bad?"

A Cold Retreat

"Very bad. Allow me." I put my pint down and walked over to them, trying to add a bit of Swayze swagger.

They stopped what they were doing when I approached them. "Can I get you a drink?" I asked politely, without swearing.

"What, just me?" the buxom one said.

"I think I can stretch to both of you," I replied, a little Jack Nicholson added in there.

"Then yes," she responded back, and the other one slipped me a smile and a nod. I took the orders and wandered back to the bar. I winked at Dave as I got there.

"You're welcome, I think is what you were about to say."

"Let's see how things go before we start smacking each other's arses," Dave replied, although he now had a big old grin on his chubby face.

Chapter 16

Penny – 2010

This was becoming a familiar evening to me. I don't wish for us to sound like loose women, but whichever bar on a Saturday night that we chose to go to, we knew at some point we would be approached by males. Often two of them. It wasn't that we're attractive, but we must have been giving off those pheromone-things that make men wild. Males, as we know, are permanently on the hunt for a mate, so all we had to do was dress up and look single.

I couldn't speak for Kate, but usually it happened that Kate ended up with the loud one or the most confident one—not always, but this was often the case. I think that this was because her boobs were more than twice the size of mine, and she specifically liked to show them off. Men are very visual and in their small little brains, a loud woman who likes to show off her skin must equate to a high sex drive. I, on the other hand was usually listening to Kate rant on and so posed less of a challenge. My

A Cold Retreat

breasts were less than average, but my blonde hair and skinny frame meant that I was seen as a happy second choice.

Kate loved men. She liked to be chased. She liked to make them uncomfortable, and she liked to be dominated by them. A Saturday night usually meant that she would not be sleeping alone. On the rare occasion that she had slept alone, it had been because her gentleman friend had suddenly remembered that he was married or had a girlfriend.

For me, I enjoyed the company and flirtation of the night. There was usually a lot of kissing, and sometimes we fondled a little bit more. But it was very rare that I slept with them. On a lot of occasions, I had met them the next day for a meal or a movie, but things had then usually petered out.

So when this guy came over with a big grin, I was sure that, as usual, he would take one (or two) looks at Kate and know that this was the girl that he would be swapping bodily fluids with for the rest of the night. But he glanced at me, which instantly brought on a wave of shyness, and it was this that caught him and won him over. His mate then sauntered over, realising that he had not been told to *piss off*, and Kate shifted around to let him into the booth.

Jim Ody

"I'm Ben," he said when he brought back the drinks and sat down next to me. "This is Dave."

"Hi," Kate and I said at once. Kate was staring at Dave, a large chunk of a man who looked like he might play rugby. He had a large build, and you could see that he was strong, but also you knew that beer and kebabs were as important to him as the gym was—probably more so.

"It's about time some nice girls were here," Ben said with a grin. There was definitely an air of confidence in him. He had a hoop earring on his right ear, which was popular about fifteen years ago, and a black-and-white tattoo of roses with a name inside that I couldn't quite make out. He had a look of someone who either worked outside or just spent a lot of time outside. His skin was dark and weathered from the sun, and he had a shaved head that suited him.

"We're here once in a while," I said before Kate could jump in.

"This is a pleasant surprise though," she added with a jiggle. This was what she did just in case the men were blind and didn't notice her low-cut top and ample breasts.

I sometimes admired the way that Kate didn't worry about what she ate. She was somewhat heavily-padded, but she wore it well. Perhaps I too

A Cold Retreat

was fooled in the way that she wore tight clothes rather than wearing bigger and baggier clothes to hide in like many other women of her size did. I suppose rather than say, *"Don't look at me; I'm hiding it best I can,"* she was silently saying, *"This is what I've got; d'ya wanna see more?"* She was nothing if not clever at this.

"I like your tattoo," I said to Ben, by which of course I meant, *"What does it say?"*

He nodded and then said, "Have you got any?"

I nodded my head. "Just a small one on my ankle…"

Then Kate piped up. "She's got her nipple pierced!"

I rolled my eyes. She always did this, like it was some great opening for me, but actually it just made things awkward. If it was Kate, she would be full of, *"Y'wanna see it?"* or *"You'll see later,"* but that was not me, and it just made me more shy.

Ben grinned. "Sound's painful," he said.

"It was over quite quickly," I admitted.

"Sounds like you, Ben!" Dave said loudly, and he and Kate laughed. Ben chuckled, but I saw that mix of vulnerability behind the confidence. Strangely enough, it was probably the point at which I fell in love with him.

It didn't take long before Kate and Dave were talking together. Sometimes, they lowered their voices and giggled, clearly enjoying each other's company. They had started talking about *Game of Thrones,* which Kate was a massive fan of, and they were lost together. It wasn't my thing, nor Ben's apparently, so we filled the time talking about a vast number of other things. Kate and Dave both smoked, so they would disappear off outside for a fresh-air break. Ben had recently given up after many years, and I had never even touched a cigarette.

"I can't believe you're single," Ben said after taking a sip of his drink. "Sorry, I know how much of a line that sounds, but it's true. Saturday night and you're not off out with some nice guy."

I smiled and said seriously to him, "Oh, but I am out with some nice guy on a Saturday night." I took a sip of my drink and left him with that thought. I guess I had just laid my cards out on the table, alcohol pumping up my courage again.

"Then I am very lucky," he said and leaned in to kiss me. It was nice, the softness of lips and tongue with the rough stubble and hands. I was glad that we were in a booth that was snuck away to the side, and also that Kate and Dave were not there. There was nothing worse than having a moment like this

A Cold Retreat

and then having your friends start to cheer. A real moment spoiler.

A little while later, my phone buzzed. It was Kate. The message suggested in quite coarse language that she would not be coming back into the pub, but would be going back to hers to engage in some pleasures between the sheets. That was typical Kate.

"The other two are not coming back," I said to Ben. He raised his eyebrows as if this was expected.

"Really?" he said, trying to sound surprised, but I think this was something that happened quite a lot. The two of them were quite well matched.

We got another round of drinks in and talked about movies. I told him how much I liked Nicholas Cage. It wasn't in a sexual way, just that he played all kinds of roles. He told me that he loved *Dirty Dancing*. At first, I thought he was joking, but when I talked about some of the scenes, he blushed slightly, and he was able to quote lines perfectly. It was incredibly sweet.

Half an hour later, he walked me home. When we got to my house, I was sure that he was expecting me to invite him in, but I was just not like that. I had been let down too many times before, so I always said goodbye there.

"You don't want me to tuck you into bed?" he said with a cheeky smile.

"Not tonight, hun. Maybe another night."

"Y'sure?" There was a tiny hint of desperation creeping in now, like he had assumed that being invited into her house was a mere formality, and they would end up naked together. Especially as his mate Dave had more than likely finished banging Kate by now…well, for the first time.

"I'm sure," I said and kissed him. His hands began to roam, but I pulled away. "How about we meet up tomorrow?"

He looked happy at this and nodded whilst pulling out his mobile and taking my number.

We kissed again like teenagers, and again, his hands tried to sneak under my top. I pulled away, waved, and headed back into my house.

I closed the door and went upstairs. I quickly looked out of the window, but he was gone.

I noticed a woman in a short skirt striding by, quickly throwing a glance at my house with a scowl. Of course, I didn't know then that this was the woman whose name was inked on Ben's arm. She would ultimately be the cause of Ben ripping out my heart and stamping all over it.

Chapter 17

Ben - 2010

Five minutes later, the four of us were sitting down together.

"I've not seen you in here before," the blonde, who I later found out was called Penny, said to me.

"We come here a lot," Dave said, jumping in. "Ask the barman."

"Kate will happily do that!" I grinned at our private joke.

"It's a nice place," I added. Women like for you to be positive about things.

"We come here once in a while when looking for hot guys!" Kate said.

"Well, I'm fuckin' roastin'!" I said, forgetting to edit the swearing. They laughed at that.

For the rest of the night, we talked and laughed. Both Kate and Dave were caught up talking about some series on SKY, and as they both smoked, they popped outside every so often for a fag. Bronwyn had finally gotten me to give up a few months back, but I was gagging for one. The third time they disappeared though, they didn't appear for what seemed like ages. To be honest, we hadn't noticed. We had been talking about movies. She said that she liked John Cusack, or Nick Cage, or someone like that, and I mentioned that I'd seen *Dirty Dancing*. I didn't mention that it was with an ex, as it was her favourite movie, nor that we had to watch the odd scene before she would have sex… But suddenly we were kissing. It seemed a little strange to be snogging in a pub in your late twenties, but alcohol and hot women make us do strange things. The vibrating of Penny's phone on the table made us giggle. I'm not sure why; it just did.

Penny looked at it and rolled her eyes. "I think that's the last that we'll be seeing of them tonight."

"What?" I said.

"They're going back to hers, *'for coffee,'*" she added her own quote marks to the last two words.

"Oh, I see," I said. Blimey, Dave didn't mess about. He was that strong, silent type. He had a cheeky face that women fell for, but he didn't talk much, which they saw as him being a good listener. That was not the case. He couldn't always think of something to say so just stayed quiet. The irony was that he didn't ever pay attention, so he really was the world's worst listener, but it actually got him laid, so who was I to criticise the young stud?

A Cold Retreat

We drank some more, and then I walked her home. There was something about her that made me want to see her again. If I were honest, I wanted to see more of her tonight but with fewer clothes on. I gave her my number and didn't make a fuss about not coming in. We made plans for the next day.

We kissed goodbye, and I watched her wave and close her front door.

I was walking down the road with a little spring in my step when a voice came from behind me. "And who the fuck was that whore?"

"Bronwyn, I just walked her home."

"And the kiss?"

"It meant nothing."

"It didn't look like nothing. You looked like you wanted to go in with her."

"Nah, I was just being a gentleman."

"Fuck off," she said, a little calmer now. She still had her make-up on. She looked good in make-up.

"How was the party?"

"Full of...what was it?" She clicked her fingers. "Shellacking!"

I laughed. "I like a good shellac!"

"So do I."

She came close, and before I knew it, we were kissing. That was how we were. Maybe that was how we would always be. She knew that we probably shouldn't be together, but she couldn't let me go. I couldn't help it. I hated her, and I loved her in equal measure.

Chapter 18

Penny - 2010

I suppose I always knew deep down that Ben was too good to be true. He was very clever in how he played it. He came off as charming and thoughtful when he was around me, but then backed off as if not to smother me. We would see each other a few times a week, and then we would have a break for a week. It was nice to be in a relationship with someone who wasn't either possessive or needy.

Of course, what I didn't realise was that he was still regularly seeing *her*. It was as if they had this invisible cord between them, and no matter what I did, it would pull them back together again.

I suppose, like all good insights into a person, I should take you back to my childhood, back to where it all began.

I had a wonderful childhood. My parents both loved me, but as I previously mentioned, they had gradually grown apart from each other. I truly believe that my dad never stopped loving my mum, but he just had an inbred desire towards other women too, however fleeting it was. My mum had remained in denial for a long time. I mean, really, how could she not have known? My dad had been almost brazen in his late nights out. I would smell the perfume on his clothes that clearly wasn't a scent that my mum owned, so she could not have missed it. I'll admit, I was not always party to his excuses and lies, although I knew of them. He could dismiss lipstick on his shirt as him catching a colleague as she fell, or an ugly love bite on his neck as a collar chafe. My mum would nod, and I would wonder what was behind those sad eyes.

This example of a husband and father to a teenager is not something pretty. It is a mould that we can unknowingly use as a blueprint for when we are looking for a potential partner. These unconscious decisions that manifest themselves as desirable traits may well be painful childhood experiences that we see as nostalgic. My dad was strong and kind, which are the main things that I think of, but he was also devious and manipulating, enjoying the hurt look on my mum's face as he blatantly lied to her.

As I got to fifteen and sixteen, he would look at me differently, and it was almost scary. I don't mean that he wanted to hurt me—quite the opposite; he had noticed that I was a woman. He hugged me

A Cold Retreat

more, and our holidays went from Wales to hot, sunny places abroad where I was bought bikinis and skimpy outfits beforehand. I cannot say that he did anything that I could ever consider wrong. But that was his strength.

He would hug me more when I was less clothed. He rushed to put sun cream on my back, with his fingers roaming a little too far, but not enough that couldn't be laughed off as an accident or an overreaction on my part.

The irony was that, by the time things did go too far, it was partly my own fault. It was the pierced nipple.

That night, my mum had gone out with some work colleagues, and I had just showered. I was sitting in my underwear applying cream, when he burst in.

"Where is it?" he said angrily.

"What?" I said. I didn't bother to cover up, as he had seen me in my underwear many times before.

"The piercing! You got your nipple pierced," he said, but there was something false about the anger—like he had worked himself up to sound angry but could no longer maintain it.

"It's nothing," I said, putting down the bottle.

He walked over to me. "Show me!"

If it hadn't been for the angry look and tone, then I would've thought this to be a strange request, but I wanted to stop his anger. I wanted him to hold me like he usually did and make me feel safe.

I took my arm carefully out of one side of the bra and exposed my breast to him. There was something in his eyes that scared me, but it wasn't fear. He reached out and touched it.

"This is unacceptable," he said, touching it. "Why would you do this to yourself?" He pulled at the stud gently, and I was worried that he would pull it out.

"Men won't want to touch you," he said with little or no conviction, now squeezing my nipple. "Do you not understand that?" He circled the areola and then quickly drew his hand away.

"I don't want to ever see it again!" Out he went, leaving me to feel violated, but worse, like it was my own fault.

This strange and disturbing memory had stayed with me for all of these years, carved deeply into my being.

The romantic side that yearned for the prince had had reality kidnap me away from a possible fairy-tale and into this harsh reality that cared not for happy endings, but a smash-and-grab, get-what-you-can-and-more mentality.

A Cold Retreat

Travis had been the guy from the teen movies. He was the senior football player, and I was the nerdy girl idolising him. From the moment he knew the roles we were playing, he had had no interest in making me the prom queen. He had just wanted to be the guy that turned the girl into a woman, and then run off and high five his mates.

So Gareth had come along, and I had tried to make him into the handsome prince, but he had been neither handsome nor a prince. He had been needy and gentle, and for a short period that felt fine. It had felt like that was all I deserved. What did I want? I had questioned. The answer, of course, was not Gareth.

Keith had been the mixture of strong and commanding but gentle and caring, but again it just wasn't what I had been looking for. It was all too nice. There was no adventure or, dare I say, drama. It was cosy and nice.

But with Ben it was different. He brought with him a passion that would sweep me off my feet. He would come over and literally rip my clothes off without saying a word, but then curl up and watch a movie with me. Then I might not see him again for a week or so and would receive only the odd text, which might or might not include an explicit picture.

This was the problem. I wanted more. He had the ability of rushing in, and we would explode together in a night of fireworks. Or we would go out for a wonderful meal and talk about everything except our future together, and then he would disappear.

It was obvious that he was with someone else. You don't get that close to someone and not suspect as much. He was open about everything except the obvious times that they were together. They weren't living together, but they were emotionally attached through time, experiences, and rose-tinted nostalgia. I could never live up to her. No matter what I did, and no matter what I tried, I was destined to be the one discarded when push came to shove.

For two years we carried on like that. Him living a life between two different women vying for his attention, and me knowing that I was the other woman but thinking that it was all I needed emotionally and physically.

But then she came round, and things got ugly. Things got smashed. People got hurt. And once again, I was left all alone.

Back to Saturday nights out, snogging the odd frog hoping that they would turn into something a little like Ben, or even Dex. Remember him? The one that could've been.

A Cold Retreat

So I threw caution to the wind and made a huge change. I took up a voluntary position abroad travelling around. It was just what I needed, exploring places and meeting guys, knowing that these would not be the princes (but that they might…) so there was no expectation.

And then I was back in Swindon, and it was a bit like the day after the Lord Mayor's Show—the excitement of the night before is over and you're left to get on with normality again. I had lost contact with Kate, so now I was back surrounded by old memories and unsure of where to go now. After three years away, I had to somehow integrate myself back into this life again.

I was sitting alone with a glass of wine in a daze of contemplation when the telephone rang.

That call would change my life forever.

Chapter 19

2000 - 2013

I had gotten used to being propositioned. It was like lads suddenly thought they had the right to come up to me and whisper or pass a note that would say, How much for a blowjob? *School had become unbearable. I had a couple of boyfriends, but they fucked off as soon as we had sex. I was not sure what the worst thing was: the fact that they used to go and boast to their mates about it afterwards or the fact that now it was done in secret, like it was taboo. Too embarrassing now to admit to having had sex with me.*

They still wanted me, if only for a night. Sometimes this was okay with me. My fairy-tales were still ground into the mud in that bush and covered in used condoms, the fantasy lost in leaves and soaked in lube.

I was lucky to get into clubs at seventeen. I say "lucky," but what I really mean is that the clothes I wore made it hard for the bouncers not to let me in. I didn't look seventeen, and for the most part, my

A Cold Retreat

face was the last place they looked when I got to the front of the queue. I was another living doll of eye-candy and a potential one-night-stand.

I loved clubbing. Men would swarm around me throughout the night, dancing close, buying me drinks, and doing all that they could to get me to be with them. I almost felt safe surrounded by people, even if it was unlikely that anyone would help me out if some guy went too far.

I danced and kissed, and if I went into the piss-soaked toilets with someone, it was because I genuinely wanted to. I'd smile, wipe my knees, re-apply my lippy, and leave. I had a liberated feeling of power within that loud, cigarette-smelling human-cattle market, covered in dry-ice, sticky sweat, and alcohol. How could I not enjoy the attention? This wasn't me trying to be with someone, stripping myself bare in order for a fantasy to come true. This was me having men of all ages and backgrounds attracted to me for however many fleeting moments of inebriation.

I had woken up and smelt the coffee. This was never going to be the ballroom in which Prince Charming would swoop in and declare a desire for us to dance, him swinging me around in a firm but gentle way as we matched each other step-to-step and my heart skipped so many beats I thought I might pass out. No, this was me dancing to The Prodigy *whilst a big sweaty labourer called Barry spat romantic words incoherently that sounded a lot like, "Tits," "Love it," "Kiss," and "Pissed!" He grabbed my arse with rough, calloused hands, and snogged me in a way that a dog might thirstily drink from a bowl. His crass gyrating was meant to pass as dancing, but equally, he was dry-humping my leg in another undignified canine trait. He then turned to a Mexican-wave of cheering appreciative mates and then disappeared with a waddle to harass someone else. A skinny guy slid in and danced a little before building the courage to come close enough to touch me. Even drunk, he was nervous. Easy pickings.*

But months of this built me up to want more. Like a drug addict, this no longer satisfied me, and before I knew it, I began to leave the club with someone other than my friends.

Tristan was okay. He was nervous and clearly thought he was punching above his weight. He got the taxi and chatted the whole journey back to his house. Only when the taxi left us there did he admit that he lived with his parents and we had to sneak in. It was great. It was exciting and naughty, and whilst the actual sex was average at best, the whole experience was something more. He went out of his

A Cold Retreat

way to please me, and he unfortunately set the bar way too high that night.

We did it again a few months later, but his parents were on holiday, and it just ended up being boring.

A couple of the lads had no other interest in going anywhere other than an alley or a hedge. I began to wonder exactly what went through their tiny little minds to think that I would leave a club to go into an alleyway to have sex. They had only bought a couple of drinks; even a prozzie got more than that!

Some had nicknames like Hammer or Big Daddy (really?!), but whatever; it was another sign that things were short term.

I fell in love more than a dozen times. I had my heart broken every single time. I had reduced my expectations so drastically that as long as they were quick and didn't hit me, I considered it a good night.

My saving grace was that I stayed away from drugs. That was the difference between what I was doing and being a prostitute. You may argue that the only difference is the monetary transactions, but no, I decided who I spent the evening with. I slept with whomever I wanted to. If I had turned to drugs, then I would've done anyone and anything just to score. I'd heard a lot of bad things said about me, but my willpower against drugs was what saved me.

One night, a guy called Pete strolled over to me in a club. He was tall and fairly skinny with a weird fashion sense that looked like he was famous or a designer. He was extremely confident (of course!) and he was slightly dismissive of me. This was obviously his play—his tried and tested play. I suddenly wanted him. He bought me drinks, and we danced, but it wasn't until later that he kissed me delicately. We left together, a couple of his friends and another girl too.

We got back to a large and expensive studio flat, which was more like some penthouse, and the party started as music filled the place. I was getting comfortable and enjoying the vibe when we moved things to his bedroom. We went at it, full of passion and excitement. This seemed to be the way, but then one of his friends appeared and began to join in, and then another. I was drunk and excited, but scared at the same time. I was lost and out of my depth. Three strong men were all over me, using me. I felt like I was in the sea, struggling to swim against the current of water that was once beautiful and tranquil. Human sharks were on me, devouring me, inside me. The girl was also there but playfully slapping me harder and harder. I wanted to stop. I

A Cold Retreat

wanted to scream. Hands ran through my hair, and my mouth was rarely free, even the tears escaped from my body in shame.

When it was over, I showered. I quickly got my clothes on and was feeling debased and demoralised when a strange thing happened. A mug of tea was passed to me, and each of them hugged me. They sat around and joked together, stealing smiles at me. But I was confused. Was this normal? Was this meant to be fun? Was I hurt?

Was...I...actually...hurt...?

Physically, no not really. A little sore and a little exhausted. Mentally, I just couldn't understand what had happened. I had been down to the lowest of lows, and I now felt elated and almost hysterical, but was the sudden release of endorphins due to a release from the depravity?

I left at 9 a.m. I got home and cried for an hour. I don't know exactly what I was crying about. Perhaps it was another example of how far away I was from my childhood dream of being a fairy-tale princess.

This wasn't to be my lowest point.

Part 2

Chapter 20

Sasha – A couple of weeks ago

I opened my eyes. My head felt dizzy, and I was suddenly disorientated as I began to remember where I was. My body ached like I had been to the gym and overdone it.

Sun shone through the window. It should've been a beautiful thing, but at that same point, I realised I was only wearing my underwear. This was strange, as I would never sleep like this if I was to take a nap in the day. I looked at my watch and noticed that it was morning.

I had slept through the rest of the afternoon, the evening, and right through the night. There is no way that I would sleep in my underwear. A bra can be such an uncomfortable thing when lying down. I had a fuzzy, thick feeling in my head as I struggled to remember yesterday, but I was pretty sure that something had been said about dinner, and I had decided to come up for a lie down.

If I was ever sleeping somewhere different, then a sleep in the day would be fully clothed, so to wake up in my underwear was odd.

I got out of bed and looked at myself in the mirror. I felt sore.

I looked tired. My hair was a mess, and despite the long sleep, my eyes looked puffy and red.

But it was the marks on my body that really scared me—small red marks on the side of my throat and on my side that looked like bruising. Finger marks.

I realised that I had begun to shake as I removed one of my breasts from the cup of the bra. I didn't need to look in the mirror to see the teeth marks. There were a couple, both deep. I had been violated, and I was then very aware of the soreness between my legs and buttocks.

My throat constricted, and my breathing became erratic as I removed my knickers. I collapsed onto the bed with the bloodied underwear and sobbed.

I remembered my phone and reached over. It was gone.

Despite being naked, I got up and went to the door. It was locked.

My head whipped round, and my eyes darted to take in everything. The windows.

Ignoring the pain, I jogged to them the best I could. Seeing no latch, I banged on the pane. Nothing. I felt a rage deep inside me, and though I struggled, I picked up the small wooden bedside

A Cold Retreat

table and threw it as best I could at the window. The glass barely even registered the impact.

I was trapped. I had willingly gone into a trap thinking that I was the hunter looking to capture the fly in my web, and instead it was me who had been caught. I was the fly using up the last of its strength to try with all of its might to escape, despite being incapacitated by the situation.

I was stupid. I was beyond foolish. I was just a woman who had thought she could take on this monster, and now I would become nothing more than a statistic. There would be no talk of my research, the way that I found him, tracked him, spoke to the victims lucky enough to have gotten away.

I will now be nothing more than another victim, a poor, defenceless female who was sucked into his world not knowing the evil this man was. But I knew. I knew. I was going to get him. And now I have failed.

I screamed. I was angry again.

And then I stopped. I calmed myself. It would do no good to roll over and give up. This was about the next victim. This was about the reasons why I was in this predicament. This was about men who thought they could use their power to overrule a woman's wants, to gradually apply pressure within a relationship to fulfil some fantasy that they had had when they were a lonely teenager, or a mark on their bedpost that they could boast about with their mates down the pub.

This was for the timid women out there putting up with the abuse because they were scared to speak out. This was for the strong women in the workplace that held power, but went home to become submissive for their man. This was for those girls who were yet to find love and would do anything to just feel wanted. This fight was for them. But more than that, this was for me. I would survive this.

He didn't know who he was dealing with. He didn't know just how much I knew about him. He was unaware that the sudden power that he felt would make him feel over-confident and cocky. That was his weakness. That was my strength. I had to play the part of the victim and bide my time.

I will fight him.
I will *fight him!*

Chapter 21

Sasha – A couple of weeks ago

I had been lying on the bed now for a while. I was dressed and had given up on catching the attention of anyone outside. My room was too high up. No one gave me a first glance up here.

I remembered the woman that I first saw—the face in the window. That as now me.

I had seen the odd people walking around down below. There was a couple holding hands, no doubt in love. Maybe equal, maybe not. They were talking to each other and both seemed completely at ease. It must have been the beginning of their relationship. Both trying hard. They were comfortable. He'd not suggested doing other things yet. They still cuddled and held each other whilst making love. His hands didn't creep up to her throat whilst he stared at her with wide, crazy eyes, only to laugh it off later. "Did that hurt, honey? Oh, I'm sorry. I was just messin'."

She would smile in relief and laugh it off. Until the next time. And the next. Before she knew it, it would become the norm... Except his grip would get tighter, and she, like the relationship, would slowly be choking and dying.

I saw a gardener. A middle-aged guy who seemed very proficient with his tools, sweeping his way over the hedges leaving smooth lines. I wondered how much he knew about Leonard. Were they partners? He looked strong, but that meant nothing. Often it was the ones who looked less athletic that felt like they had something to prove.

I made a failed attempt at waving at the gardener, and at one point, I even flashed my tits. I had a notion that men had some sixth sense when it came to naked or half-naked women that helped them to seek out these snapshots of titillation no matter how brief. I guess I was proved wrong, or that groundsman had no interest in boobs. Perhaps he was so fixated with superb bush trimming that he was able to quash the distraction. *A true professional,* I mused, digging deep with the gallows humour.

And then I heard the voice.

"Sasha." It was Leonard, but it was coming from the wall. "There is a speaker behind the picture on the wall." My eyes immediately shot to it, not that it made a blind bit of difference to anything. "I am about to unlock the door now. I ask that you sit on

A Cold Retreat

the bed facing the window. Do not attempt to move. I have food for you. If you move, then I will leave and you will not know if or when I will ever return."

There was a silence that felt large and almost swallowed me up.

"Sasha. Say, *"Yes, Lenny"* if you understand. Alright?"

I tried to compose myself, but then I remembered that I wanted to sound scared—make him think that I would do anything for him. "Yes, Lenny." My voice naturally quivered. I couldn't have hidden the fear in my voice if I had wanted to. It was the only positive to this whole thing. Some positive.

I heard two clicks, and the door opened.

Leonard walked in with a massive grin on his face and handcuffs dangling from his hand. "Put out your wrist." His voice then was stern.

I reluctantly thrust my wrist out, glancing briefly out of the door that had already begun to close on its own. Was it a fire door or a way to slow me down should I try to make a break for it?

He clicked the metal bracelet on, the sides biting into the sides of my wrist. "If you have any thoughts of running, then be advised that beyond that door is a hallway with another locked door at the end. I am the only one who knows the code. So your chances of escaping are even slimmer than you thought they were!" He wheezed out a horrible chuckle.

"Okay," I said in a pathetic voice. "What do you want from me?"

He clipped the other handcuff to a ring that he produced from the bed. "Only that you are never too far away from the bed!" He laughed again. It was a haunting sound. For a second, I thought I was going to throw up.

"I have been a fan of yours for a while, Sasha. Or should I say @sasha_sex_kitten!"

I tried to look shocked. "You...knew my profile?"

"I thought I knew your profile. That's not you then? Those tits are not the ones I've seen before." He looked hurt, like I had let him down.

Of course I hadn't really stripped naked. I had used some other woman's account that had only had a hundred or so followers. Her figure wasn't massively dissimilar to mine, although our "intimate bits" were not alike in any way. He may've liked my face, but he loved her tits and pussy. I could live with that.

"Who is this woman then that you stole the body of?"

A Cold Retreat

"I dunno." My head hung in shame. I wanted to get out of there, not discuss the merits of photoshopping someone else.

"Well, think! I wouldn't mind checking her out! She might have a prettier face!" There was that awful laugh again.

I couldn't help it. Despite myself, I was stung by his words. His obsession with me was almost dismissed at the thought of it being someone else younger and more attractive. *Well, get that bitch here instead of me!* I wanted to shout. But of course, I remained quiet.

"Well!?" He pushed, getting close. Too close.

"Tammy someone, from Alabama."

"She's American?"

"That would be my guess." I tried not to be sarcastic, but it was hard.

"Well I never. Tammy from Alabammy!" That laugh again. I wanted to rip out his voice box and shove it up his arse. "I love American women!"

"Really," I mumbled.

"Jealous, huh?"

"Green with fuckin' envy… Now let me out of here, you sick fuckin' arsehole!"

"Well, well, have we got a filthy mouth." He grinned. "And how is your arsehole?"

I shot him a look and was about to swear again at him, but I glanced at the door and then looked away.

"There ain't no escape, Princess. Remember the other door!" he said, and then he got out his phone. "Tell me, what is she called?" I couldn't believe that he was suddenly hung up on this. It only went to underline everything that I had come to understand about men. They wanted you from afar. They dreamed and fantasised right up until the point of capture and then suddenly they were no longer interested.

I told him. His face lit up when he saw her, and I could see that he suddenly wished she was here in place of me. I hadn't thought I could have any more hatred for him, but at that point, I did.

"Well then. I'm off." He put the phone away, walked to the door, and then came back in with a tray. "Your breakfast," he said, putting it on the side. He turned back and uncuffed me before a little skip in his step took him out of the room without so much as a goodbye. The door slammed, and a clicking sound could be heard.

I looked over at the toast and the mug of something that smelt like coffee, and I wondered how long he would keep feeding me before he decided to do something more drastic.

A Cold Retreat

I rubbed my wrists and took a bite of the toast. I hadn't realised just how hungry I was until the smell of the toast and coffee hit me. This was not how I had planned things.

It just goes to show you. You spend all that time researching and planning, looking to take someone by surprise, when *hey presto*! They catch you out instead. Bloody typical.

Before I had headed to Leonard's house, I had thought about writing a post online, about where I was, that would be timed to go out in a few days' time. If I was back, then I could cancel it, but if something happened to me, then it would raise an alarm. But I chose not to bother.

So here I was alone, and no one knew that I was even missing.

Chapter 22

Sasha – A couple of weeks ago

An hour had passed since he had left me. I was trying hard to keep my spirits up. I was just so disappointed in myself. I had researched him. I knew that he stalked women. I knew that he had attempted to force himself on women, but he had never been successful. I knew that he had been imprisoned and then had taken over this B&B. I was also aware of a number of attempts to force himself on women working here.

But just how stupid could I have been not to see what was right in front of me? He had been caught before because he had been making random attacks. He had followed women and then suddenly pounced with little or no plan. Then here he employed women with no ties, and had gradually made it seem like his actions were just another part of the job, another role that he expected them to play. Here, he could plan, adapt, and cater towards the needs that he had.

A Cold Retreat

I thought that I had researched him carefully. But what if he had researched me too? This had never occurred to me.

I had thought that I was the one holding the cards. I could waltz in here pretending to be a naïve woman looking for a job, teasing him with knowing that he already knew who I was. I could get him alone and then show him exactly what it was like to be dominated; in his own lair there would be no one around to help him.

But what if he knew me already? He had found out that I now lived alone. My previous relationship had been so toxic that it had severed all ties with family and friends.

I was suddenly rich pickings.

I felt myself getting worked up again. It wasn't hard. I was so pissed off that I was here locked in the tower like some stupid fucking bimbo princess. He was stalking around the castle ready to come and do whatever he wanted to do with me. These princess fantasies had come in full circle. It was like I had wished upon a star—or when I blew out the last candles on a birthday cake, my wishes had come true. But someone had tweaked those fantasies into the macabre version where I was imprisoned with a beast that could only turn into a monster.

I screamed loudly until my throat hurt. It was stupid, I know. When it comes down to it, we have little control over our emotions. I suddenly hoped that he hadn't heard me, as this would only give him more power and, again, give him the upper hand. I ruefully smiled at that. He certainly had the fuckin' upper hand on me alright.

I took a deep breath and scanned the room. My mind looking, searching, analysing. I was *The Terminator* highlighting objects and categorising them into weapons or helpful tools quickly. There was little in the room though. It had been stripped of the books and comforting touches of the day before. But I had to remain confident. *Just how secure is this room?* I wondered. Would he really have gotten a bunch of labourers or contractors in to secure a room? This was a man who had just been released from prison for rape however many times. People would pick up on that. These would be the first people to say, "*Sure. We secured this room upstairs for that guy just out of prison.*" Everybody had a price, but everybody had a conscience too. Therefore, I was looking at the likelihood of him carrying out the work himself. He was not qualified as an engineer, so this brought me hope. Somewhere within this room was a weak point. It stood to reason. It was part of the main structure,

A Cold Retreat

which again could mean that this being a completely rebuilt room was unlikely. So that meant that he had reinforced the current structure. That left a risk of those weak points.

I just had to find them.

I knew that the windows were reinforced and didn't open. I knew that the door was locked. These were the obvious places. The floor and the ceiling were my next choices. I also had a thought about the speakers. These might have wires, which would need holes for them to run through. Holes could be made bigger or could lead out to somewhere.

I suddenly felt the adrenaline flow again.

There was at least one good thing with how this had played out. My biggest fear—or what I had thought was my biggest fear—would no longer matter. I had been scared that I would get this far and—despite everything that I had read, researched, or had been told—maybe wouldn't be able to go through with hurting someone who had done nothing wrong to me.

I had asked myself: Could I really build up enough anger to murder somebody based on what could always be a set-up or hearsay? If he was nice to me, offered me food and friendship, then whilst I would not be held against my own will, perhaps I would develop a kinship with him, respect, or some sort of Stockholm Syndrome where everything that I knew before I dismissed, letting down all of those women.

But now I knew first-hand this was an animal, a sociopath with no care for other people's feelings. I wanted him deader than dead now. I wanted him to suffer.

But first I had to get out of this room.

Or perhaps all I had to do was make a plan to attack him when he next came in?

***

More time had elapsed. I had pressed walls and the ceiling, but nothing seemed obvious. I laid down and closed my eyes.

I coughed, and when I opened them, my eyes went wide with fear. There was smoke in the room. I looked down and saw it coming from two vents on the side of the bed. I turned over to the other side and saw two more pumping out the thick, white, odourless smoke.

My head went light, and everything in my world went black. *I've lost,* was my final thought.

Chapter 23

Travis – A week ago

The day was quite serene. A gentle breeze glided through the air, and I was in a contemplative mood as I strolled through the woods. This was my sanctuary, a place that had become familiar to me.

I tried to draw comparisons with my life and that of a former rock star or footballer. There were of course few similarities on the face of it, but it was the psychological scarring that struck a chord with me, living in the past, a regretful reverie of nostalgia from a time when I was something: a desired male by females from afar resulting in many relationships, affairs, liaisons, and encounters—some fleeting and by chance, others planned and predictable.

I smiled to myself. I had enjoyed those times even though, for the most part, I had been an arsehole. I had an overconfidence that for the most part could be backed up. I wasn't necessarily mean or outwardly horrible to anyone, just a little dismissive of those that didn't live up to my standards. I would take advantage of the fact that women saw me as a figure of fantasy, participating in dates that I had no intention of following up on after bedding them.

That sounds pretty bad. I realise this now. But I didn't force anyone to do anything that they didn't want to do in the first place. We talked, laughed, and enjoyed each other's company. It just so happened that more often than not we had sex. And after that, my interest began to disappear. Familiarity can be comforting for some, but it lacked the jolt of excitement for me, as I had Chanelle for that. I liked to see the different reactions that women had to my touch. Some would quiver at the very thought of it; others couldn't wait and would strip themselves naked the minute we were alone. Some played hard to get or unleashed a dominatrix side, and others seemed so nervous that it felt like a crime. The differences were what excited me.

For a lot of this time, I had Chanelle. My memories of her and our relationship were incredibly mixed. She was a nice girl. She was also annoying. But there was no excuse for the cheating that I did on her.

Back then, I was able to shift the blame from myself to her quite unashamedly. I see-sawed back

A Cold Retreat

and forth from accusing her of not noticing my infidelity due to her own selfish pastimes, to then being frustrated by her incessant naivety. Of course, these were both incorrect conclusions. I was to blame. I wanted the familiarity of a long-term relationship, with the flashing excitement of the other women on the side.

But we all change—sometimes for the better, and sometimes for the worse. By the time I realised that I wanted to settle down, I'd been forced to close down my company and was working for someone else. He was now the old me, and I was fading, slowing down, adding a few pounds and greying around the edges. He was the new generation, and I was the one cast aside.

I walked further along the track, minding out for the odd piles of faeces left possibly by irresponsible dog-owners (or wild animals), and towards the lake. Sitting on the slight hillside was a couple deep in conversation. The guy reminded me of John Cusack with a long coat and a hoodie underneath, sharp facial features, and a cigarette in his fingers. The girl had shaggy dirty-blonde hair and wore a summer dress that was certainly more fitting for the weather than the guy's clothes. I looked away just as they clocked me. I pulled out my phone as a sign to them that they no longer held any interest for me.

At one stage, I might've thought about flirting with the girl, but now I was a little out of my zone. I was unsure of exactly what it was I was looking for in a woman now. The attractive girls from my past were now too young, and whilst I could still feel the attraction, it just ceased to be the right thing to do anymore. I was now in my late thirties, chasing twenty-year-olds, which fell into that same category as the nineteen-year-old males revving their cheap cars at the school gates in the hope that they would be seen as cool.

The collection of available women my age was full of divorcees, single-parents, widows, or women that should probably remain single for the good of mankind. I knew that I was no longer the catch that I once was, but I'd always struggled in relationships. With Chanelle, it was fine. We didn't live together, although she did stay with me often, but she was too caught up in her own life that she didn't care what I was doing. As long as I spent money on her and took her out, then that was all she had needed. Until one day it wasn't…

I sat down and gazed up at clouds that had once seemed so exciting. Even though I had commented a number of times that they were mundane, the truth was that each one was different, their shapes unique and the speed at which they moved governed by a

A Cold Retreat

different wind each time. Now I looked up to them and saw that those previous throwaway comments, like a lot of things, now came back to haunt me, as I longed for that carefree notion that they were nothing of importance against the excitement of my life.

It was now after the Lord Mayor's Show. In fact, it was more like the Lord Mayor's Show was over a year ago, and I was no longer invited. The excitement was happening elsewhere, and I was left looking in from the outside.

I was so deep in thought that I didn't even see the ball roll near me.

"Hey, old man!" a whiney-voice of a child piped up. I looked up and saw some short ginger curls atop the face of a boy now scowling at me.

I frowned. "*Old man*? What, *me?*"

The kid looked like I was the one being an idiot. "Yeah, now give me the bloody ball back!"

"How old are you? *Five?*"

He looked back at another kid. "Listen to Gramps! Thinks he's funny, don't 'e!"

"You want your ball back, or do you want me to burst it?"

"I don't reckon you got the strength! Haha!"

This was the last fucking straw. I got up and kicked it behind me straight into the lake.

"You fucker!" the ginger-kid shouted, then turned to the other kid. "Go and get my mum!"

"Sorry," I said in a fake apologetic voice. "At my age, I sometimes lose my bearings."

"You'll lose more than your fuckin'…"

"Giles!" a woman shouted, trotting over. "What's going on?"

"This paedo kicked the ball into the lake, didn't he?"

I held up my hands in innocence. "Look, I think there has been a misunderstanding. These lads kicked the ball to me, and I tried to kick it back, but it hit this tree here and rebounded back behind me into the water."

"What a retard," the boy muttered.

The mother, who was possibly a similar age to me, nodded slowly, possibly believing me or possibly making a mental note of my features for a photo-fit ID later on when she reported me. "Really?" she offered.

"Yes. I'm afraid I'm not the player I once was." For the first time in the whole of my life, being completely honest about my age and decreasing abilities felt good.

"A liar is what he is!" the boy said in disgust.

"Giles!" his mother scolded. "That's no way to speak to an adult."

A Cold Retreat

"You're not the one whose ball is in the pissing water!" He stomped his foot and suddenly sounded like he might cry. It was all I could do not to laugh.

I made a show of pulling my wallet out. "Look, I'll happily buy the lad a replacement ball?" Thankfully she was already waving this idea away. Bloody good job, as I didn't want to give the annoying little shit anything.

"No, no, that's fine," she said, although she stared at my wallet like she might make a play to snatch and run.

"Okay then," I replied, putting it away quickly.

"I'm sorry if he's been bothering you," she said.

"No problem." I paused. "It's…it's just since Hendrix, my dog, passed away last week… I… I just like to come here along his favourite walk and think about those good times."

"Oh, I'm really sorry for your loss," she said, walking over. She looked like she might hug me but then remembered that we had only just met and flung an arm around me instead.

"It's just a dog," the little sod Giles muttered.

"Giles! You say sorry now!"

"But, mum!"

"Giles!"

He bowed his head, a little embarrassed. "Sorry, mister."

"It's okay," I said, and as his mother turned away, I winked at him.

"Fucker," Giles mumbled and ran off to where his mate was.

"Look, I really am sorry," she said. "My name's Helena."

"Thanks, Helena. I'm Travis… I live on my own, so without Hendrix, things are a little quiet, ya know?"

She nodded. "Only too well. It's been a few years on my own now since Giles's dad walked out on us. When he's asleep, it gets very quiet." She paused. "He's…a bit of a handful sometimes!"

"Really?" I grinned.

She held my gaze for a second, up until that awkward moment, and then looked back to where little Giles was. Then she said, "Well, it was nice meeting you."

"Likewise. Look…maybe if…" I started, but she had a look of horror suddenly come over her face.

"Sorry," she said. "If I don't watch him, he'll get into some serious trouble."

I nodded and held up a hand as a goodbye, but she was already jogging away, and it hung there awkwardly, a little like I suddenly felt inside. It was another confirmation of how life had moved on. For a second, things had looked good, and years gone

A Cold Retreat

by sealing the deal would've been a formality, but now it was a missed opportunity, or perhaps it was just that I no longer was half the man that I used to be.

I walked home and thought about calling in sick to work tomorrow. I was turning into one of those sad, single middle-aged men. No doubt I would soon take to wearing cardigans and leaving stubble on my chin from neglect rather than style, drinking alone and growing lonely day by day.

I fucking hated life at that moment.

Chapter 24

Travis – A week ago

Ten years ago, I would wake up early and go for a jog. I would use this as a warm-up and then do a round of push-ups and pull-ups before slowing with a couple of bicep curls and dips. Then I would finish with some work on the heavy-bag. I trained like a boxer without stepping into a ring.

I enjoyed the feeling of pushing my limits whilst experiencing the healthy glow and lactic acid-induced hardness of my muscles, and of course, it maintained my weight and helped attract women.

I now enjoyed the extra hour in bed that I had throughout the winter, and come summer, I would jog the odd day and sometimes paw at the punch-bag until my knees and back hurt. Dips, curls, push-ups, and pull-ups had packed up their routines the other side of the grey hair and re-homed themselves with a younger version of myself in another street. We held on dearly to our memories but didn't miss each other that much.

A Cold Retreat

I sported the look that was often described as post-athletic but now "gone to seed." It was probably still considered quite good for my age, but I was a shell of my younger self, with more than the odd wobble creeping in, pushing my weight up a stone.

I then reminisced on the times that I would walk into my own office in charge of my day—in charge of my life. There was something incredibly motivating about being your own boss. Despite the dream and assumption that you will cut loose, you actually find that the opposite is in fact true. There is an addiction in seeing with your own eyes your hard work bringing in the money. You stay late in the office because you know exactly how much money you will get if you put in that effort.

I longed for those times again.

I now worked for a guy called Ian Tillsman. Most people call him Mr Tillsman. I struggled with this, as he was ten years younger than me. The whole role-reversal thing was a bitter pill to swallow, and he knew it. He smiled with just the one side of his mouth. I'm sure, in his head, he called me a loser and used me as an example to stay focused and not slip into that middle-aged abyss where you no longer called the shots, but picked up all of the shit that no one else wanted to do. He tried to sugar-coat the shit by pointing out that it was considered too important for the young female temps whom he employed purely as something to please his eyes and line the sheets of his bed with.

At some point, I had gone from being Leonardo DiCaprio in *The Wolf of Wall Street*, to being Christian Slater in *He Was a Quiet Man,* plotting to shoot all of my colleagues dead.

I hated going in to work, and I was beginning to make this obvious. I was yet to bring in any new business this month, and the danger lights were already flashing.

If I lost this job, then I really didn't know what I would do.

And that is what really pissed me off!

I couldn't even pinpoint the moment when things had shifted. Yes, back when I had been my own boss, making lots of money, there had been that one deal that fell through. I had invested a lot of time into it, assuming that it was a done deal. But I'd had other contracts in place.

I was almost a failure due to my own success. I was doing so well, then suddenly I was working on too many contracts at once. Time was running out on them, and there just wasn't the ability to hire and train other people. I had gotten too big too quickly. I had been greedy. I had agreed to all business, and

A Cold Retreat

pretty soon I was agreeing to contracts with a turnaround of six weeks whilst working on another four similar contracts. I became blinkered, blinded by the profits and potential earnings without fully appreciating the financial penalties for failure.

I had been unlucky that I had missed the deadline to the first one by a couple of days. However, the company had decided that they would sue me for breach of contract, and again, instead of just paying up, I had chosen to fight the case. It wasn't the financial costs that crippled me, but the excess time that I then became obsessed with. This had put me behind on another contract, and then there had been the snowball effect that eventually forced me to close and file for bankruptcy.

This had been the final straw for Chanelle, who had been happy to turn a blind eye and remain ignorant of my philandering, but the embarrassment and social bubble-burst of bankruptcy had been too much for her. When I broke the news to her over dessert at the exclusive restaurant *The Pear Tree*, she had excused herself to visit the restroom and had never returned. Even today, I struggled to eat a crème brulee with the same gluttonous gusto as before, without a wave of nausea unexpectedly washing over me like a creamy tsunami.

So, an hour into the day, I had a couple of leads that I was following up on, but I had lost my enthusiasm. Sales for another person lacks the motivational pull when you work on a percentage rather than for the whole profit. I was still struggling with this. I was an IT programmer and designer; I was not a salesman.

I let my phone ring twice before answering it. We had the three-ring policy, so I would always pick it up at the very last minute. This was what seemed to be one of the few areas that I could still control. Small wins and all that.

"Hello?" I said, trying to muster up something that could be construed as enthusiasm. "Travis speaking, how can I help?"

"I saw your ad," a confident female voice said. "About website designs?"

"Yes, we offer a professional service at an amateur price," I replied. It was a corny patter but one that had been advised to us as a good response. I used it in a slightly sarcastic way with humour, and I think it sounded better than if you tried to be completely serious.

"Really?" I could picture the grin as she said it. I also began to picture the rest of her, and suddenly I was able to find and open the box of charm that I

A Cold Retreat

had shut away inside at the same point that my pride had left town.

She went on to explain that she was the owner of a small Bed & Breakfast business looking to join the twenty-first century with a full all singing-and-dancing website. I assured her that this was exactly what we were the market leaders at, and in fact, when singing, we hit notes others couldn't whilst our dancing produced flare without missing a beat of the rhythm.

"Very good," she replied, clearly impressed with me.

"We like to think so!" We then had a little tennis match of ideas back and forth, as she served me a couple of fast backhands, and I was able to volley them straight back.

"Look," she then said as we were finishing up, "why don't you come and spend a weekend here, and we can discuss what we need. Business is so much better when done face-to-face. Don't you agree?"

Uncharacteristically I paused and actually felt myself turn around and look to see if anyone else was listening. This was an ethical tightrope. It was a benefit being offered by a potential client, so technically that was okay. Had I been the one to offer her the free weekend accommodation, then this could have been seen as bribery and/or a conflict of interest.

I agreed and sent her my details. She mentioned that she belonged to a group on Facebook in the B&B sector and that if this went well, it would guarantee more than a dozen other requests. They would all go through me, of course.

This was too good to be true.

In two weeks' time, I would be staying there. Of course, what I didn't know was that this was not about the weekend. This would affect me for the rest of my life.

Chapter 25

Sasha – A week ago

My head pounded like a wine-induced hangover the day after a girl's night out.

I was naked and cold. He had not even bothered to put my underwear on this time.

As I lay on my back, tears welled and then escaped from the corners of my eyes and trickled down almost into my ears. I went to rub them and realised that one eye was bruised and puffy. That made me sob like a child. I was rendered helpless, and yet he had still felt the need to hit me. What sort of an animal would do that?

I tried to sit up, but all my muscles screamed for attention. Down below, I felt as though I had been completely and utterly used and abused. I was sitting in a pool of blood that was now tacky to the touch. I felt stretched and ripped.

It dawned on me about the same time as I saw the writing on the walls, the words smudged in my own blood:

I AM THE MASTER!!!

This was no longer sexual. I had never thought that I would long for that to be the motivator in this. But the good and bad thing about a sexual deviant is that sex and power are connected and, in the same token, last for the period of the act. The obvious downside to this is that behind the abuse is a desire fuelled by excitement. Excitement wanes through familiarity, and so when the object of desire is no longer desirable, then they are no longer of use. For somebody who has been kidnapped or held against their own will to no longer be an object of desire, means that they are now a risk and a liability, so they must be gotten rid of immediately.

The writing on the wall may well have been my death warrant. I had to do something because this was more than likely the last time I was to be sexually abused. The next time I was attacked, it would be in order to take my life.

I hobbled to the window and looked out.

I could see the handyman again. He was working on the pond, cleaning something. I banged on the glass. If he would just look up… If he would see a battered and distressed naked woman, then maybe he could raise the alarm.

"Hey!" I shouted. My throat was sore and raw. It was almost impossible to form words to start with. "Help!"

A Cold Retreat

He worked on, transfixed with his current job, unaware that whilst he made everything beautiful on the outside of this place, on the inside, something ugly and evil was happening.

He stopped and looked back at the house. For a second, he glanced up, and I thought that he had seen me. He even shaded his eyes with his hands. But he was determined to finish his job, perhaps also forced by Leonard too.

I was determined too. I banged again and again until my palms hurt.

But then he packed up his wheelbarrow and walked away towards the outbuilding.

Exhausted, I almost slipped down to the floor but instead made it over to the bed. I had to rest and take stock of the situation. I had been blindsided, but now I had to be ready.

I gave myself a good ten minutes of rest where I tried to completely relax. I used all of the breathing techniques that I had learnt through yoga, Pilates, and meditation. It was incredibly hard to clear my mind when, deep down, I knew that I had to remain alert. Relaxation and alertness was a fine oxymoron.

I used the pillows to cover the air-vents, pushing furniture up against them. It was by no means airtight, but it might give me a few seconds extra to try something else.

As before, a sudden wave of anger grew up inside of me, and I felt humiliated that I was in this predicament.

And then I heard the door unlock…

Chapter 26

Dex – A week ago

It had been a funny few days for me. Yesterday, I had met a girl in Devon whilst parked in a secluded car park in the sand dunes. She had been one hell of an attractive girl who had been more than a little flustered when I opened up the van without my shirt on. I liked to live a nomadic lifestyle travelling around in my campervan and pretending that I was a surfer. I was not. I was far from it.

For some reason, I had told her that. It was something I almost never did—spoiling the illusion that I'd built. I might have looked like a surfer, but the truth was that I was more like a slightly below average body-boarder than a surfer. I could just about get up onto a surf board once in every twenty attempts, but after an hour of swallowing salty water and rubbing burning eyes and shoulders that feel like they may give up on me, I would come back onto the shore and hang out at some beach-café. The great pretender. I think Queen wrote a song about that once.

Jim Ody

I grew up in Swindon and for a while worked in a large corporate company wearing neatly pressed white shirts and sensible ties, but the truth was, I had hated every minute. My only release had been the band that I played in, but that was just a little fun. Our singer Marco had been the only one who was serious about making it big, and it wasn't long before he had moved to London. I heard that he had at one time had a solo record deal, figuring he was some sort of Billy Idol-type radio-friendly rocker, but like most serious musicians with any talent, he was dropped due to poor sales—or more likely a lack of promotion and marketing from a record label that was only interested in funding their own established cash-cows. That had been in the early stages of social media, so Marco was just slightly before his time. He had gone on to have a couple of small parts in musicals, but the last I heard, he had managed to get a name for himself writing catchy songs for up-and-coming boy-bands. I guess that's success.

I had been known to still play the odd gig on my guitar with friends in small cafes, but it was for entertainment and impressing girls rather than for any income.

I was lucky to have inherited some money, and whilst I had wanted to travel around America, my

A Cold Retreat

mum had talked me into investing it. I think she had in mind property that I could gain an income with, but I had put it all into my mate's surf-shack, a place that sold surf gear and also offered burgers and drinks. The business model meant that we could turn over a steady profit stream, via the food, to help us with the up and down of the surf-gear.

My mate, Slam, designed and built surfboards & skateboards, and these over the last year had begun to sell really well—in part to their quality and cool designs, but mostly because two locals had begun to win tournaments in their respective fields whilst sporting the brand: Stevie Valentine in the surf and Omar DeShante on wheels. Slam had looked past the graffiti and shop-lifting of these two mouthy punks when he had seen just how good each was, and he had given them free equipment. If nothing else, it had stopped them from stealing ours. This, of course, was nothing new, as skate kids especially had been signing brand endorsements for years over in the States. Nothing sold a product as well as a winner wearing your gear and holding your board whilst grinning with a trophy.

I started making burgers and pouring coffee, then moved onto a bit of local sales and promotion before wandering around the coast increasing the reach of promotion. This mostly led to hanging out shooting photographs and dating women.

I was scared to commit to a relationship. This had happened early on in my life (I was eighteen) when a girl called Cindy declared her love for me one day and then left me the week after. I had already begun to think about a perfect proposal idea, some huge set-up to declare my love. I had been thinking so long term that you would've needed a time machine to see just where my mind was at. I had been past the wedding day and the two-year anniversary. I had been past the birth of our first child. It was ridiculous to think about this now, but I had fallen hard for this girl—so hard that I had been unable to pull myself back up for years.

I had fallen into a pattern of meeting a girl and instantly becoming friends. The first few weeks would be special, and then I would need to move on with nothing but my mind's Polaroids to remember them by. I had driven around Norfolk, then Suffolk, Sussex, through Dorset, then cut up and around Wales, and then back down through Devon and Cornwall. Now I was heading north again.

Each relationship felt special, but I was careful never to get too close. I made a lot of friends and had a really good time.

A Cold Retreat

But then things had almost changed, and I had nearly stayed in Falmouth with a hippie called Moon, a beautiful woman of mixed race who painted portraits and enjoyed yoga. She had improved my surfing and helped me to forget about the taste of the sea water and the burning of my eyes. It was ironic, that the one I had loved the most had been the easiest to leave behind. She could look deep into my soul and see exactly what I was thinking. Then, one day, before I could mention my plans, she had held out her hands for me to hold. She looked away for a second, and then when she looked back, through tears she loudly whispered, "You need to go, don't you?" I had nodded, feeling the lump in my throat with the finality of the scene hitting home hard.

"It's what you have to do. Follow your heart…" She kissed me on the cheek, then said, "You'll be back one day."

That was really hard, but somehow, I had felt that I had her blessing. I left the next day.

That was a month ago. I had stopped off in Devon for a few weeks and was going to head back up to Swindon. My mum had been ill for a while, and whilst I popped back up every few months, watching the difference each time was too much. She was angry at how she felt I had squandered my money, and each visit was less than pleasant. She had died six months ago, and whilst I had been back for the funeral, I was heading home to finally clear her house. I had put this off for too long. It was a job that needed to be done, but my feelings for Moon had been too strong for me to leave her. And now? *Maybe I needed a break.*

It was not going to be an easy thing. Clearing out the possessions of someone who has died is heart wrenching. They may've stuffed something in the attic meaning to send it to the tip, but now you come across it and assume that there is some deep sentimental value in keeping it, and not just pure laziness. But then there are the things that will bring tears to your eyes—trophies, medals, wedding dresses, pictures, these things that have been put here for safekeeping—and now you have to decide what to do with them. Nostalgia and pragmatism locking horns to see who will win for every single item, meaning that the task will take weeks rather than hours.

I didn't have anywhere to stay, but I thought I'd worry about that later on. I was driving a campervan after all.

The girl in the car park had been nice. I would be lying if I said that I hadn't fleetingly thought about her in a sexual way, but she wasn't buying my

A Cold Retreat

bullshit, and had taken off, and I think that was the best thing for everyone involved.

I then saw someone looking to hitch a ride. It was strange, but when it was a female, I always thought I must give them a lift just in case the next person to stop was an axe-murderer.

She was bouncing around, and all I could notice was her dark top and brightly-coloured tights under denim shorts. There was something about her that made me think she might be fun.

I pulled over and she jogged up to the van, her breasts jiggling like slightly deflated water balloons.

"Goin' north are yer?" she said loudly in an Irish accent.

"Yeah," I said. "Hop in."

"Ta very much. Name's Kim, if yer were wonderin'."

"Hi. I'm Dex."

"Really?" she asked, then added excitedly, "Yer wouldn't believe what has happened to me, so you wouldn't!"

"Probably not," I replied, thinking that perhaps this had been a mistake.

"I can't say though." She made an action of zipping her mouth shut. *Oh, if only*, I thought.

I nodded and slowly pulled out onto the road.

"Even if I did tell, yer. Yer'd think I was a crazy bitch!"

"Are you?"

"Cheeky fucker!" She slapped me playfully on the arm.

We drove for a good five seconds before she felt the need to break the silence once more.

"I was heading south yesterday. I thought that it would be good."

"Not turn out that way?"

"People around here are fuckin' loonies! Fuck me, matey, they are." I could see her twirling a pointed finger around the side of her head in the universal "idiot" gesture. "Cuckoo!" she added for effect. She didn't need to. I wasn't one of them.

"Ah ha."

"Do you come from around here?" she then asked, but not in a tone that sounded like she was worried about my feelings.

"No, Swindon," I said.

"Fuckin' 'ell, not much better, so I heard!" She grinned.

I took a deep breath. I'm not sure why. I was always a little protective of my birthplace.

"And what have you heard?" I tried to say without feeling.

A Cold Retreat

She nudged me, which caused me to swerve and almost kiss the central reservation of the dual carriageway. The Peugeot that I was overtaking suddenly disappeared in my rear-view mirror, having braked suddenly in fear of my suddenly erratic driving behaviour.

"Testy, fucker!" She laughed. "High teenage pregnancies is what I heard!"

"That was from some study in the late 90s, which I'm not sure had any truth. It's probably some rumour started by someone from Oxford."

"Why Oxford?"

"Never mind," I replied, not wanting to get into the discussion of football rivalry with her or indeed in a discussion about anything with her. It seemed that she had a lot to say about everything.

"Be like that then," she said, and I secretly hoped that she was going to give me the silent treatment.

This time the silence lasted almost two minutes before she mumbled, "Seriously, you would not believe what I have just witnessed."

I turned on the CD player and let Brian Wilson sing about Good Vibrations. God only knew that we needed some of them in here…

Chapter 27

Dex – A week ago

"Yer thinking of stopping anytime soon?" Kim asked. "We could change the music too."

"To answer your first question: yes, I can pull over at the next services or even at the side of the road here, if you want?"

"Nah, I can wait. I have a bladder like a steel drum, but it's been like seven hours since I pissed, so not wanting to clean your upholstery, it might be nice to stop."

"Sure."

"And the music?"

"You don't like The Beach Boys?"

She hesitated. "I mean, they're like, okay, right? But it's been a while that we've been listening to…what's this, their greatest hits or something like that?"

"Or something like that," I said, fighting hard not to roll my eyes. There was something about her that I felt was incredibly annoying. Maybe I was being sensitive over going home, being unsure at what I

A Cold Retreat

wanted in life, the emotions that would flow when I cleaned out my mum's house, or Kim's jab at Swindon and now messing with musical legends like The Beach Boys seemed too much. I'd always liked them, and they appealed to me for everything that they were. A band that sang a lot about surfing but never surfed… shit, that was me to a T. Sure, I went out once in a while on a board, but it was for show, for a slice of lifestyle specifically cut out like a desire from a magazine or a clip of beauty from Pinterest. The band knew that people would lap up songs revolving around sun, surf, and girls. These were three of my favourite things…

"So what else have you got?" She not only snapped me out of my reverie, but kicked down the door to my log cabin and fired a shotgun at my tranquillity.

I took a deep breath—twice—and then pointed to the glovebox.

"In there is a selection of CDs."

She popped it open and greedily grabbed the CDs like they were muffins. "Let's see…"

She flipped through the sleeves of discs, making noises like she was suffering from indigestion. "You holding these for someone…? Like your granddad?"

"Eh?"

"Johnny Cash, The Kinks, Mamas & Papas, Joni Mitchell…and who the fuck is Conway Twitty?"

"Underrated."

"Undiscovered, I'd say! Fuck, at least there's some Aerosmith. Let's put that on before me hair starts to fuckin' fall out!"

She remained fairly quiet for the first song but then suddenly piped up to "Walk This Way."

"Where's Run DMC?"

"This was the original," I said.

"Without Run DMC?"

"Correct."

"Feck off! White boys rappin' before their time, eh?"

"Something like that."

"That's the name of The Beach Boys album we were listening to, is it not?"

I glanced over just in time to see her grinning.

"Good one," I said in a way that suggested it was good for a three-year-old and not a grown woman.

The rest of the song played out, and I can only wonder to myself why I decided to engage in conversation with Kim. Perhaps I felt sorry at the fact that she appeared to need to talk constantly, and so I was denying her these simple human rights by remaining a silent witness to her.

A Cold Retreat

"So why are you moving around?" I asked, putting down the can-opener to the tin of worms that I had undoubtedly just opened.

"It's a long story, Dex, my man."

"Don't tell me—I wouldn't believe you if you told me?"

She seemed to chuckle to herself and then uncharacteristically seemed pensive before saying slowly, "Nah, this one's a little different. I'm a little worried that yer might just kick me out if I told ya."

I nodded, keeping my eyes on the road in front of me. There were a million images flying through my mind's eye—everything from the amusing and the bizarre to the reckless and the criminal. Looking at her, and the mouth that was on her, it really could have been anything.

"How about I promise that I take you at least to the services?"

"So you'll still kick me out?"

"I never said I would kick you out. All I'm saying is that if I feel that it's a risk riding alone with you, then I reserve the right to decline to take you any further on your journey."

"Still sounds like you're kicking me out."

"Nope. Not true. Go on, shoot."

And so she told me exactly why she had been hitching a lift for the past three weeks all around the country. What she told me left me with an open mouth and unable to wonder exactly what it was that was sitting next to me. She almost looked at me as someone to help her, but had concluded that perhaps I was not quite the one.

She had been through a lot, more than most people would ever see in movies let alone experience themselves. She stopped at the point of going to Huntswood Cove. She said that not even I would believe what had gone on down there.

By the time she reached the part of the story where we met, we had been parked up in Exeter services for twenty minutes. She had been through a lot. That wasn't even including what she described as the most unbelievable thing. She glanced at my face and my lack of words.

"It's been a fuckin' ride alright!"

I nodded. "You... *Blimey*, is all I can say!"

We both got out and used the toilets. She was relieved (if you'll pardon the pun) that I was waiting for her when she came out. We got coffees and snacks and silently walked back to the van.

I idly checked my emails whilst still thinking about what she had said.

Then I noticed that one of the B&B's I had enquired about had come back to me. I found it in my SPAM folder and responded straightaway.

A Cold Retreat

Oddly enough, they said that due to a promotion they would give me two nights for free! Money wasn't a massive issue for me, but it was always nice to get something for free.

Using all of my dexterity skills with big fingers on small phone keys, I tapped out a positive reply, every now and then having to go back and change the word that the predictive text decided to amend for me, and then pressed send.

"Looks like I have free accommodation." I grinned and instantly felt like the biggest fool. "Shit, sorry... I wasn't thinking."

She nodded and waved dismissively. "No matter. Not your issue."

"You can come too, you know?"

She winked. "I probably could... but I won't..." she paused and looked far off out into the car park where a family was clearly shouting at each other and flapping their arms. The joys of being crammed into a car together.

She then said, "I've got a plan." But it didn't seem like she was going to tell me what it was.

Kim sipped at her fancy coffee and ripped the cellophane off of her newly purchased CD.

We pulled out of the car park with Katy Perry singing loudly for all to hear. I still felt like the world's biggest arse, so I suppose karma was in full effect…

A Cold Retreat

Chapter 28

Christian – A week ago

The feel of the cool beer as it hit my mouth was a wonderful thing. The sun was shining brightly, which was a beautiful thing for most, except for those of us who worked outside.

"Terry! Go get the ladders and pack up the van," I shouted to my apprentice. We were working on the grounds of a wonderful old country house called Caulfield Hall. It was set back from the main road with a boathouse and large lake behind.

Sometimes it was hard to work when the large house with its great tower stood there almost beckoning me to come inside. It certainly made a change from the usual gardens on housing estates or council land that needed tidying up.

This place seemed like it was full of history. I couldn't help but wonder what life might've been like if things had turned out differently.

"Chris? You gonna stare at that place all afternoon, or are you coming to the pub?" Jack called. I turned to see him grinning at me whilst Terry struggled with the ladders.

"Tough one." I winked but pictured the landlady Gaynor, a woman that promised so much and delivered fuck all. We'd had something of a flirtation for a few weeks now, and I was beginning to think that this was just a game to her. It had been a while since my marriage had broken down and my ex-wife Nina ran off with the kids. I say kids, but they were adults now and had moved out a while ago. But she had convinced them that I was a bastard and she was Mother Teresa, so they had slowly forgotten that they once had a dad.

So all I had was my landscaping and grounds clearance job, which had proved to be successful. I had been a fireman once. I was also an adulterer and part-time bastard. I didn't mean anything by it; it just seemed that I was often swayed by female attention. It was ironic now when you think that I struggled to get any of that now. I guess I had lost my mojo. I was never James Bond, nor Austin Powers for that matter, but of late I had turned into a bachelor. Not a Hollywood playboy bachelor like Jack Nicholson or Warren Beatty, but that lonely, slightly-given-up-on-life bachelor.

We pulled up outside of The Pig In The Blanket pub and, through lines of banter, rolled inside.

A Cold Retreat

"Lock up your daughters!" Gaynor said loudly in her West Country accent. She was just past forty and had a husband somewhere, although we had never seen him. She wore a shirt with a couple of buttons undone to show a cleavage that was plentiful. Her dark-red hair was swept back and held tight by a large silver clip.

"Hi, Gaynor," I said, suddenly feeling confident. "Usual, please."

"And for yer workers?" She nodded, knowing that I would pay for them too.

"Tap water." I winked.

"Golden tap water it is," she replied, tapping the local cider brand. Then she looked at Terry. "And the young lad, he'll probably want a glass of milk, yeah?"

Terry blushed a warm shade of red, something he did a lot around Gaynor. "I'll have one of them too." He nodded and bowed his head almost in shame.

"You will, will ya?" Jack and I both laughed.

A few minutes later, we were all sitting down in the corner just far enough away from the darts board to be in relative safety of some of the locals' wild, moonshine-induced miss-throws. These were legendary. Two windows, one television, and a cat had all at some point fallen victim to a pair of old boys who should probably have known better, but probably couldn't have cared less. Gaynor took pity on them—which is more than could be said of the cat owner who refused to bring her cat out to the pub until they apologised. The old codgers had more chance of being picked for Swindon Town that coming Saturday than she had of receiving any form of apology.

I had given up on any romantic notions with Gaynor a while ago. Sometimes you get the feeling about people, and she was of the sort that, if she flirted with you, then this was actually a sign that she was *not* interested. I knew this because she did this to me all of the time. However, a couple of days ago some new guy waltzed in, and suddenly her brash loud comments had packed themselves off somewhere and she was suddenly all sweet small talk and blushes.

Sometimes you have to just be honest with yourself.

And this was the reason that I was fumbling with my phone.

I was new to this technology lark. I didn't mean a phone—I was quite capable at using one of those, as long as it was for phone calls or text messages. Finally, I had decided that, since I had grown up in a time that went from typewriters to computers and

A Cold Retreat

memos to emails, there was no reason why I couldn't now surf the net on my phone.

It had taken some getting used to, I can tell you. The screen was small, and my fingers were big. I found myself looking around at other people and wondering just how they moved their digits with such dexterity and precision, whether it was two hands balancing the phone on ring and little fingers whilst thumbs sprinted over the screen or the single pointy-finger digit pecking away like a chicken with ADHD.

"'E's on it again!" Jack said, nudging Terry and spilling his pint. "Careful, lad."

"I'm just looking," I said. I couldn't help it. I had to check to see whether she had replied to me. I'd started chatting to this girl online—woman, I should say. Her name was Penny, and she looked really cute. We hadn't met yet, but we had both hinted on it, so it was only a matter of time.

"Is that Tinker, or whatever it's called?" Jack grinned.

"Tinder," Terry mumbled.

"Tinder? Oh, right. So what do you know about this Tinder then, Terry-lad?"

Terry shrugged. It was in a way that said he knew a lot but wasn't sure how much he should admit.

"Come on," Jack pushed. "Don't be shy."

"It's not Tinder," I said, but this fell on deaf ears.

In a small voice, Terry said, "It's where you find women and stuff."

"And stuff, eh? What, like jump-leads?"

"No. Just women."

"Just women?"

"And men."

"Just women and men? Hmmm?"

I looked up. "Why are you repeating everything he says?" I looked back down to my emails and saw that she had sent one. Jack responded with something that made him laugh, and Terry also sniggered, but I couldn't multi-task, so it was lost on me.

She wanted to see me this coming weekend. Not only that, but she had booked a hotel nearby. My pulse immediately quickened. I pictured her, or rather, the two pictures of her that I had seen. In my mind the two-dimensional pictures came to life, my imagination filling in the blanks of what I couldn't see.

I didn't know what else was said then. I didn't care.

I couldn't wait for this weekend.

I really couldn't wait.

Chapter 29

Sasha – A few weeks ago

Outside of the windows clouds moved silently with the wind, birds sung songs that I couldn't hear, and the colourful flowers in the garden teased me, hinting at their beauty but too far away for me to know except from memory.

I had hope deep inside of me growing like an unborn child, and I tried to build myself up with strength and optimistic thoughts so as not to miscarry. This was the difference between survival and dying. The moment you are resigned to losing, that is the moment a part of you dies. I had to remain focused. I had to get into that combat mindset of a soldier captured. You had to know that the chance of survival was slim, but every extra moment was a bonus and built up your positivity. This was no place to be sensitive. I had to switch off my emotions, compartmentalise everything into pragmatic actions, not dwelling on the situation or long-term regrets.

Jim Ody

My heart leaped as I heard the door unlock. I was still naked but felt no need to cover myself up. He had seen me like this before and taken full advantage of me, so to cover up now would tell him that I needed to be covered. I had to dig deep.

When he looked at me, I saw the register of surprise in his eyes that I was still naked.

He shuffled in with the tray.

"Hands behind your back," he said sternly.

"It's okay," I said, a little upbeat. "I'm not going to do anything." He ignored me as the door closed behind him and walked over to the bedside table.

"I mean... What would be the point?" I said, suddenly aware that I was babbling. This could be a sign of misdirection, so I stopped.

He clipped my wrist in the handcuff and fastened it to the bed. He let out an audible sigh and then said, "What do you mean?"

"We both know that the gas didn't properly knock me out, right?"

He remained silent, his eyes darting back and forth between mine. He was trying to look deep inside me, trying to determine the lies and exactly what I might be up to. He still remained completely in charge of me, but a flicker of doubt was now evident. This is how you dent strong armour. Such over-confidence must be reined in. Allowing his

A Cold Retreat

over-confidence had not produced the mistakes that I had first thought, so now I had to change tactic.

"I've never had that done to me before...and so well! You must've realised how much I was enjoying it too?"

He gulped, a clear involuntary signal of the body that he was on his back foot.

"You do know how good that felt, right?" I pushed again.

"I...I know what I'm doing," he said in a small voice. It was hard to detect what else was there, but there was something. Was he excited? Was he disappointed? Was he confused? Was he all of these?

The biggest issue, of course, was the endgame. What was this all building to? I knew what mine was, but I was a long way away from that.

Did he even know?

"When are we going to do it again?" I asked, and it took everything I had to bury the natural feelings that I had. My stomach dropped, and a lump tried to form in my throat as a flash of my predicament washed over me.

"I dunno." His eyes looked around the room, like he was nervous that I had set up a trap.

"Why not right now?" I said softly and laid back on the bed as far as the cuffs would allow me. I slowly opened my legs wide, even though they still stung and my muscles ached.

"Can't," he replied, embarrassed, and scuttled away, fumbling with the lock. Then he was gone.

At such a time of great despair, that was one hell of a victory.

The problem now was what he would do next. This game of chess might have been fun if we were two strangers in a bar, but being held captive by someone and then making a move that made him embarrassed and nervous could very well prove detrimental to my health and well-being. He would be sitting down somewhere mulling over his next move, and it could well be murder.

I was yet to fully understand his mind and motivations. He had been caught many times with actions of intent, and this told me that he enjoyed risk without fear of repercussion. He also liked the idea of power. Whether that was in general or over a woman remained to be seen. If I now became a willing participant, then this might make me a real turn off. You couldn't force someone to do something that they already wanted to do themselves. I would no longer be a challenge or exciting.

The flipside of this might be that he would not bother with gassing me or drugging me, so I might

A Cold Retreat

be coherent enough to fight back. Or for ease, he might gas or drug me to make it easier to kill me. I had to accept that I might have decided my own fate.

I wandered over to the window again. Would this be my only ever view of the outside world now?

He will not beat me.

This mantra repeated through my mind over and over.

He will not beat me.

He would not beat me.

Chapter 30

Ben – A week ago

I was glad to be a foreman now. This was about as managerial as you could get whilst still dipping your toe in so to speak. A few years ago, I had suffered a slipped disc, and I'd had to start going easy on carrying heavy items. I hadn't of course, and this meant that many days I would end up being laid out on a hard floor or visiting a chiropractor.

I had to smile at that—how misfortune could turn into fortune, and because I thought I was still young enough to carry two-dozen bricks further than I should on my shoulder.

I smiled at the receptionist, who politely showed me to my seat in the waiting room. I was expecting the chiropractor to be a knuckle-cracking butch woman who enjoyed inflicting pain on alpha-males whilst spinning some tosh about how it was helping. What I got was an attractive middle-aged cougar who was gentle, for the most part, and forceful and painful when she needed to be—apologising each time.

A Cold Retreat

It was very hard not to fall in love with someone laying their hands on your near-naked body when they looked like that. Unfortunately, she was happily married. She told me this when I asked her out for a drink. I fully expected *"professionalism"* and *"not wanting to mix business with pleasure"* lines, but instead, as I was buttoning up my shirt, she simply replied, "Under other circumstances, seeing you button you shirt up might be a pleasurable thing, or even disappointing, but currently I am happily married. I certainly have no plans to change that." It was by far the best knock back that I had ever received. I was thankful that the receptionist did not hold these same thoughts and agreed to come out for a drink later.

And so it began that every week I would meet Tilly the receptionist and we would go out for a drive or a meal, but ultimately end up back at her place going at it like teenagers. Well, she was only twenty, but I was now the wrong side of forty and struggling to change my ways.

I couldn't explain it, even when I tried. I had been with Bronwyn for more years than I could remember. She was everything to me, but she was *too* familiar. We were a train-wreck sometimes, but I thought there was this chemistry about us. It was not in the sense of romance that others talked about.

Jim Ody

It was not two chemicals coming together and slowly merging to produce a nice colour or smell. No, I was the potassium perchlorate, and she was aluminium powder, and somehow we ended up coming together and BANG! We produced a flash bomb explosion of either lust or hate.

The tender moments were rare, and maybe that was why I felt the need to get it elsewhere, but the passion of us was immense and intense. It was the stuff of movies: clothes ripping, feverish movements, a cardiovascular explosive workout ending in two sweaty and out-of-breath lovers.

But then I would go and say something wrong, or perhaps she would push me too far with a cutting remark, and we were suddenly shouting at each other and spitting out insults with sharp tongues and peppered expletives. We would split up. We would get back together.

So, Tilly was beautiful but young. This was something that I had always done. Bronwyn always remained the same to me. We grew together and accepted our changes, but I liked to have my cherry on top. And there had been plenty. I guess the only one that almost changed things was a girl called Penny. She had felt like more than a cherry on top. At times, I had felt like we were the ones in the

A Cold Retreat

relationship and I was being pulled back to Bronwyn by means of loyalty or routine.

I had spent a few lonely nights sitting with some bottles of Newkie Brown, weighing up both women. It had almost felt unfair that I'd had to decide. I was no psychologist, and this might have been me trying to make excuses for my actions, but honestly, letting Penny go was what had kept me seeking out other women whilst being with Bronwyn. I was, in a way, punishing her for making me choose her. It was completely unfair, and by no means a justification of my actions, but maybe I was saying: "*I chose you, so you have to let me do this.*" I didn't know sometimes. Maybe this was just all of my own bullshit. Maybe I was still that teenage boy that wants it all.

I didn't know how long I was going to carry on with this. That was the thing; I rarely thought long-term in relation to my girlfriends. After Penny, it had just been Bronwyn and me for almost a year. Then I had met Susie, a twenty-year-old finance clerk. We had dated for six months. Then I'd had a break for six months, and I met Gemma who was a Personal Trainer with bright red hair. She had also been twenty. Okay, so somewhere along the line I had turned into the Matthew McConaughey character Wooderson, from the movie *Dazed and*

Confused, kept back year after year at school and proclaiming in his strong Texan drawl, "I keep getting older, but the girls stay the same age!"

Maybe it truly was an homage to Penny. Or maybe I was full of shit, looking for excuses as to why I still liked to fuck twenty-year-olds but stayed with a woman that was my own age.

I had never wanted kids, but perhaps that would've stabilised the boat so to speak. If I was hankering after credit, then you could look no further than to say that, without kids, I could ultimately walk away whenever I wanted to, but I hadn't, and that should tell you all you need to know about my commitment to Bronwyn. Okay, so we were not married—or even engaged—but she had never once hinted that it was something that she would be wanting to do. We were both the products of broken homes, parents with failed marriages, so what sort of an example was that? We both had friends who had married and divorced.

I was sitting here with Tilly, looking at the lithe body, and there was that natural desire there, but I also knew that this was not for the long run. One of us, probably me, would get bored and move on.

She smiled at me as I sipped my wine. I then caught a glimpse of a lady at the bar with blonde shoulder-length hair and a figure-hugging dress.

A Cold Retreat

She was closer to my age, and for a fleeting moment, I hoped it was Penny…

Chapter 31

Ben – A week ago

The next day at work, everything that could go wrong did go wrong. One of the granite worktops fell from the delivery lorry and broke—an expensive mishap, and one that would put us back a day, as we couldn't finish fitting the kitchen without it. We were on a tight deadline, and I would lose a lot of money every day we missed that deadline. To add to this, it was pissing down with rain. Typical bloody British weather!

It was late before I left the site, which meant I would turn up back at home at the time I had told Bronwyn. The problem, of course, was that I had planned on dropping in on Tilly. It was her birthday, and I had bought her a gift. It's embarrassing to say now, but it was underwear. I didn't often buy underwear for women, but she was a great lover of things silky and expensive, and to her, new underwear was what shoes and handbags were to others. If I was honest, I had no interest in shoes or handbags. They all seemed similar to me.

A Cold Retreat

The same could be said about underwear, but it was the person wearing them that made them special, and Tilly had a body that suited them.

I dropped her a text, but didn't hear anything back. I assumed she was not happy that I was working late. I sent her another one in the afternoon, and she replied almost instantly. This seemed strange, and when I looked at our previous conversations on my phone, I couldn't find it.

And then I realised exactly what I had done. I had sent the text intended for Tilly to Bronwyn.

I stood around fingering my phone, unsure exactly what I should do, for what seemed like half an hour. Had it not been Tilly's birthday, I would've made my excuses and faced the music, but to not see her on her birthday would have felt like I was letting her down twice.

My phone buzzed. I looked at the sender and saw that it was Bronwyn.

You had better see her then if it's her birthday, was all it said.

I responded with **Okay x.** I knew the kiss was pushing things.

There was silence and then the buzz again. **Make sure you come home to me.**

And then a few seconds later, another text with a simple **x**.

Again, I thought maybe I was pushing my luck. What the hell did I think I was doing? She knew what I was like, but still allowed me to go and do these things that a normal person wouldn't. Maybe, deep down, this was what annoyed me. Surely she should care, right? I would go mental if I knew she was shagging other men. Yes, that made me a big fat hypocrite, I know that.

I grabbed my mug of tea. I was the king of excuses. Could I really convince myself that my infidelity was Bronwyn's fault? That was the skill of a master manipulator.

I didn't know. I couldn't answer these questions, because I had never before given them much thought. I'd not felt the need to dissect that good fortune from the gift horse.

Throughout the rest of the afternoon, I was wrestling with the dilemma of what I should do going forward. Tilly had always been mentally immature for me. Not against other twenty-one-year-olds, but against a guy over forty, her outlook on life was a lifetime away. She had not known a world without computers, satellite TV, or mobile phones. A band like Nirvana was seen as old fashioned, and to her, the two remaining members of the Beastie Boys looked like granddads. Our lives were growing further apart each day, and it

A Cold Retreat

was inevitable that the remaining sands of our relationship were heading rapidly for the neck of the timer.

I pulled up outside her flat. My heart beat faster, but it was out of desire rather than love. I skipped up the outside steps to her first floor flat and rapped lightly in the beat that I had made my own.

I heard the quick steps and the way she flung open the door with a grin and a squeal both saddened me and made me happy all at once.

I kissed her softly and handed over the flowers that were so hard to hide behind my back. Then I gave her the bag with her presents.

She took the flowers into the kitchen to find water and a vase, but her gaze was drawn to the presents more. I liked that about her. Finally, she looked into the bag, and her eyes grew big as she saw the flimsy fabric.

"Wow," she said, holding it on the hanger. "Shall I put it on now?" I shrugged but with a big grin. It was hard not to smile when asked a question like that.

And so she did. She looked fantastic, but as usual, the price seemed slightly pointless, as within minutes each item had been discarded onto the floor.

I would never see her wear those items again, but I would remember the vision for a long, long time to come.

The drive home that night was long. My heart beat hard as I left my van, but this time there would be little chance of desire or such a happy ending.

I walked into the house tentatively. Life with Bronwyn could sometimes be like walking along a beautiful Caribbean beach—one with many hidden landmines.

"Hi!" I called out, not so much in a salutation but to set a gauge at the response.

"Up here," was the slightly cheerful response. It felt like a trap. I don't know why, but it did.

I was tentative in my steps as I walked with caution up to our bedroom.

"There you are," she said. "You came back."

"Of course I did. Why wouldn't I?"

She dropped the covers slightly to reveal naked shoulders. "You still gonna see her?" she said seriously. It wasn't a warning, but it seemed like a question of general interest.

"I don't think so, Bron," I said, and that was the first time that I think that I actually meant it.

"Really?" She seemed surprised but dropped the covers even more to reveal the breasts that I knew so well.

A Cold Retreat

"We're always together, aren't we? Me and you, Bron. We're a team!"

She grinned and flung back the covers to reveal the rest of her naked body. "You'd better still have something left for me, or there will be trouble!" She winked, and I couldn't get out of my clothes quickly enough.

The difference in the two women was unbelievable. There was a large part of me that wanted them both. Sweet and sensual, and hard and passionate. They were polar opposites but gratifying in their own right.

The next day was not great. I hated to break up with people, but Tilly took it particularly badly. She was crying hysterically down the phone at me. Yes, I know I should've done it face to face, and honestly it was me taking the easy way out. It was me being sensible. If I had gone there, then there was no way that we would've had the talk. The minute we were together, my brain would've scrambled, and before I knew it we would be circling parts of each other's bodies with fingers and tongues. Then I would be left there in bed, guilt-ridden, whilst she freshened up. I would then actually be finding it hard to still do then, or I would go for round two. It was just the way things were.

So that was that. I then found myself scrolling through a few hotels I thought we could get away to. "Mess up someone else's sheets" was a phrase that Bronwyn had giggled a few times before when dropping hints.

I wanted to take her to the coast, maybe to Bournemouth or Weymouth, but money was tight at the moment until the project was completed.

I looked at the email that I had received a few days back for a local B&B twenty miles away. It wasn't exactly exotic, but they were doing some sort of promotion and said that I could stay there for free for a few days. This might be exactly what we needed to get back on track, even if it killed us!

Chapter 32

2014 - 2015

I felt like I was made from plasticine. Perhaps at one time, I had been a cute little child, adorable and innocent. Gradually, as I got older, I had become misshapen from being mishandled, dropped, and abused. I had picked up things that I could no longer get rid of. I was forever tainted. Now I barely represented something that was anything like the version of what I might have been if I had been loved and looked after.

I am not sure how it happened, but I had become friends with Pete. Our relationship was unorthodox, as we would rarely do couple things, but we would somehow end up together. We weren't exactly together, but we were something.

Sometimes I would go out on my own or with friends, and I would be kissing some guy, and then I would look over and see Pete. He would wink approvingly at me, and even if I didn't go over to him, eventually at the end of the night, we would leave together, slowly acquiring other people as we got back to his. They would just appear.

Pete and I would go off alone, and again, we would suddenly be joined by others. I cannot say I totally enjoyed it, but then I also cannot say that there wasn't an element of excitement to the whole thing.

There is a fine line between excitement and fear. Both strong emotions are built around the unknown. The lack of predictability is what raises our adrenaline levels and makes us feel alive. I am not saying that this is something everyone should try. It isn't. Not by a long shot. But it opened me up to some of the best sexual feelings I have ever had. But like all good things, you had to take this with the bad. I had no control over who joined us. There were considerable differences in the participants. It is shameful to say now, but some people appeared and had sex with me and left, and I am not sure I even knew what they looked like.

After a few months of this, I became depressed. The actual act and evening was okay. It was a rush and an experience. I was satisfying a number of men, and perhaps the odd woman, and it wasn't like they would kick me out naked and chuck my clothes from the door behind me. No, we would talk and chat, sometimes even watch a movie.

A Cold Retreat

But then I would make the lonely journey home. The taxi driver would look at me with sadness, assuming that I was a prostitute. Who knows, on some level, maybe I was?

I would get into my house and close the door. I would pop an anti-depressant and wash it down with vodka, and then I would cry.

I would cry for me, now, at what I had become, but mostly I would cry for the cute little girl who had clasped her dreams tightly in her tiny hands. She had looked into the future and seen only wonderment and excitement. She had travelled the world helping people, reading poetry, and making her parents proud. She had looked great and worn a smile with every outfit. She'd had a boyfriend, who turned into her loving husband and then a wonderful father. There was sunshine, dancing, and even when it rained, a huge rainbow arched overhead to remind her that if you looked hard enough, in everything you would see beauty.

But that little girl was the glass of milk that got discarded and left out too long in the sun. She ruined and went off behind the backs of those that should've been watching over her. The silent cries for help were ignored. The innocence within her escaped through sweat glands as she fought the weight of those on top of her, numbing her soul with each and every thrust, a sneer and grunt of a teenage boy's own selfish satisfaction, all at the expense of her ability to ever feel like anything other than a worthless whore.

For a while, I had felt special. I was the girl that attracted the men on the walk back to Pete's place each time. People would look and feel a desire towards me. I was a female magnet pulling men from any visual range, and they would follow like a lost puppy. This felt powerful. I almost felt like Eros, or some such love goddess.

Then one day, I had pulled myself out of the house to go to the cinema. I watched some cliché tripe about a girl that gets a guy after he firstly barely acknowledges her, then misses the opportunity, and finds that she is actually the love of his life. I forget what it was called, but there are about a dozen movies that fit this synopsis so let's not think too hard... So in the darkness with a coffee, I had sobered up (I'd been drinking all day on my own). The feel-good movie had done just that: recharging that small part of optimism in me that I had assumed had been traded-in carelessly for something that I had already forgotten about long ago.

I walked out, and I saw Pete. He didn't see me, but he was striding along with a pretty younger version of me, and behind him a better quality of hangers-on were evident. I was filled with jealousy and then envy, rage, disappointment, and finally a deep sadness.

It wasn't me who attracted everyone. It had never been me. It was Pete—who he represented. He was the God figure. I was the doe-eyed girl by his side that everybody fucked to make Pete happy. All of those people hadn't desired me. They had actually, on some level, desired Pete and what he represented. I had just been a stepping stone that they could lie on, poke, prod, and ejaculate with. I had been absolutely nothing to them.

Then they were gone, and I was left sobbing next to a group of teenagers who must've thought I was on drugs.

I almost ended my life that night.

But I wondered whether the only way to get my life back was to go through everyone and everything that had ever made it bad. It was drunken stupidity at best. I stopped at an off-license on the way home. The guy at first refused to serve me, thinking that I was on drugs, as I cried the whole time I was in the shop. He tried to usher me out, but at some point, I flashed a boob and he served me quickly, looking embarrassed and none too pleased with my bargaining techniques. I had stopped crying if nothing else.

I must've opened the bottle then, as the next thing I knew I woke up face-down in my own doorway. I had opened the door and passed out, not even shutting the door behind me. Surely someone must've seen me lying there? But not one person had ventured over to see if I was dead.

Over tea and toast (and throwing up) I began to make plans...

Chapter 33

Sasha – A few weeks ago

I ate up my food, conscious that it could be laced with poison or a sedative. I had to accept that my life was in the lap of the gods now. I had made my decision to push on and had to suffer whatever fate was handed to me.

The bread was surprisingly good. It was cut thickly from an unsliced loaf. You could tell this, as it started thick one end and was quite thin the other. I thought he must've cut this himself, as the part-time chef would never have made just a sloppy show of culinary skills no matter the simplicity of the task. I tried to second guess what this meant. It could mean anything. I could literally decide any outcome, good or bad, and make this scenario fit perfectly to it.

I drank my tea, which was strong but sweetened. It was lukewarm, and I assumed that this would never be scolding hot just in case I decided to throw it at him. I then wondered whether he had thought of this or whether it was just me with the abundance of spare time on my hands that would think such thoughts.

I sat back and looked ahead at the wall and door in front of me. I was a prisoner, except now I felt like I was awaiting a decision on my death. My usage was slim now, and we all knew that I was in a bad position. I had been held against my wish. I had been raped repeatedly. I had been abused, both physically and sexually, and I had seen his face. My chances of not being murdered were less than slim. I suddenly thought of a surprising fact that I had recently heard of: If you were involved in a plane crash, then the chance of you dying was less than 4%. I had a feeling that my chances of dying, over the next 48 hours, were somewhat higher.

I got up and put on my clothes. I was almost preparing myself for some sort of fight, and so I for one did not want to be doing this with pendulous tits and my arse out.

I felt lethargic, which was only to be expected. I had been here a couple of days now, with no fresh air or sunshine. It was easy to see how prisoners went mad. The restrictive nature of the room and the unknown future was incredibly demoralising. I was speaking more and more to myself as if I were now two people.

A Cold Retreat

This time, I had to be ready. As soon as I heard the door, I needed to be on him.
I sat and looked at the door and waited.
Focused and waiting.

Chapter 34

Sasha – A few weeks ago

At one point, I nodded off. I suddenly woke myself up with a start. I think my head had suddenly flopped over to the side. I gritted my teeth, determined that this would not happen again.

Hours must've passed. I started off in an almost meditative state. I may have even slept with my eyes open.

And then the door clicked open.

He came in slowly, tentatively, like he expected me to be hidden behind the door with an axe ready to behead him at the first opportunity.

"You've put some clothes on?" he said, a tinge of disappointment creeping in.

I smiled and tried to remain calm even though the adrenaline was pulsating through my body.

I stood as expected and then suddenly turned and threw the whole of my weight at him. He stumbled backwards unexpectedly, and I jumped and clawed at his eyes. He covered up, and I fell on top of him,

A Cold Retreat

my knees coming down with all of the force that I could muster onto his crotch.

I expected him to buck and throw me off like he was some UFC cage fighter, but instead, he howled and covered himself. I was left with a choice: fight or flight.

I wasn't going to run anywhere. I saw the weak spot in him. Whilst he had thought I might try something, in thinking that I was submissive and compliant, he had let his guard down. I had timed the attack perfectly. Was it luck? Maybe. But I had been left in a room with only my thoughts to imagine a way to get out of this. I had played out as many scenarios as I could, and really, as long as no gas was pumped into the room and Leonard came alone, there was a good chance that this would work. Yes, the probability and risks of failure were still too great, but to hatch the perfect plan would have been hard.

I punched him once and then twice in the face through his hands. I was possessed, swinging wildly at him.

But then suddenly what must've been an elbow caught me in the nose, sending a flash of pain through me, and my eyes watered. It was enough to lose my momentum. As a natural response, my hands flew up to my face. Suddenly I was falling sideways. I crashed down on my shoulder and felt his weight move on top of me. I clawed my fingers again in desperation, using all the knowledge I had researched for self-defence. As with everything in life, understanding the theory was one thing, but putting it into practise was completely different. Like with cage-fighters, when it came to grappling, it was essentially a physical game of chess—second guessing your opponent, getting them into a position that they could not get out of. Every single placement of a hand, arm, or leg completely changed the game plan. Hundreds of scenarios practised in slow motion, and then reactively at normal speed in the gym. And now I was following instructions only ever practised on a submissive instructor in a self-defence class I'd taken a few years back. And to be fair, this had been enough until I was struck in the face. The shock of the pain was disabling. It was not the first time that I had been hit in the face, but it was still a shocking experience.

He was then pinning me down, and I could feel my fight draining out of me. I half expected to see it pooling around my body.

Then the door burst open, and a figure charged in, knocking Leonard off of me. He swung

A Cold Retreat

something that made contact with almost a comedic clang.

As I looked up, the guy pounded Leonard with some sort of metal bar once, then twice.

He stopped, and I could hear his rapid breathing. He turned to look at me.

"Are you okay?" he said with real concern. I recognised him. It was the gardener.

I nodded, but I was struggling with what was happening. I was overwhelmed with emotions that I was unsure of. I was free. I was happy. I was surprised. I was tired. I was confused.

"I am so sorry. So, so sorry…" He turned around and helped me up. "I tried to get to you sooner…but… Look, I've been here for a year since I got out… He…he said that if I didn't do what I was told, then he would tell my probation officer and I would be back inside…" He showed me the door. "Let's go… After you."

Walking out of the door of my prison was too much, and I had to stop for a second as tears streamed out.

"Come on," he said. "Let's get you downstairs and get a drink or something. I nodded and took a deep breath. My legs felt heavy and tired as I almost stumbled down the stairs. He held out his hand to steady me.

It was such a long way down to the ground floor. We walked in silence, him knowing that I was struggling with things.

"I saw you," I said as we walked into the large kitchen, "out of the window."

He nodded. "I know. I couldn't look up..." He paused. "I didn't need to be cleaning out the pond. I just thought that if you were to look out then it might offer you hope. Y'know, to see someone."

"It did." I nodded.

"I'm Charlie, by the way."

"Hi," I said, although my voice was slightly more than a whisper. "I'm Sasha."

His head dropped in guilt as he replied, "I know."

He went over to the side and picked up the phone. "D'you want me to ring the police?" he said, but I could tell he didn't want to.

"What will happen to you if you do?" I said.

He shrugged and looked somewhat defeated. "I've killed a man. They won't care about the circumstances. I'm a criminal, so they'll just send me down."

"Why were you in prison?" I asked, it suddenly occurring to me just how important that was.

He pulled up a chair and gestured for me to sit in one of the others.

A Cold Retreat

"Causing Death by Dangerous Driving. It took me a while to be able to pronounce that correctly." He allowed himself half a smile at that. "My girlfriend had dumped me. I was completely distraught. I just never saw it coming. I… er… I took some pills, a few actually, and went for a drive. I stopped at a pub and had a couple…only a couple, but I suppose, mixed with the pills, it messed my head up. I got into the car thinking that all I had to do was guide the car home and I would be okay.

But at some point, I went for the brake and hit the accelerator and lost control of the car. I careened into a bus stop, injuring a young mother and killing an old man. I hit my head and was knocked out, which meant that by the time my blood alcohol level was taken, I was definitely legal—I might've been anyway…" He paused, and I nodded him on encouragingly.

"The barrister later used this to plant the seed that I was under the influence but pointed out that quite conveniently this couldn't be proven. Again, the toxicology reports were issued, pointing out the other things that were evident in my system, but again, there was nothing illegal. The conclusion was that I knowingly got behind the wheel having taken a concoction that could have had a bearing on my ability to drive, and whether it was this, tiredness, or the break up, my actions lost control of the vehicle and injured and killed someone."

"She meant that much to you?" I asked, although it sounded like more of a statement.

He nodded. "We were engaged. She'd been planning our wedding… It's just…" He appeared to choke up.

"Look, we don't have to call the police. He's dead now. I would have to go through all of this again with interviews… I just don't think I could do it."

"So…what now?"

I sighed. There were so many things running through my head. "I guess we go and bury the body."

He nodded. "Really?"

I shrugged. "What else can we do?"

"I guess that sounds like a plan."

Chapter 35

2016

I despised who I was. I had changed so much that I was unrecognisable from even my own memories. I felt like one of those women who change their appearances with surgery—subtly at first, smoothing out here, cutting, and plumping, but soon tightening, reducing, then masked in fake tan and make-up. Slowly the natural beauty is changed and hidden by press-on nails, sticky eye-lashes, and pencilled eyebrows into something devoid of character and resembling a generic woman fresh off the trend-fed gossip column production line. The lack of expression is evident with skin so tight that a smile is painful, making it hard to gauge their emotions. We only see a permanent grimace, which is deliberate, as not only is it the only expression, but ultimately how they now feel as they realise that after all the pain, suffering, and money spent, they actually feel no better about themselves.

I went back to Pete.

I tried to live normally. I flirted down the pub and in other clubs, but things were just not right.

Pete knew the magnetic charm he possessed. I could see why lost people got caught up in cults. He had that ability to make you do things without asking you to do them. He might suggest something, and before you questioned whether or not it was something you wanted to do, you were doing it.

I didn't know how he did it, but I was able to turn off my emotions. There were those who questioned why I was doing it, those common-sense voices that would tell me that I would be full of regret the next day.

The fact that I had come back to him told him that I was psychologically broken down. I would do exactly what he wanted. I needed him.

It was all completely backwards. When I was alone, I felt down. I felt completely regretful of what I had become. I was working in an office throughout the week, adding data into spreadsheets and databases, numbed into looking acceptable and programmed to act normal to get through the week. I needed that excitement. I craved the fear of what would happen to me. I was addicted, completely caught up within it, unable to see the wood for the trees anymore.

A Cold Retreat

I was living my own Fight Club *scenario, maybe more* Sex Club *or* Drug Club, *anything to get that pain to help me to feel something.*

I guess you could say I crashed. It was my version of overdosing.

I turned up at Pete's. No longer did I go through the whole charade of going out to a club for the evening first before joining the depraved and sordid human carnival floats as they waltzed back to Pete's expensive apartment. No, now I headed straight there, smudged make-up and laddered-tights. It didn't seem to matter.

Pete opened the door in mock surprise, which eventually became a look over my shoulder for fear of embarrassment. I sauntered in, a lustfulness building out of anticipation. But I was not taken to his bedroom. I found myself down the hall in another room, cuffed and blindfolded.

At first, the excitement of not knowing what or whom was touching me was almost too much, but the once-gentle, soft touch and the tickles of fingers tracing shapes lightly over my body gave way to strong, rough fingers scratching over my body sure to be leaving bloodied lines. The once-gentle breath on my neck that led to heavy breathing was now animal grunts. The tickles were now hard slaps that left my skin stinging.

Jim Ody

There was laughter from men and women as they verbally mocked me. I no longer wanted this. I was sore and felt like I might be bleeding. I was about to say something, maybe try and buck off the person that was currently inside me, when something very nearly suffocated me. A large, heavyset woman sat near my head. She draped herself over me, her size almost cutting off all of the air supply. The last thing I remember before I passed out was my body being shoved with each thrust and the rough lace material of her knickers on my lips.

I woke up cold. I was no longer handcuffed but still blindfolded. My tears dried but left black streaks down my cheeks towards my ears. I hurt everywhere.

Everywhere.

I struggled to get up, my arms and legs weak and my eyes adjusting to the light again. It took a while to find my underwear.

I left that morning never to return. I had been beaten, with large bruises and welts all over my stomach and legs. My breasts had teeth marks on them.

I got help the same day from a women's refuge. Even though I wasn't escaping from a violent lover, husband, or partner and I had a safe place to live, they helped to counsel me. For the first three weeks,

A Cold Retreat

I just wanted to leave this life. I had had enough. But they convinced me that life had more to offer.
  I was going to make it.

Chapter 36

Pete – A week ago

I had never really understood what the fuck life was all about, and more to the point, why so many people decided to moan about it. It was what you make of it, was that not what the old adage said? I was fed up with people whining and doing jack shit about it. What bloody idiots.

My parents were rich, that wasn't my fault. There had always been more than a suggestion that I was removed from normality due to this, my expensive education giving me an unwarranted advantage; which in many eyes, I had gone and thrown away. This, of course, was utter rubbish. Riddle me this, which scenario enjoys the fruits of life more: the man working all hours of the day so as he can retire early or the man living off his parents' fortune and partying like every day is New Year's Eve?

I'd never looked to be appreciated, nor had I sought the affirmation of popularity and acceptance of others. Ironically enough, my nonchalance was

A Cold Retreat

seen as some sort of swagger, and I was able to gain a number of followers and admirers. I was always happy to have people around me, so I never discouraged anyone from coming by. There had always been people here in my flat.

My flat was large and part of an expensive apartment building. My parents owned the building, and this was the largest and most extravagant flat, or maisonette actually, with its two floors and roof garden.

I was sipping my third gin of the day even though it was barely mid-morning. Two women were snuggled down under separate duvets on the large wrap-around sofa. Most of the others had left. I never know. I happily left the house with strangers still here. They would let themselves out, and they rarely took anything.

A guy with long shaggy hair walked in, buttoning up his shirt and yawning. "I can't remember anything, mate," he said.

"That's a good sign, my friend."

He nodded and smiled. "This your place?" he asked, looking around like it was the first time that he had laid his eyes on it.

"It is indeed."

"It's a beautiful place, mate. I don't remember much from last night, but I smell of sweat, sex, and alcohol, so I'm pretty sure I had a good time!"

"Yeah, you fucked one of these," I said, nodding at the sleeping beauties. I didn't know if he had, but it was more than likely.

"Really?" he said, impressed. He was good-looking, so it shouldn't really have been such a surprise. "You think they'd…um…wow!"

"You want me to find out whether they want a repeat performance sometime?" I chuckled. He was a first timer here, a child unleashed into the corner shop facing tubs of sweets for free. He liked the look of the sweets and wanted more.

"Would you?"

"I can do better than that. Come back here in a few days. They'll be here. It's inevitable. Serendipity."

"Yeah, okay."

"You hungry?" I asked. I always fed my guests.

"Sure."

"Go grab a shower, and I'll cook something up." He nodded and disappeared. He neither asked where the shower was nor about towels. He would find it all for himself. They usually did.

I felt something a little different. I think the cocaine had been cut with something different, or

A Cold Retreat

perhaps it no longer did it for me. Our bodies easily become immune to things and we crave stronger and stronger things, be it caffeine, sugar, alcohol, or drugs. We ignore the signs and increase the dosage until one day our bodies give out.

The pain in my chest started as nothing—wind or indigestion—but soon spread like a fiery heartburn, and with a tightness that felt like compression, I started to sweat.

I blacked out.

Voices spoke in the distance like a dream. Panic-fuelled chatter in higher-than-normal octaves. My body wriggling within itself. My clothing loosened. The sense of flying before being laid down.

Sirens and screeching tyres. Authoritative calm voices demanding things. Darkness.

A dream. A vivid dream about a girl covered in blood. Laughter and pointing. Blame and shame in my direction.

A house. A party. A doll with a missing eye and a red dress.

And then nothing...

Chapter 37

Pete – A week ago

I was in hospital for ten days. Apparently, I was lucky. During this time, not only did my heart almost fail, but I became sick through withdrawal from drink and drugs.

By the third day, my dealer came in to visit. He was caught trying to slip me some pills and quickly ejected from the premises by security. This wasn't an NHS hospital where you could wander in and out when you wanted. No, this was private. The same doctors and specialists worked here, but they were paid a lot more, and therefore you were considered of higher priority than others. No, it was not fair. But lying here, what was I going to do about it?

The thing with hospitals is that they completely screw up your routine. Worse still, you have extremely long periods of being on your own and thinking. I would try and charm the nurses, but this wasn't some teenage fantasy. The nurses couldn't have cared less about me. To them I was almost self-harming—knowingly consuming toxins and

A Cold Retreat

chemicals to fool my brain into thinking that I was no longer lonely.

I realised that I had missed out on a relationship, a single wholesome, romantic relationship. I had traded it for a hundred fleeting acquaintances inherently satisfying a need to be loved—the single thing that I thought I didn't need.

I had girls come and go. We would go out for meals, watch movies, and have sex, but nothing was exclusive. I had at some point chanced upon the life of a polygamist. I was never going to marry any of them, and I was happy that there was a production line of woman that came into my life in groups of three or four, stayed for six months, and then moved on. I couldn't speak for them, but I rarely felt any twinge of jealousy when other men had sex with them.

The men brought me company and male companionship, and I now realised that what they also did was stop me from feeling like I was Hugh Hefner or some other type of playboy that lived in a lavish domicile decked out in half-naked women. The men made it feel a little more normal and like a party.

Things had calmed down a little too. Years back, only one or two women would be around at any given moment, and back then, I had an army of disciples that followed my cash flow, laughing at my jokes, taking my drugs, and mostly just fucking my women. Some of the men had been animals. I couldn't condone all of the things that had happened, but neither could I deny that such things had gone on or scorn the acts. It was a free-spirit love that I promoted. It was harking on back to those hippie-love-fests of the sixties: sexual awakening, pushing boundaries, deviance, and decadence. Our parties were myths, and we attracted everyone.

But there were drug raids, and the odd negativity that seeped out of the top floor and dripped down into the poor society below, and soon numbers dropped. But I was still attracting two or three women at a time, and the men just moved on. They grew up. They got married. They gained a conscience. Whatever it was, it had made the place a little bit quieter and lonelier. I took more drugs. I drank more gin. I was filled with much more regret.

The scary part was the things that the drugs did to me. I was paranoid. I began to panic when surrounded by strangers. The touch of others raised my heart rate. Whilst in my own surroundings, I was happy to be part of strangers all over each other, but out in the real world, and fully clothed, I became unhinged.

A Cold Retreat

On buses and trains I would see faces—blurry and sinister, making me look away, but when I dared look back, they were gone. I also began to fear going into dark places, down into cellars, or even the London Underground. Perhaps it was horror movies or my drug-addled mind that now produced more thoughts of fantasy but with less rationale. A scary prospect.

It made you think of The Verve song with the Stones intro. It was a warning that, after a while, the drugs didn't work. The reasons for taking them were no longer relevant. What was once recreational and an added bonus, somehow developed into necessity and a sole need to have any ability to function. When a treat becomes a need, then something is wrong. And with flashes of faces that I could no longer distinguish as real, mixed with feelings of blind panic and the thoughts that something bad was going to happen to me, I was beginning to lose it big time.

So maybe the overdose was a blessing. Maybe my subconscious took control and forced me back to reality. But here I was.

At first it was just an email, addressed to me and looking legit. I dismissed it quickly as junk.

I had been offered a free weekend retreat, a chance to recuperate and fill my time with introspective meditation.

I mentioned it to one of the nurses on my last day, and she thought it was a very good idea. I wasn't sure.

"Go for it, and I might pay you a visit when you get back." She giggled. Her short hair was pinned up, which seemed a little pointless.

"A house call?" I smiled. She was a little sturdier than I was used to, but I was never one to turn anyone away.

"If you like." She waved as we exchanged numbers.

Fuck it, what did I have to lose? A few days in a countryside B&B. What was the worst that could happen?

A Cold Retreat

Part 3

Chapter 38

Sasha – Two weeks ago

I sincerely felt no remorse as we dragged the lifeless body of my captor down the stairs, through the back of the garden, and to the side of the old cowshed.

The fresh air felt wonderful as it tickled through my hair, a fine example of a simple pleasure in life that is taken for granted until it is stolen away from you. The outside world seemed clearer when fully immersed in it rather than through the smeared glass of an upstairs room.

"Are we going to bury him?" I asked, having not wanted to broach the subject earlier. The fact that we didn't have spades had made me wonder.

We slung down the body into a broken heap, then he replied, "Nah, that's too much like hard work. Believe me, I've had to do that before for him."

I should probably have suspected as much, but I had honestly thought that, until me, Leonard had only made a few improper advances—lecherous brushing from his hands on women's behinds,

A Cold Retreat

maybe even as far as trying to kiss them, but suddenly my stomach dropped as a memory exploded into my head: the face at the window saying "Help me". The reality of the situation hit me hard.

"So he's done this before?" My voice was flat.

He nodded. "You're certainly not the first, although it would seem you're the last!" We smiled. Perhaps we could've said a little more, but we didn't have the time for that.

He pulled back some corrugated tin, the sort used on old barn roofs, and revealed a set of double doors.

He looked up at me with a wicked grin as he opened it up, pulling back his head with a deep breath as he did so.

The foetid aroma escaped and attacked me unapologetically. My eyes watered, but it was the thick smell that got me and almost made me gag.

The thick smell of death.

"This is where they go," he said. "It smells a bit!"

"What is this?" I asked. Normal places didn't have hidden holes in the ground to dispose of dead bodies.

"These weren't built for that sole purpose…or maybe they were." He paused and looked thoughtful. "They were built as secret bunkers for the second world war. The idea was that people hid out down here. The threat of ground invasion from the Germans was so great that this was a last resort kamikaze attack. They would sit in the small rooms and try and shoot as many German soldiers as they could before being overwhelmed."

"Jesus! That's some role!"

"Well, of course the threat never materialised, but those men sat there waiting like sitting ducks."

"So this isn't just a big hole then?"

"Nah. It might sound better, but these are old structures."

"I never even knew that they existed, let alone were around here!"

"They were kept secret until recently. Well, this one is still secret, but the ones in other parts of North Wiltshire and Gloucestershire have been revealed."

"I'm not sure I really want to ask this, but…"

"How many bodies are there?" He grinned. He seemed to enjoy the uneasiness that this was causing me.

"Well…yeah."

He bent down and pulled Leonard's arms, dropping his upper body over the hole before pushing his legs until he suddenly disappeared.

A Cold Retreat

There was sickening thump of him hitting something else that wasn't hard and then another release of gas. If this had been a cartoon, then a cloud of green would have shot out around us.

"Not many," he said, pulling up the door and slamming it down. "Three or four."

"Three or four?" I was surprised. I was scared. Even though the witch was dead, so to speak, the realisation of just how lucky I had been was not lost on me.

"Who are they?" I asked when he just nodded to my previous acknowledgment.

We began to walk back towards the house. It looked so much more beautiful from out here than from inside that room. As we walked around the corner towards the pond, I looked up at the window, half expecting to either see myself or to see another lost soul.

"Leonard was clever. He was able to employ or choose people that wouldn't be missed."

"What about me?" I said, suddenly thinking that perhaps he had begun to take risks.

"What about you?"

"How did he know that I wouldn't be missed?"

"He knew," he said, looking at the house. "Believe me, he knew."

The one thing that sprung to mind was why Charlie hadn't gone to the police. He must've realised that the longer he stayed here, the harder it would be to convince someone that he was not involved. He was the younger man, and he appeared to have been given full rein of the place, so to run off, or even drive off, didn't appear to be too hard.

"Did you not think to just leave? Or phone the police?"

He was already shaking his head. "He said he would blame me. He said I had no proof and it would be his word against mine. What could I do?"

He was probably right. It was easy to try and point the finger and tell someone what they should do, but he was fearful of going back to prison. Perhaps on some level he assumed that if he kept quiet it would help him, turning a blind eye, but there was a part of me that couldn't quite believe his fear outweighed the guilt he must've felt as people were imprisoned and killed.

"What about the people who died?" He looked confused.

"Did you not feel guilty that they were suffering?"

"No," he said. "Leonard told me things that they were guilty of. Y'know, child neglect and stuff. I could never hurt them myself…but…it was easier

A Cold Retreat

to turn the other cheek and pretend that it wasn't happening.

Chapter 39

Sasha – Two weeks ago

We talked together for a long time. I don't know why we sat and poured out everything that was in our minds, but that is exactly what happened. I got the feeling that he felt the relief of it all, as the emotion overflowed, bringing us both to tears at one point.

I can't explain how it happened. We were both feeling each other out, but also becoming more comfortable together. We were tentative as to what the future would hold for us, but there was something familiar and almost exciting about this.

I shouldn't have been feeling like this, *but I was.* How was that possible?

I think what made this a little different was that, whilst I had been through something bad, I had come into this knowing that there were risks. I had walked into the lion's den assuming I was the lion tamer. Then the lion had attacked me, so part of me knew I had no one to blame but myself.

A Cold Retreat

There was such irony in this. This was, of course, the line that I had told myself ever since I was a teenager. The blame always stopped with me.

I had thought out this plan months ago. I had chosen Leonard from a random news article that I found on a website. I had spent a whole evening reading up on his rape attacks. This normal-looking man with a sharp nose and thinning hair could suddenly become an animal towards women.

I found him on Twitter and noticed that he had a few admirers, a host of women taunting him with provocative messages. But this was the internet. No one was who they really were on the internet, were they?

Were these women any worse than me? They were being suggestive, posting pornographic pictures and movie clips that more than likely were not themselves. There was no suggestion here, no innuendos, or flowery come-ons that needed you to read between the lines. These were graphic depictions of what they wanted with words that said as much. All of this to a guy with a history of attacking young attractive women.

But he hadn't been a lurker. He hadn't just had an account and followed people. No, he had interacted, replying to comments and offering suggestions of what he would like to see or what he would like to do. For the most part, a lot of people on these sites were harmless. They were living out fantasies, speaking to people that they would never meet, and often both parties were putting up pictures that were not themselves. It was a strange friendship based around small seeds planted by one and growing into a fantasy that was hard to distinguish from reality for the other person. If that person then did the same, then these two were in effect corresponding with perfection. Often, this could go on for years. It was only when one person got into the realms of obsession that these loose games of lies untangled into disappointment and anger—a truly fascinating case study of psychology.

So this was one of the easiest ways possible to become friends. I could see his type, and it wasn't massively different from me, although there was no way in Hell that I was going to pose naked. Luckily for me, I had found someone on Twitter who was more than happy to post herself naked daily, so I had used any of her pictures that didn't have her head on them. I had also posted head shots of me so that his imagination would automatically put the two together.

I had known Leonard ran a B&B from the research, but his advertisement for the job had been

A Cold Retreat

a stroke of luck. I had planned to stay at the B&B and try to carry out my plan from there, but the job had suddenly given me a reason to stay there, with no rush carry it out. That had meant that I could form a friendship and gain trust, which would have made it all the more easy to execute the plan, if you pardon the pun!

So here we were. Sitting down in the lounge, drinking wine and eating pizza. Charlie had ordered it in.

We were an unlikely couple brought together as captives. Our stories couldn't have been more different, but our paths had collided, and now we paused together, analysing, wondering... Deep down, neither of us knew if we could trust the other.

"I've thought of doing that before...killing him, I mean. But it was when he had you... I couldn't let it carry on," Charlie said through the mouthful of pizza that he hungrily chewed on. "He didn't even offer a reason this time."

I nodded. The food was good. It had been a few days since I'd enjoyed some great comfort food. The wine also slipped down. This was the longest period I had been without alcohol in a long while. So now I frivolously knocked back glasses of the stuff. I just didn't care, as we drank our way through whatever we found.

"So what now?" I said. It was the question that we must both have been thinking for a while. It was a little like a night out meeting someone special, enjoying their company, snuggling into them and stealing a few kisses. You wanted it to be for more than just one night, but you were too scared to bring it up.

The question held much weight. Both of us were killers. I might not have actually killed Leonard, but given the chance, I would've. I certainly planned to kill in the future. Charlie had killed Leonard, and I couldn't be sure it was the first time he had done such a thing.

"Up to you, I guess?" he said, taking a gulp of wine.

"How so?"

"Well, I want to stay here. I'm not sure what I'll do, but here is a house, a business… I've helped run it for a while now."

"You want to carry on with a B&B like nothing has happened?" I was surprised, but it was a happy surprise. I wondered whether this might just make things work so much easier.

"I don't see why not. I'll give it a go." He took another bite of pizza, stopping momentarily to lick some melted cheese from his fingertips. "I've got nothing to lose, right?"

A Cold Retreat

I nodded. "What about your probation officer? Don't you need Leonard to sign something or speak to someone?"

"Yeah, but I'm sure I can get round that." He winked.

"So," he said after another generous swig from his glass. "What about you?"

"What about me?" I said. I realised that I was trying to put a brave front on, a blasé demeanour to show that I was non-committal about things.

"You got somewhere else you want to be? You got a life out there?" He nodded to the wall, but it was obvious that his gesture was meaning the rest of the world.

"Maybe I should stick around," I said, slowly looking at my hand as it was twirling the glass ever so slightly with my thumb and forefinger. I looked up, and he smiled ever so slightly.

"Maybe you should," he said. "Maybe you should."

And that was how it started.

I walked the house looking into the rooms. There was a sudden excitement about this large empty house that I had *sort of* acquired.

And Charlie?

I didn't know about Charlie. But I hadn't known about a lot of men who had come and gone in my life. The difference now was that I was no longer going to take any shit. He had to earn my trust. If I didn't like something about him, then he was going to be taking a closer look at the bunker.

But there was something slightly enigmatic about him. He seemed confident but never backed this up with words. It was in his eyes. It was the comfortable gestures and the way he appeared amused like he was two people sharing a joke.

I found a bedroom on the second floor that had a large bed and windows facing out to the front of the house. I wanted the opposite view from what I'd had before.

"A good choice," Charlie said as we went up to bed.

"It'll do for now. I guess we have a lot to talk about tomorrow…partner!" I held out my hand, which he duly accepted and shook, quickly and firmly.

"Until tomorrow." He winked, and for a second I thought he might hug me, or even kiss me, but then the moment was gone. He turned and walked away.

I opened my door and slipped inside with the things of mine that Charlie had retrieved for me. I slowly closed the door behind me…and slipped the bolt through to lock it. I didn't really know Charlie, did I?

Chapter 40

Two days ago

I looked up at the doll in the red dress who stared back at me with an empty gaze. I had had her since I was a child. To others, there was a sinister look to her face—specifically, a pensive look that was neither happy nor sad, but slightly cold and uncaring. Of course, to me she was an imaginary friend who had spent far too long having to hear my tales of woe throughout my youth.

Even in my teens I had found myself talking to her. I would sit up in my room with a hot chocolate, blowing the steam away and rambling on to my doll about the boys that had never known I existed. She sat patiently, never uttering a reply, not wondering why I didn't hold her close to me, undress and redress her, or brush her long brown hair.

As an adult, she had come with me whenever I moved. She was never boxed up or stuffed in a bag, but was often one of the last things to be carried out. She would sit in the front of the car—not in a seat, but laid down just where I could see her.

Jim Ody

She had become something more to me. She had begun to be a symbol of strength. I didn't even know where she had come from. My parents couldn't remember ever buying her, only that one day I had appeared holding her, and from that day forth, I would talk to her.

When I got back from late nights out, parties or such, I would talk to her about the boys or men that I had met. She would look at me again with empty eyes, but wouldn't blink at the things that I had gotten up to. She wouldn't judge me or try to get one over on me. I trusted her, and I hoped that she trusted me too.

Her name was Sasha. It was on a small tag inside her red dress.

When I came out from the women's refuge I decided that I needed to be stronger, more focused, and to take no shit.

That was the day I changed my name to Sasha.

That was the day that I decided to get back at all those bastard men that I now knew to be worthless. I had learnt about forgiveness and strength. I knew that the only way to get over this was to forgive and to move on. I got that this was the right thing to do, and for everyone else it was—but not me.

A Cold Retreat

I would not be happy or able to move on until they knew exactly what they had done to me. They had to pay.

That was the only way that Sasha could ever truly be free...

Chapter 41

Sasha – A week ago

It had been almost a week now. I found it hard to really think about what that meant. We had started off slowly, hanging out and getting to know each other. It had been a little like a very long first date, where you think you like that person but you try to not think too far ahead. I was also conscious that this was quite *possibly a business arrangement*—or at least to him it might be.

This was the first time in a very long time I had met and spent time with an attractive man and not ended up sleeping with him. Perhaps this suggested that he was someone different. I loved the way that he never boasted about anything. What you see was what you got.

Charlie was comfortable with me. We really thought we could make this business work, and we agreed to pretend that we were a couple.

"We should go and get some pictures taken together!" I said to him.

A Cold Retreat

He nodded, but then replied, "Let's just take some selfies, or we'll set the camera up in different types of weather. It'll look like we've been together forever!"

I think we both felt the same. It was as if pretending we were in a relationship meant that we could play a role, and this insulated our hearts, stopping us from getting hurt. Charlie didn't talk much about feelings, but there was something slightly vulnerable about him bubbling just under the surface.

I began to clean some of the rooms in preparation for guests. I almost thought about not going through with my plan—maybe try to forgive and forget—but I just couldn't.

It was the thing that loomed over me.

Not the police turning up after some tip off and discovering a bunker full of dead bodies. No, it was the potential fuck up of this whole idyllic situation with a new partner, as I unravelled mentally with talk of payback and possibly murder.

Who was I kidding? If I was to go as far as to bring them here and force them to stay, then this whole situation would be compromised. There would be no choice but to kill them.

But what did I really know about Charlie?

He had talked at length of his time locked up, the break up, the pills, and the car crash. And last night, he told of how he was sick of being blackmailed, how he had been made to dispose of bodies. He had been in deep, and perhaps that was the key.

I needed to really get to know Charlie. Was there a chance that I could become the new Leonard? Could I be the one that subtly dropped hints of calling the police if he didn't help me? I felt guilty about this thought, but it couldn't hurt to have a plan. He had shown that he could be manipulated, and I had to remain focused, which meant I had to be the one in charge.

But he had a charm about him. Maybe we could be a couple, our love binding us together into a strong trust, but maybe that would take too long.

And then I thought about killing him.

I could do it now before I became too attached to him, use the drugs that had been used on me, and then bang! Smack him over the head with something and send him on a one-way trip to the bunker.

The truth of the matter was that I had feelings for him. The way his green eyes twinkled when he whistled a tune. The manly smell emitted from him when he got hot. The way he flicked his hair behind his ears when he spoke about something from the

A Cold Retreat

past. I saw those big arms, and I wanted to feel them wrapped around me.

Again, it had only been a week.

I worried that I was nothing to him. We had spent all those nights under the same roof chatting, snuggling up, and drinking wine, and yet he had not made any advances to kiss me or to touch me other than a quick kiss on the cheek. But that seemed slightly too platonic. The sort of kiss posh people do as a greeting but barely even touch. A grand gesture of nothingness, completely pointless.

I had cooked up a light lunch. It was nothing fancy, just a tossed salad with some chicken pieces and splashed with vinaigrette. Charlie had been working on the website, giving it a refresh.

"Smells good," he said, smiling and sitting down opposite me. "We need the website updating. I don't have the programmes to do a great job."

"I might have an idea. Let me think about it for a while." We ate in the kitchen around the small table. It was more intimate than in the dining room. That was for the guests, even if we didn't have any yet.

We began to eat. At first, it was in silence, but this was normal for us. We liked to enjoy the first few mouthfuls of our food, giving it our undivided attention, before we started with the small talk. It was another of those things we realised we had in common.

"I think this is going to work, Sash," he said. His abbreviation of my name made me smile.

"What, us?" I said, leaving something unspoken hanging there.

He looked me up and down slowly, his eyes feasting on what he saw, and he nodded. "I don't see why not." He took a drink, which was a can of lager, and then added, "But I meant this business. I think we can make some good money."

I opened my mouth to tell him about my plans…but the words got stuck in my throat. He was sitting here in a kitchen bigger than one I could ever imagine, in a house that was huge, and this handsome man had rescued me from being locked up in a room.

The little girl inside me began to cry. Through everything that I had wanted and ever dreamed of, it seemed that reality was destined to be too far away. Each turn in my life produced not just a dead end, but poisonous apples and wicked witches, and the palace and prince disappeared forever.

But despite the pain and suffering, just as I thought I was almost ready to give up, he had come along.

A Cold Retreat

"Excuse me," I said, pretending to cough as tears streamed down my face.

But deep down, I knew I still had to go through with the plan. I had to be strong, or I would never be truly happy ever again.

Chapter 42

Sasha – A week ago

Tonight, we went out for a meal. We hadn't left the house together very often, choosing instead to go out separately, still thinking about what we should and shouldn't be doing.

We took a drive out to a pub called The White Hart in a village called Compton Bassett. We were sure nobody would know Charlie there.

"I've been meaning to ask you," he said, looking up from the flickering candle on the table for two. "How did you come to go for the job in the first place? I mean, you seem like you would be good at most things you put your mind to."

I took a sip of my wine, a standard stalling trick that I had learnt from days of interviews. Should I tell him the truth or lie? We were at the awkward place when to lie could mean having to admit as much in the future, but telling the truth would somehow make me feel too vulnerable.

A Cold Retreat

"I've had high-pressured jobs," I started, which was true. "But I wanted something different. I wanted to change my life."

"You have family around here? You can't have always been single, right...?" He then stopped and looked at me strangely. "You *are* single, right?"

I nodded. "I've been treated badly by men." I left it at that.

"And I've been treated badly by women!" He raised his pint of bitter, and we tapped our glasses gently.

The meal arrived not long afterwards, and we chatted about the world and the beautiful places within it. We talked about travelling and the places that we would love to see, whilst being careful not to analyse our relationship too much.

Charlie talked about Peru and the Inca pyramids that he would love to see one day, and I talked about the white sands in Bermuda. This was where I was comfortable—not specifically in Bermuda (although you would be hard pushed not to be comfortable there!) but talking in fantasy. It was make-believe, and expressing my desires to be in a far-off place was something that I was very much used to. I had been known on many occasions to be doing this exact thing whilst a stranger was naked and panting on top of me, my mind ten thousand miles away whilst the rest of my body was limp and being forcefully jerked with each one of his thrusts.

We joked at an old guy who was wandering around, approaching all the young ladies like he was a real catch and then swearing at them when they turned him down. Eventually, the landlord had seen enough and showed the old guy the exit.

We were still laughing about him as we were driving back in Charlie's BMW.

Getting out of the car and looking up at the house, a sense of achievement washed over me. I had overcome something others would remain traumatised from. Fleetingly I wondered whether the shock of it all might suddenly hit me at some stage in the future like some PTSD. For me, the difference from what I had been through before was being locked in a room. I considered many times that I had been raped, even if each time it was by a boyfriend or someone that I had thought I wanted to be with.

"That was nice," he said, taking my hand. I nodded and smiled at him. It was all a bit goofy and teenage, but that was exactly how I felt.

"I enjoyed it," I agreed as we walked into the house.

We stopped and looked at each other. I'm not sure exactly what happened next, but suddenly our

A Cold Retreat

lips were touching gently. It felt really nice. And then our tongues came together in hungry, open mouths, and his hand wandered over me. I realised that I was already grabbing his bum tightly.

This was perfect.

We moved slowly against each other, and it almost felt a little anarchic to be doing this in an area that we would have others around in the future.

We shed our clothes. We took things slowly, as I was still sore and bruised.

At one point, Charlie stopped and, out of breath, whispered, "Is this okay?" I nodded even though I felt red raw, and I suddenly realised that this was exactly what I had been doing for the whole of my life…except now, it felt good emotionally, even if physically it hurt, which was the complete opposite of what I had experienced before.

Later, we lit the fire in the lounge and snuggled next to it naked under a blanket. I had never done anything like this before.

"Charlie?" I said. "What if I told you that I wanted to do something bad? What would you say?"

"What, like support Oxford United?"

I chuckled. He knew how to lighten the mood. "Maybe not that bad…or maybe worse."

"Worse than Oxford?" He grinned but then noticed that I was serious. "I'm sorry."

"I've always wanted to get them back. You know, the men that treated me badly."

"Okay."

"What if, before we open up here again, we…sort of invite a few of these bad men here?"

"You want to invite a load of your exes here whilst we wait on them? What? Are you going to smother them in kindness?" It was hard to gauge whether he was being sarcastic or serious.

"Not exactly. I want them to know what they did was wrong. I want them to pay…"

"You really—" I cut him off.

"I want to hurt them, Charlie. I don't know, maybe I even want to put them in the bunker."

Charlie turned and looked at me. "They were that bad to you, yeah?"

I nodded. "They really were, Charlie. They really were."

"I…I just don't know…"

"I was forced to have sex with men that I had never even met before. Not one at a time either. Sometimes it was only when they'd finished that I saw their faces!" Tears had welled up in my eyes. I hadn't meant for that to happen, but it had. The

A Cold Retreat

feelings, when I remembered, always made me this way.

"If we did this, Sasha..." He looked off into the flames that danced in what now seemed to be a morbid ritual that only lacked the beats of a tribal drum. "Then we have to plan this thing down to the last point."

I nodded, and the rush of relief glided over me.

He got me. He understood what I had been through and was still willing to help me.

This was all too much. My eyes once again flooded out tears, and I struggled to speak to reassure Charlie that it was happiness.

"I'll help you, Sasha," he soothed, and I wondered once again whether I held the upperhand. Then I wondered why I had suddenly felt such a thing.

We kissed softly and returned to our separate rooms for the night.

That night, when I closed my eyes, I once again thought of Bermuda, except this time Charlie was there with me.

It was the best sleep that I'd had in weeks, months, and possibly years.

Chapter 43

Sasha – A week ago

A slight rap at my door woke me up the next day. "Come in," I called, and I heard him struggle with the door. It opened, and in he came with a tray of breakfast, including a small vase with a flower in it. It was the clichéd sort of thing that you see on the telly in some cheesy movie, but it was the sort of thing that I happened to also like, even if it had never happened to me before.

"I could get used to this!" I smiled and sat up. For a second, I was a little self-conscious that he could see my naked breasts, but then I remembered the night before and thought it silly that I would be bothered at such a thing.

"Sorry," he said, suddenly looking away.

"Were you sorry for looking at them last night?" I asked.

"Not at all."

"Then don't be now."

A Cold Retreat

And so began our plans. It was so nice to share this with someone else and also to be actually putting this into motion.

"So, I was thinking," he started. "We need a list of names, contact details, and ideas on how we can get each of them here."

"I can give most of those details to you now," I said. "I've already thought about this for a while."

"We need a way to get them here so there's no trail, so I spent some time ringing an old buddy of mine who sent me a programme that I can use as a sort of filter for emails."

"You have been busy." I smiled. I couldn't believe he was already up and onto it. "So what does this thing do?"

"Well, not so much do, as doesn't do. It means the email only stays in the person's inbox for a certain amount of time, and then it deletes it, but not just from the email, from the history and the hard drive too. My mate reckons it's untraceable."

"What if they tell people where they're going?"

"This is the great thing. Any reference to the name of the B&B will be wiped from their computer, phone, or whatever device that they have the details on. It also cannot be forwarded or printed out."

"You really think this'll work?"

"I don't see why not!"

"Come here." I motioned, pulling back the covers and placing the tray onto the side. "Breakfast can wait."

My smile was wide between kisses. I giggled like an excited child, the elation of the moment getting the better of me. I had lived in the shadows of a dark place for a long time now, and this felt like a release. I made no apologies for this over-the-top hysteria that had gotten the better of me, but I figured Charlie thought it to be fuelled by his lustful touches, and so would not notice.

A few minutes later we were done. My heart rate was still high, and my breathing was trying to get back to normal. His arm was slung over me as we cuddled, two lovers bound together with naked skin and sticky moistness, open to each other with a reckless abandon, nipples, wobbly bits, and pubic hair open to silent wonderment and critique. A moment of serenity floated over us as we each flittered between memories and future plans. The small touches and smiles, finger walking across each other, pokes and prods, then nipple kisses before more stirrings below, a hardness felt against my thigh, and a shuffle into position. I opened up my legs to welcome him in again. We were teenagers again in a feast of exploration, singing the

A Cold Retreat

same song but changing the beat and the melody, a remix rather than a reprise. With a shift in position, I turned over and pulled up to be on all fours. I pushed back on him as he entered me, wanting to be used hard. It was what I knew. It was what I was used to. It was what I now craved. He obliged, grabbing my shoulders and pulling me up with one hand, whilst the other snaked around and grabbed a breast tightly. A silent understanding saw us finally come together in a way that bounds us through a mutual, animalistic understanding.

It was an hour before breakfast was finally eaten.

"You wanna talk about it?" he said vaguely, but I know what he meant. "You don't act like someone who has been held captive and raped."

"And how should I act?" I said a little dismissively. I could see he was intrigued by me.

He shrugged as I drank some cold tea. "You don't act like a victim…you know…?" He faltered slightly, and I saw that he was worried he had overstepped the mark.

I pulled my hair back, mostly for fear of getting it in my toast. "I'm not a victim, Charlie. And d'y'know what? I'm never going to be a victim again."

He nodded in acceptance.

It was not long before I jumped out of bed quite literally. I stretched, enjoying the feeling of every muscle and ligament pulling. I pulled back the curtains, unfazed by my nakedness, and glanced at the sunny day outside.

"We've got some busy days ahead of us, Charlie-boy!" I said in a sing-song voice. I was happy.

I was actually well and truly happy.

A Cold Retreat

Chapter 44

Sasha – A week ago

This last week or so had been busy. We had talked and planned like a business couple. We were still taking things slowly. I was not sure we would call us a couple, but currently we had no one else, so at least I knew that we were exclusive.

I had researched the bastards from my past life. The first one I tried was Christian Raney. He had been the hunk who had taken me into the bushes at school when I was thirteen. He was my first crush that I had naively given up my virginity to, only to then be molested by his mate Barry too. I suppose I had been raped. I mean, I knew I was raped, but I had never told him no; I just laid there and accepted it. It was at that moment that the whole world had changed for me. That one indecisive moment had spoilt me. After it had happened once, then a second time was nothing. The third and fourth time had become the norm until I could barely remember what it was like to have an opinion of my own.

Christian was proving to be quite illusive—not appearing on Social Media anywhere—however, I did manage to find a friend of his, and through *his* pictures I found Christian. A bit more digging, and suddenly I had enough details. His slim athletic build had bulked out into that of someone who had befriended beer and never missed an opportunity to socialise with it.

Then I wanted his mate, bush-hider Barry, but found out that he had been murdered in prison by an unknown assailant.

And so it began. Some of the information I already had, and I was soon able to set up a weekend that everybody invited could come along to. Each one of them thought they were going there for different reasons. This didn't matter. Before they found out, it would be too late.

Charlie brought me a cup of tea as I was tapping out a reply confirming an unexpected surprise. A guy from my past needed a place to stay and was looking for quotes. I knew who he was because, today with Facebook we can search against the name and location. His VW campervan was the same. I offered him the weekend for free to seal it.

"Maybe we should charge them?" he said, rubbing my shoulders. It was a gesture of affection

A Cold Retreat

that he showed once in a while, the merest suggestion that we were perhaps a couple.

"It's not wise," I replied. "We don't want any trail to be left that will bring the police here."

He nodded. "Good thinking."

He then left. He was sorting something out in the outbuilding. He told me there was a generator there that he was trying to fix up. It was something Leonard had wanted him to do before his demise. When I asked further, he just told me that it was a surprise. I was sure it was something sweet, but I just hated surprises.

It was funny, but I had been going around the house like we were opening it to paying guests. Maybe I was just playing a role, but I was trying to tweak every detail in order to make it look just right. Part of it was that I wanted this all to appear authentic. If someone thought it was a set-up, they would run. Not only would that mess up my plans, but it could bring other people here to snoop around.

I walked around the attic, but I wasn't sure how this could be used. Charlie and I had yet to discuss how we planned to *get* them when they were here. Part of me fantasised about scenes from 80s horror movies: picking them off one by one without the others knowing—shower scenes, stakes through beds, out-buildings, cellars—but the truth of the matter was that this only worked in movies...

The floor below had our bedrooms. The only room I hadn't been in was Leonard's. The door was locked, and I hadn't wanted to ask Charlie about it. I wasn't sure why; it just seemed weird to ask. Then, like a lot of things, the longer it went on, the more strange it might seem, so I just stopped thinking about it. Maybe I'd bring it up later, or in a day or so.

The bedrooms were clean, and I wondered who I would put in the room I had been held captive in. It had taken me a couple of attempts to go into that room again, even if I could never bring myself to close the door. It had been cleaned and now seemed fresh.

I walked to my room and sat on the bed, drinking in my surroundings. In some ways, this was a little like college, staying in the dorms. I knew this was my home for a while, but I couldn't fit that into a timescale or decide what I would do after.

I knew my shell wasn't that thick anymore, and underneath was a confused little girl. My dreams to be a princess had been pushed further away from that becoming reality. Whether my abilities to make the right choices were flawed or I had been too trusting, wanting to believe things in people that

A Cold Retreat

weren't there, I had left behind me memories lined with regrets. My experiences had left me confused, hurt, and ultimately alone. *"What about Charlie?"* You may ask. Well, what about him? He was a similar person to me, forced down a path he didn't want to be on, First caged up in prison, and then blackmailed on his way back into society after having lost contact with his family and friends. Together, we had decided to invite people from my past and do away with them. He should have been talking me out of it. He should have been telling me that we could make a fresh start somewhere else when he no longer had to check in with his probation officer, maybe offer to help out in society, but no, instead we carried on poisoning ourselves along a darker path.

Did either of us know where this would take us?

What would happen when the excitement from this wore off?

I felt like I was spiralling deeper and deeper into something I couldn't control.

I took a deep breath.

A week to go before we finally got this party started. I smiled to myself, but deep down, I still didn't know whether it would be enough…

Part 4

A Cold Retreat

Chapter 45

Travis – Friday

My Porsche Cayenne was all there was to mark a time that I had money and when the word success was my middle name. I now resented it to a point—the way it taunted me whenever I had a need to drive it. The purr of the engine used to excite me when the motor started and I made my way to the house of whichever young lady I had chosen to date that night.

But the backseat also held fond memories with Chanelle, like the time she had wanted me to take pictures of her in her underwear so she could post them on the internet showing off the leather interior and Porsche badge. She would try to poke fun at me driving such a car whilst secretly enjoying it. Her friends' boyfriends drove Golfs, Clios, or four-year-old BMWs. She loved what it represented.

The Porsche was now eight years old with more than a generous helping of wear and tear. I had washed it yesterday and was now making my way to the B&B on the other side of Wiltshire. This was make or break. I had to gain this contract to show that I still had some business brain about me. My boss couldn't wait to see me fail.

I stopped at a drive-thru Starbucks, which was an obscure notion that I had not seen coming in life. I had always thought that the point of getting a coffee was to take a break from your driving for a while and load up on enough caffeine to keep you going for the rest of your journey. To now be able to stop and get your coffee without even leaving the car seemed to miss the point, and yet here I was doing exactly that.

I wondered to myself whether a better way to cut down the length of time of stopping was to wear a catheter and order your coffee with a push of a button on the car screen. It would instantly go to the nearest coffee service station and, with number-plate recognition, would mean that as you pulled up, someone could hand you your coffee order without you even pulling to a stop. This then got me thinking about designing an app for your phone that could also download to the car.

I glanced at myself in the mirror, quickly smoothing over any part of my hair that looked thin or showed my receding hairline. At one stage, my hair had been perfect. I had felt like I ruled the world.

A Cold Retreat

Leaving Swindon behind me, I was engulfed by the countryside, everything becoming greener the further out I went. There was a mix of houses from communities tied together through tradition, and the private estates of those with money. Their gated properties hinted at the wealth within whilst wagging a finger to deny access.

I twisted along the road, momentarily enjoying being away from everything that I had known, and opened up the engine. The sun was shining brightly, even if in the distance like a dark blanket, rain clouds rolled in.

At first, I almost missed the turn down the private road. I slammed on my brakes enough to slow the car right down but without the wheels locking.

The lane was cracked slightly, but still the surface remained in good condition. I was looking at it from a visitor's point of view. This helped when designing the website. What did I feel when I turned up there?

As the house came into view, I knew that this was a great picture for the title page. It showed the grounds and how far out into the countryside it was, and it also showed off the house from a slight off-angle, which made it look bigger than it probably was.

I pulled up around the side next to a couple of cars and took a deep breath. I couldn't blow this. If I was to keep this car and turn my life around, then it all started here.

I was wearing a suit. I didn't have to, but this was business, so it seemed apt.

I felt nervous and anxious, feelings that recently had become all too familiar, ones that, up until recently, I had never experienced.

I strode up to the door and was met by a smiling lady with medium–length red hair. Almost instantly, I thought I had this in the bag, and then once again, the realisation hit that this was not me from ten years previously, but the one now marred by age.

"Hi." She smiled, holding out her hand to shake. "You must be Travis?"

I nodded and took her hand, matching the firm grip. "I am indeed," I replied, trying to sound confident again. Somehow, I had to channel the old me, but in a more business-like tone. "You must be Sasha?"

"Guilty!"

"You have a lovely place here. The setting when you come down the lane is wonderful. I really think there are some wonderful picture opportunities for the website here."

A Cold Retreat

She seemed to wave this off, and for a moment, I thought I had already blown it, but then she suddenly said, "Never mind that now, Travis. I want you to come and relax for tonight and tomorrow. We can get down to business after that. This place is certainly somewhere that you have to experience first… Breathe in the ambience…" She took a deep breath to emphasise this point, waving her arms as if thrusting smells up her nose. "Then, and only then, can you fully appreciate exactly what it is that we have to offer!"

"Right you are then," I said. "I'll just get my bag."

Bag in hand, I followed her up the steps into the house. My eyes danced over a well-formed behind, and once again, I wondered whether my charm might win out for this contract.

Chapter 46

Dex – A week ago

It had been an interesting ride with Kim. There were good and bad things about picking up a hitchhiker, I guess. The long roads of the A38, M5, and then M4 certainly went quicker with someone like her in tow. Kim wasn't a person for silence. My assumption was that humans have the ability to form words and communicate better than any other animal, and so Kim obviously felt that to remain quiet when in the presence of someone else was to somehow deny evolution and the way that man had progressed himself.

I dropped her off at Leigh Delamere services between junctions 18 and 17 of the M4. For a minute, I enjoyed the silence, but before long, I had plugged in my MP3 to the stereo and was singing along loudly with Mötley Crüe. I refuse to apologise for listening to some classic Hair Metal. Thick in nostalgia, it reminded me of a time when I was the opposite of the bands and their melodic boasts.

A Cold Retreat

At junction 16 I came off of the motorway and went round the roundabout to head through Royal Wootton Bassett. A few minutes later, I was in Thornhill.

I went around another roundabout, noticing the traffic slowing in front and also a lad on a bike about to cross the road.

I slowed to a stop behind the white transporter in front and then heard a thud on the side of my van.

I glanced in my mirror to see that the lad was off his bike and lying at the side of the road. It looked like he hadn't realised I had stopped and ridden straight into the side of me.

I turned on the hazard lights and got out. Straightaway I could see that the lad was okay, more than likely a little embarrassed.

"You okay?" I asked.

He looked at me like I had just told him that he was a fucking idiot—words that had travelled through my mind but I was sure had not come out of my mouth.

"D'I look okay, wanker?" He was about ten with shocking orange hair. He probably didn't like it described as ginger or strawberry blond.

"I think you rode into the side of my van," I said and then realised that it probably hadn't been the best thing to say.

"No shit. You slammed your brakes on. I didn't have a chance!"

"Not strictly true, is it?" I half-grinned, hoping to join the banter.

"Fuckin' wanker now blames me?" he said to nobody but himself. "I could sue you! Where there's pain, there's money!"

"A claim? Where there's pain, there's a claim."

"Fuckin' right there is, mate. You better take me home, and you and me mam can sort out the compensation."

"The compensation? What, for my van, the dent that your hard head caused?" The little shit.

"Dangerous driving, drink-driving, using your mobile, driving like a wanker." He was counting them off on his fingers.

"None of those are true though."

"Don't matter none." He grinned, thinking that he had me. "I'll say what the fuck I want, paedo!"

"Paedo? Okay, and how do you work that out?"

"Easy. You was looking at me being sexy on my bike and didn't see that car in front and nearly hit it!"

"The car in front was a transporter, and I didn't even see you, even with your bright hair."

A Cold Retreat

"I tell you what," he started, looking like he might ask me for a fight, "I would lamp you if it wasn't that I need a lift back."

"Where do you live?" I conceded.

He pointed through a break in the path to a street on its own with fields behind. "Over there."

"Righto then, let's get your bike in, shall we?"

He jumped straight into the passenger seat and left me to put his bike in the back.

"So, you call me a paedo and then jump into my van. Would you say that's a wise move?"

"Just start the van and get me home, perv."

"A perv is not as bad as a paedo, so I take it that I have been downgraded." He said nothing…until Mötley Crüe began singing about Dr. Feelgood.

"What the fuck is this?" he said, screwing his face up.

"Does swearing make you feel more manly?"

"Does picking up small boys make *you* feel more manly?"

"Touché."

He looked at me funny again. "Fuck's that mean?"

"It's a bit like saying *fair enough*, or *good point*."

"So say that then, and not something gay like tush."

"It's touché, not tush. It's French."

"Whatever, I live over there. Next right."

I took the right turn and drove almost to the end of the street before the lad said, "Just here."

I turned the engine off and helped him get his bike out. No sooner had the wheels touched the ground than a woman came rushing out of the house.

"What's going on?" she said worriedly, her fierce brown bob bouncing with each step. The lad made a show of walking dazed and then fell over when he got to the grass.

"Giles!" she shouted. "What happened?"

"Mum…" he said, sounding dazed. "He hit me with his van…" I had to hand it to the little shit; he was a great actor. He should've been in bloody *Bugsy Malone*.

"Actually, he rode his bike into the side of my van," I corrected.

"Giles? What's the truth here?"

Giles looked guilty, and suddenly I knew that he must've had a history of this.

"He slammed his breaks on! I had nowhere to go!"

His mum shook her head slowly. "So you weren't paying attention again, Giles?"

A Cold Retreat

"'snot my fault!" Giles spat, but the spite soon disappeared, and he then looked his age for the first time.

"What about the last time?" his mum said.

"Weren't my fault either."

"And the van before that?"

"Fucksake, mum! Why'd ya have to make such an issue out of it!" He stormed off, miraculously recovered.

She stood there, a little embarrassed, but there was also something else. She fussed with her hair.

"Look," she said. "Let me cook you dinner as an apology. I don't know what's got into him since his dad left."

I smiled, half wondering how he could get out of it and also trying not to say out loud, *the answer's in the question.*

"I can't send you off like this," she said. "I'll whip something up for us."

I wasn't sure how it had happened, but suddenly I was walking into a stranger's house.

Perhaps this was a dream and I had fallen asleep at the wheel. Or perhaps I had crashed and was in a coma.

Whatever, life couldn't get any worse than this—surely.

Chapter 47

Christian – Friday

Love is about being completely irrational. It's also a touch of fantasy. But I stared at my 2004 Honda Civic and wondered exactly what this said about me. It shouldn't matter. I knew this. I got that what someone thought about my car was completely irrelevant to what they thought about me. But perhaps it planted a seed. Did that seed grow and blossom into love, did it wilt and die, or did it never even bother to shoot at all?

It was just a car after all, practical and reliable without too much wear and tear—exactly how I would like to see myself through someone else's eyes.

I wondered whether this was fool's gold. Was I now entering a mid-life crisis where, despite not conceding to a sports car, I was now tailing younger women? Sasha was my age and looked gorgeous. Was this some sort of honey-trap?

I'm not sure that, outside of supermarket detective novels, the word "honey-trap" was a part

A Cold Retreat

of everyday language. Perhaps today it would be a hustle, with me being the mark. And her a con-artist.

My self-esteem was not like it had been in my teens, when I was cock-sure approaching women with the knowledge that they were on the edge of passing out with me looking at them. Those were times that you couldn't buy back. And if you could, at what cost?

Nowadays I had an ex-wife who cost me more since we were apart than she had as my wife. I was not sure how I managed to get caught up in a dire economic struggle that saw the price increase as the benefits reduced. She had played her hand well, and as usual, I had thrown my cards away in the hope that the next hand would be mine.

We had been together since sixth form, and we had become parents at eighteen, so we had two kids that had left home by the time we had split up.

I had loved Nina a great deal. In fact, I still loved Nina, but somewhere along the line, we had both taken different paths, and as we had gotten further away from each other, neither had had the enthusiasm to turn and try to reconnect.

We saw each other once in a while, mainly at family parties and anniversaries, and on the odd occasion, we had been known to meet up just for a chat, but we were deeply ingrained in the past and not in the future.

I chucked my holdall in the boot. It had a couple of changes of clothes, toiletries, and a large and hopeful packet of condoms. I didn't know what to expect, but I sure as hell didn't want to not be prepared, just in case things went well.

Maybe it was my time to find true love?

The static on the radio spoilt my enjoyment of Bob Marley singing "No Woman No Cry," and I wondered whether I should be reading more into this or not. I turned the radio off and sung my own version of the song, before my own rendition of The Animals' "House of the Rising Sun."

The journey was a blur. My mind was packed with pictures of Sasha, and both my heart and stomach felt the way they hadn't felt in a number of years. This was all about expectation. It was lust. It was hope.

I turned into the lane, glancing at the trees on either side and noticing that I had suddenly slowed down. As I got nearer to the house, the car was almost crawling.

The gravel crunched under my tyres, making it obvious to everyone that someone had arrived. There were already a couple more cars there, but I didn't even take in their makes and models. I looked

A Cold Retreat

in the mirror one last time and walked into the house.

Chapter 48

Ben - Friday

Bronwyn had gotten up and pampered herself. She had spent an age in the bathroom washing her hair, scrubbing, cleaning, shaving, waxing, exfoliating, and whatever else a woman could do before spending the next hour rubbing lotion all over her body, doing her hair, and painting the nails on her hands and feet.

"You will be the beneficiary." She winked, slipping on some brand new underwear that I'd not seen before. Many years had passed since we had been together and we both bore the scars of time, but that was always to be expected. Like me, she had smoked for a number of years. We'd drunk too much and had pulled way too many all-nighters, so it was inevitable that more than a few signs of aging would be evident. The laughter lines now were permanent lines that only time-reversal or surgery could fix. But she still had that cheeky grin and a skinny body that looked good both in and out of clothes. I was lucky. She had always been there for

A Cold Retreat

me, turning her cheek when I needed to work weekends and evenings, even though she saw my workmates up the pub. She always made an effort with her appearance too, which was something that couldn't be said of some of the wives that my mates had ended up with. They had ballooned in weight and lost teeth, and making an effort meant a clean, shapeless baggy t-shirt over their leggings.

Bronwyn had been in a great mood ever since I had suggested this short-break, although I was more than a little worried.

I had seen this look before. She was being extra gooey and lovey-dovey. I am certainly not saying that I didn't like this, I did. In fact, I bloody loved it—the flick of her hair, the flirty looks, the way she would suddenly touch me in an arousing way...

It was just that I had been here before. It didn't last. It couldn't last. This was because it was leading up to something, and that would either happen before or after a complete sexual explosion. It was like it built up this sexual tension, and we could have just had sex now, but we knew that waiting until later would make it all the more euphoric. We had been known to make noises so loud that the police had been called.

Once, when we were younger, the only way Bronwyn had thought she could prove to the police that I was not abusing her was to show them the video we had just shot of us having sex. The police had declined to watch any more than a few seconds of it, accepting that the noises from the laptop were indeed noises that could be construed by those not party to the situation as being somewhat animalistic and violent. I'd never felt such a mix of being proud and embarrassed at the same time before, and possibly never will again.

So what was it that she was expecting? One of two things, neither of which I had much enthusiasm for: Marriage and/or a baby.

I had married friends. Most had been married twice, some three or four times. None of them appeared happy. I also had friends with children. You knew these as the friends you didn't see anymore. They had decided upon a friendship hiatus determined by their offspring that would last the duration of their childhood. My ex-friends neither had the energy nor the enthusiasm for anything that didn't revolve around their little mucus-makers.

So despite Bronwyn's happy mood now, we knew that come two days' time when she was neither engaged nor impregnated, we would slip back into our usual routine of her watching *Love Actually*, *Cocktail,* and *Pretty Woman* for the hundredth time, whilst I slipped off to have sex with

A Cold Retreat

someone ten or fifteen years or so younger than her…

"We should do this more often," Bronwyn said, getting into the car. I was still worried that she was reading into this trip a little more than I had planned. A good relationship is based on communication, and at some point we had decided that, actually, for us, it was better to just bury our heads and pretend that things didn't happen.

I wondered how we had made it this far. Logically we should've parted company years ago. I knew that I had a straying way about me—and before you start feeling sorry for Bronwyn, what you don't know is that she had also gone off with other people. She fucked her boss a few years ago, and every time we took a break she found someone else within days.

But here we were, still together. We might not be married, and perhaps that was why we both were able to find solace in others, but we were connected on some level.

"Maybe this could be a more regular thing," I said, starting the engine.

"Really?" she said, and I knew that, again, I had offered her hope. I mean, I was not against marrying her; it was just that I didn't feel pressured enough just yet. There might even be a day when I thought that kids were a good idea, but I also wondered whether the bloodline should stop here. Was it right to bring someone like me into the world?

"So what's this place like?" she asked me.

"I'm not sure," I replied. "The pictures looked nice though, so I thought, *why not?*"

She fumbled with her long hair, and I then felt her eyes burning into me. "Ben? I love you, you know?"

I smiled. I liked to hear it. Sometimes our relationship was like a takeaway meal that you had put in the fridge for the next day. You heat it up, and whilst it's never quite as good as the first time, you're still glad that you went back to it. There are also the bits that got overcooked; you put up with them because there are other parts that you still enjoy.

"I love you too." We could still get a bit mushy too. We were almost too familiar with each other, but part of that was okay for me. It meant that, later on, in the privacy of our room we would do the things together that we both enjoyed. It was the part of the relationship that we were the most open with. Neither of us was scared to suggest something or get the other person to change angle, position,

A Cold Retreat

pressure, or pace. So was this the true secret of our longevity?

The Jam were on the radio singing about going underground, and there was something in my stomach that suddenly dropped and made me feel sick. It was the feeling when you know that something bad has happened, but you cannot remember what it was. On a few occasions, your body tells you this, but when you remember, you realise that it wasn't that bad after all. Silently you tell yourself to stop being silly... Other times, you remember, and it feels like the bottom has completely fallen away from your world.

I couldn't remember. I just assumed that something had happened, but I had forgotten.

"You okay?" Bronwyn asked, noticing my change.

I nodded. "Yeah, sorry, just something to do with work that I had forgotten," I lied. How do you begin to explain to someone that it was a feeling? I was not a hippy-type or anything.

She rested her hand on my thigh, and things got a little better.

"Next left," Bronwyn said, looking at the Sat Nav. I, of course, missed it and had to turn round in a gateway.

We turned right and went down a long drive that rattled our fillings a bit, before the large house came into view.

"Wow, this is nice," Bronwyn said and then winked. "You've just earned that thing you like!"

"Good stuff!" I said, parking the car next to some others.

We got our stuff together and walked towards the main door. I still had that song in my mind as we were met by the smiling face of the woman in charge of the place.

There was something about that smile that seemed so very familiar.

Chapter 49

Pete - Friday

I woke up with a pounding head from dehydration and a lack of sleep. A dark cloud was outside the window, and to me this seemed rather apt for the way I was feeling. I was recuperating, getting used to a clean lifestyle, when Jas turned up on my doorstep. I don't mean to be mean, but Jas looked like shit—a real shame as she was a pretty girl. Her skeletal body was a clothes hanger for her skin, as it draped sadly over the bones. Her long, stringy hair had already started coming out, and her teeth had seen much better days. Welcome to the life of a drug addict.

And here was the difference: I had money. I could afford the drugs and the prostitutes and still eat three square meals a day.

I had first met Jas five years ago when she was standing on the corner a few streets down. She hadn't been on the game long, and she was still pretty and carried decent weight.

We forget all too often that the majority of these women were already victims. Most grew up with physical or sexual abuse, and so this was a means to make money from doing something that they had already been forced to do for free anyway. Some felt empowered by it. For the first time, they had rules that men had to abide by, and at the end of the night, some of the shame was dampened down by cash or drugs.

Then there were the girls who thought that this was the first rung to a life as a model or actress, either ending up in porn or selling themselves out on the street. I found this even more saddening, as these girls often came from backgrounds that were run-of-the-mill. They were pretty but deluded by a guy stringing them along. He would ask them to do something for him. He would buy them booze and eventually give them drugs. The idea was to get them hooked on the drugs. Once that happened, he owned them. They would do anything for him. Anything.

He would send them out on to the street all day, every day, and as long as he kept the drugs coming, he would take all the money they made.

Their mind would die and their bodies were not far behind.

This was the life of Jas.

A Cold Retreat

I had brought her home one night, and she joined in with a party. I'm not sure why I picked her up, as there were other women coming to my house. Perhaps I felt sorry for her. Perhaps I saw her standing there and decided that I wanted to have sex with her—pure and simple.

So she had come to the party and seemed to have fun.

I saw her out and about, and whilst she had managed to get out of prostitution, she never quite shook the drugs.

We hung out once in a while. She often came to the parties, but would begin to get depressed and pass out in a corner rather than joining in the fun.

You might try and point the finger at me and say that I never helped her if I was still giving her drugs, but don't forget, I wasn't a dealer or a pimp making money off her; I was an addict too. I was sharing what I had with her.

"What are we doing today?" she asked, her eyes hooded as they usually were. It had been years since I had seen those blue eyes wide.

"You don't remember?" I said. "The retreat? We're gonna get clean."

"Really," she said in her slow speech. She struggled to sound fully conscious now, which was becoming a worry. "Like, for real, and shit?"

"Yeah." I nodded.

She stood up naked in front of me. Breasts drooped like small deflated balloons. Hip bones protruded above her pubis, which appeared more prominent than it should, with thin, wispy hair neglected like the whole of the body it was on.

We had gotten drunk last night. We'd smoked weed and taken speed. Pumped up with an adrenaline rush, we had feverishly fucked for what seemed like an hour, her skinny frame quashing my desires and almost making me limp at times. Her eyes had been alive with large pupils even though the lids had stayed at their usual half mast, and as I thought back, I didn't remember climaxing. I wondered if at some point I just passed out.

Here I was trying to turn over a new leaf—getting away from it all on a retreat to cleanse my mind and body—and yet somehow, I was still able to have a debauched night of drink, drugs, and sex with a junkie-whore.

Visions of my parents' disappointed faces filled my mind. All of the money and all of that education and class could not stop me from being a complete and utter fuck up.

"Are there going to be…like…drugs?" Jas asked innocently.

A Cold Retreat

"No drugs, Jas-baby. We're gonna get clean, remember?"

She stumbled as she pulled on knickers that looked like they could fit a child. At that point, I was pretty sure I had been unable to climax with her. She looked small and innocent with a small thong on that was baggy and not sexy in the least. I was going to help her as well as me, I decided.

"Have I got anything?" she asked, but seemed confused by her own question.

"What do you mean?" I pressed.

"Clothes and shit? Drugs and booze?"

"No, none of that, Jas. We can stop in town and get you some clothes though. What d'ya think?"

She had pulled on a vest that, again, was baggy, and she looked at me for a moment almost trying to remember how to speak. "Yeah?"

"Sure."

Was I wrong to want to grab Jas and shake some sense into her? I knew that this would achieve nothing, and the likelihood was that she would pass this off as normality, unable to question something that appeared severe and violent to others.

We got into my Range Rover and headed off to the local TK Maxx. A flash of my credit card, and Jas had a wardrobe of clothes for the weekend. There was something a little Richard Gere and Julia

Roberts about the whole thing though. I saw the odd glances from those who saw this excuse for banal gossip as a treat. The posh, well-dressed guy with the drugged-out hooker.

I suddenly felt incredibly sad for us both. Perhaps that was my intention.

We left the judgemental simpletons behind us as industrialisation gave way to the simple life of the country. It was a splash of blue and white collar combining—never so easy to distinguish between the two anymore. The blue-collar farmer had, for the most part, merged into the aristocrat farming as a hobby, at first so his high-maintenance wife could have the horses that she so desired, and then they could have dogs, cats, chickens, a couple of goats, and a huge vegetable patch screaming out *"organic and sustainability"* at every man who would listen.

I had never wanted to be part of this idealism. It was a crock of shit to me. Dreaming away in isolation felt foolish. Perhaps I was just of a generation that enjoyed the hustle and bustle of a town. The sound of cash registers, the honking horns of disgruntled commuters, and police and ambulance sirens almost became melodic in their delivery.

But it wasn't to say that I couldn't quite happily venture out to the countryside once in a while,

A Cold Retreat

specifically to a fancy hotel where I could be waited on.

I turned off onto a road full of potholes that, thankfully, the suspension of the Range Rover was able to absorb the shocks of. Jas had fallen asleep—or was unconscious. Sometimes, the two were not too dissimilar.

It had rained earlier, but now the sun was high in the sky like a giant spotlight shining on us, making us feel like the stars of this situation. Jas looked at the house with eyes that squinted from the brightness, and I had to wonder whether she remembered why she was here.

"Is this your dealer's house?" she asked as we started to walk towards the entrance, our shoes crunching on the gravel.

"No, Jas. Let's not talk anymore about drugs, dealers, or getting high, yeah? We are here to get clean…remember?"

"Clean, huh?" she muttered.

In we went.

Chapter 50

Dex – A week ago

"Dinner will be ready in ten minutes!" she said with a big grin on her face, and she turned back to the kitchen again.

I looked at my phone for the time. It was late afternoon. I had been hoping to be at the B&B by now. I couldn't believe I was sitting in a stranger's house as she cooked me dinner. It was a classic case of not being strong enough to say *"no."* The inability to want to hurt somebody else's feelings.

"Can I use your loo?" I shouted, walking towards the kitchen. I noticed that the food appeared to consist of beans on toast, although she hadn't started yet and was messing around with eggs too. For some reason, I felt a little disappointed. I was not sure exactly what I had been expecting. It was never going to give Gordon Ramsay a run for his money, but not being a kid anymore, I thought it might be something a little more…er, grown up.

A Cold Retreat

"Sure, love," she replied. "Up the stairs. You can't miss it; it's the room with the bath in!" She snorted as she laughed at her own joke.

"Got ya!" I said in mock humour.

The bathroom did indeed have a bath in it, so it was not fooling anyone. The colour was a diarrhoea brown, which had been popular about the time that ABBA were singing triumphantly about "Waterloo," a song that was historically incorrect as not being where Napoleon won the war at all. Mind you, I was not sure how involved the Swedes were in it, and Google hadn't been invented back then.

As a standard procedure in another person's house, I locked the door. I never wanted to be caught with my pants down, especially not in such an unfamiliar environment as this, and I also didn't trust that little shit of a boy, Giles.

I had just flushed when there was a bang on the door. Not a bang like a hand or fist, but more like that of a tool. I took no notice and washed my hands in an act of cleanliness.

I unlocked the door to find the lock jammed, and I pulled on the handle. In a swift move, it flew out, and I stood there with the handle in my hand.

I was locked in the bathroom. Great.

"Hello?" I shouted. I then heard the giggling. "Giles? Are you out there? Can you open this door?"

There was more giggling, then footsteps running away. I could only hope that he was about to get his mum. This was not an ideal situation at all.

I waited…and waited.

"Hello!" I shouted. "I'm locked in the bathroom!" Again, I waited, but nothing.

I suddenly had a montage of horror movie clips all surrounding innocent people being enticed into the homes of deranged killers, imprisoned and then turned into somebody's play-thing before being brutally tortured whilst dirty inbred folk giggled and chewed on fingers from a cloudy jar.

"Help!" I shouted as loudly as I could, but this time rather than at the door, it was out of the window.

It could be regarded as an overreaction, but I pulled out my phone. I considered ringing the police and then realised just how stupid that sounded. I rang the only person I knew who lived nearby, my old band mate Jez.

The phone had barely rung once before it was answered by the excited voice of Jez.

"Dexy! How the hell are you, mate?"

"I've been better, Jez…"

A Cold Retreat

"Haven't we all, mate! That battle-axe a few doors down keeps giving me shit. I've told her that if she wants me to knock her on her arse, then I will..."

"Jez, listen!"

"Calm it down. What's up?"

I was massaging my forehead as I replied, "I'm sorta locked in a bathroom."

"You what? Locked in a bathroom? Whose bathroom?" He was laughing now.

"I'm not sure... Look, can you come and get me?"

"Sure, where are you? A coffee shop or summat? I was locked in Coffee#1 for five minutes once, before I realised I was pulling the door instead of pushing it. Bloody easily done, my friend."

"Right."

"So have you tried pushing it?"

"I'm at someone's house."

"Why don't you call them?"

"I have. They don't seem to be answering."

"Whose house?"

"I can't remember her name..."

Jez laughed knowingly. "Ahh, I get ya! You don't want to wake her, ya dirty dog!"

"No, no, it's nothing like that. I brought her son home..."

"You did what! Er…is that what…y'know…you're…"

"God, no! Will you listen to me?"

"Right, okay…sorry."

"I'm in Hazel End."

"Okay. What number?"

"I don't know the number. My van is parked outside though. You know, my VW campervan."

"Orange and white?"

"That's it."

"I'm on my way."

It was an awkward ten minutes. I was surprised that the boy's mum had not come to check on me. Perhaps she thought that I had a dodgy stomach or something.

Then suddenly I heard the thumping of someone heavy loping up the stairs, and then there was a banging on the door.

"Dex! You in there, mate?"

"Of course I am," I said. "I can't get out!"

"Right," Jez said, and suddenly there was the sound of tools tinkering. Suddenly the door swung open and the large figure of Jez grinned at me and pointed to the handle that I was holding.

"There's your problem, mate. You wanna leave that attached next time you want a dump in a pretty lady's house."

A Cold Retreat

"I wasn't... Oh, never mind."

"You should've called," Giles's mum said, surprised, like this wasn't something that I had thought of.

"I did. A number of times."

She suddenly looked ashamed. "I'm sorry. You really are having a bad time with us. I don't blame you if you don't want to stay for food..."

"Food," Jez jumped in. "We're not going anywhere before we've eaten, right, Dexy?"

I shrugged. "I guess we'll stay."

She beamed. "You'd better come down then."

We sat down and tucked into the beans on toast with fried egg and some sort of potato mix that might, or might not, have been hash browns.

"Nice place you have here...er..." Jez started.

"Helena."

"Yes, Helena."

"Thank you... Jez is it?"

"It is indeed. With a J, not a G."

"Good to know."

This was classic Jez. He was married, but he was a terrible flirt. Terrible because he didn't always mean to, and I had never known him to cheat on his wife. He talked about it, but anyone who knew Jez was aware that he talked a good talk about a lot of things, but he rarely acted on it. I suppose, in some ways, we were alike. The only difference was that I was not married. I was happy to portray myself as something that I was not. I wasn't looking to fool people…or perhaps I was. Or maybe the person who I was really looking to kid was myself. I wanted to be the surfer, and I wanted to be the skateboarder. I could just about do both, but I was far from being able to execute each in any way that didn't scream *novice*. I had been doing both for years, but still looked like a ten-year-old who had just taken them up.

"That was great!" Jez said.

"Yes, thank you," I said.

"Don't mention it." What I really wanted to mention was the fact that I had not seen or heard from the little shit Giles since he had fucked around with the door handle and laughed at me. I let it go.

"We had best be off," I said.

"Really? I could put coffee on?" she said, and it was almost a desperate attempt to keep us there.

"Yep, I've got the wife to get back to. Give her some Jez-lovin'! Haha!"

Helena looked at me.

"Me too. I've got to go see her too."

"What, his wife?"

"No, I mean…"

A Cold Retreat

"Actually, yes," Jez said grabbing my hand. "We have a special relationship."

I was lost for words.

"Oh, I see," Helena said as we walked towards the door.

"Thanks for bringing Giles back," she called as we left.

"You're welcome."

We stood outside.

"Did you have to say that?" I said.

"No, but it made you feel uncomfortable and was a good excuse to leave."

"True, but still…"

"So where are you off? Over to your mum's?"

"Tomorrow I was going to venture over. Today I was meant to be staying at a B&B. They said I could stay there all weekend for free."

"Really?"

"Yep. Looks a nice place too."

"You want to come over to mine for the night?"

"I'm not having sex with your wife," I added.

"You're not the only one," he mumbled under his breath before saying: "Come on, she'd love to say hello. She loved the band. We can watch a movie and drink some beers. You can go over to that B&B gay retreat tomorrow."

"Why is everything gay to you?"

- 315 -

He shrugged. "Just is, really."
"You coming over then?"
"Fuck it, why not?" And off we went.

Chapter 51

I looked out of the window and saw the cars below. I had mixed emotions about this. How should I be feeling? I was more than confused with the whole situation.

I needed answers, but I was too scared to ask the questions.

She stood silently at the door. Her stare tried to penetrate into me and search for words. This was exciting and uncomfortable all at once. She was like a pet that had brought a dead animal as an offering and dropped it at my feet. She stood back, unsure whether I would praise her for the present or scold her for taking an innocent life.

I broke the silence first. "It really is good to see you again," I said, holding onto the doll, smoothing the red dress.

"It's been a long time, Penny."

"I've not been called that for what seems like a lifetime. I'm a very different person now."

She fussed with her hair, possibly conscious that it was now short and nothing like I remembered.

She had always had long hair and had told me stories of men yanking it back when taking her from behind. She had always been so open with her sexual exploits, and I wondered whether on some level she had enjoyed trying to shock me. But now she looked different. Not just physically—she was of course ten years older than the last time I had seen her. She had lost a lot of weight, which changed the way her face looked. Her cheek bones were now prominent, and her skin was less smooth now, showing subtle wrinkles.

"What is this all about?" I asked. "I feel like I'm missing something here, Kate."

"Like you, I am no longer Kate. She was the woman that men were resigned to fucking when women like you were already taken…"

"So this is revenge on me? Jealousy?"

What I had first taken as a spiky edge to her words suddenly softened, her eyes opening up in horror.

"God, no! What I mean is I can understand why I attracted the men that I did. *But you?* You were always so nice and kind…and yet…" She went off into some reverie. "And yet they still treated you the way that they did."

"Boys are boys, and d'ya know what? A lot of men can act like spoilt boys too. They want

A Cold Retreat

something, and they think that they can have it, and then they get cross when they don't get it."

Kate's look changed. Her face seemed suddenly filled with anger, screwing up and becoming suddenly ugly with rage. "That's abuse, Penny. They cannot get away with that!"

"What d'you mean?"

"You changed your name. You went into hiding. Was that not enough?"

I tried to smile, not sure whether it would add fuel to her anger. "I went travelling. I changed my name to Hope. I did it to reinvent myself. I became more liberated and sexually empowered. It was nothing to do with the men in my past, but more to become the person that I wanted to be. One with self-worth and a focus to succeed."

"But don't you see? Those bastards are the ones that took your self-worth from you. They made you do things that you wouldn't normally have done. They cheated on you. They forced you to do those horrible things... They used and abused you!"

"Kate, look, calm down. Yes, those things happened. But they made me stronger. I got myself into situations that I shouldn't have..."

"It wasn't your fault, Penny! That's my point!"

"I am not saying that it was my fault. I wanted to be loved. Was that *so* wrong?"

"But they took advantage of you!"

"Yes, and at other times I took advantage of them. We all do things that we are not proud of… Look, Kate, I don't see why you're going on about these things that happened so long ago."

Kate stopped and looked at me. A sly grin appeared on her face. "They're here."

"What?"

"I've invited them."

My stomach dropped, and my heart beat fast. "Who?"

"Travis."

"Travis? Who's Travis?"

She looked shocked. "The guy you met at Starbucks. The one that made you do those things, then fucked his girlfriend in front of you!"

I couldn't believe what I was hearing. "That was twenty years ago!"

"But you were devastated!"

"He was my first love. As brief as it was."

"He stole your virginity!"

"I gave it up to him. He didn't steal it."

"But he forced you."

"Kate… Look…it was scary. It was exciting. It was disturbing. I was broken hearted. I felt abused, but I never told him to stop…"

"But that doesn't—"

A Cold Retreat

"...*Matter*. I know. But it isn't so black and white. It happened, I wish it hadn't...although," I paused to collect my words. "There is a part of me that is glad that it did."

"How can you say that?"

"I'm not condoning anything, but I am ashamed as much of the person that I was back then as of the way I was treated."

"I don't understand how you can be so forgiving." She came over and leant down. We were almost face to face.

"Kate. We cannot live in a world where we hold everybody else responsible and accountable for our own mistakes."

"There you go again! Blaming yourself."

"Look... What am I doing here? What do you hope to gain?"

"I want them to apologise. I want them to understand how bad we have been treated."

"I don't know, Kate. I don't know whether I can be a part of this."

"What? How can you say that? How can you let them get away with this?"

"Who else is there?"

"Dex, remember? The guy that you got with at the gig and he went off with someone else?"

"Dex? We weren't even seeing each other! Kate, I didn't even remember his name."

"He led you on, and then the minute your back was turned, he was off fucking someone else!"

"That was one night!"

"That's as may be, but you were upset for weeks over it!"

"And now I look back and I'm embarrassed that I was so upset over someone that I only kissed once!"

"What about Ben, *huh?* He strung you on for bloody ages and still kept going back to that slut of his!"

"Okay, yes, he hurt me the most, but I'm over it, Kate."

"I just can't believe that these bastards are so easily forgiven!"

"I'm not forgiving them, Kate. I've moved on. I've forgotten about them…"

"What? *Even* Ben?"

"No, I haven't forgotten about Ben, but I knew what was going on. I was the one that turned a blind eye. I made the decision to stay around even though I knew it would never last."

"Right!" Kate turned away and walked to the door. "I'm Sasha now, by the way! I did this for you!"

A Cold Retreat

"Look, Kate... I am grateful, I really am."

"We'll talk later. Just think about it, yeah?"

I nodded, and she disappeared. It felt a little like an ultimatum. I was scared at what might happen if I didn't agree with whatever plan she had.

I thought about just slipping out and running away. I missed Kate, but I really didn't want to be part of this.

She had emailed me out of the blue. I had been so pleased to hear from her. She had told me that she now owned a B&B and that I should come over for the weekend. I had thought it would be just the two of us, and again, this showed how much I was still that person—the one who wanted to believe.

When I had arrived, I had been quickly ushered up to my room. I had sat here for what seemed like ages before she joined me.

Again, I felt used. She didn't want to reconnect so much as to commit some crime together. The truth was, I had seen that look in her eyes before. My room was a couple of floors up, with corridors and stairs before getting outside. I was scared to make a break for it. I felt almost paralysed inside this room.

I took out my phone.

Of course, there was no signal.

I hoped that this was just one big joke on me.

Chapter 52

Sasha - Friday

I just didn't get it. I had gone to so much trouble to try and put things right. I had done everything for Penny, and she just didn't seem to care. Yes, I had thrown in some people myself that had done me wrong. Christian had always been the one that I fully held responsible for how I turned out. I didn't subscribe to the notion that I had just been naïve and had gone along with the situation. He was the one who had known that I was vulnerable, and he had done everything he could to force me into doing exactly what he wanted.

To me, the question was all about control. Who was the puppet and who was the puppeteer? He had always been the one who held the power, and so he had known exactly what he was doing. He hadn't cared about my feelings and what I had wanted—nor the repercussions of his actions, the fact that my expectations from future relationships slowly lowered until I was crawling along the bottom, happy just not to be beaten.

A Cold Retreat

I sat down on my bed and began to cry.

"Hey, hey," Charlie said, coming over to me. "I don't want to make you feel worse, but Sasha, what did you expect from her? She doesn't get it, does she?"

Through the sobs I managed to say, "But she was the motivation. I thought if I felt the way that I did, then surely she would too? I don't understand why she doesn't feel the same."

"Remember what I said?" he pressed. This was the real reason that he was remaining calm.

"But would I not end up being just as bad as them downstairs?"

"They were never trying to help you, were they? All they thought about was themselves. They just wanted to take, take, take. You wanted to help her. She's thrown that back in your face." He stopped and grabbed my hand. "You knew the risks beforehand, didn't you?"

"But this was about her... How could I then not tell her? I thought that she... I don't know... I just assumed things would turn out differently."

"Sash, that's life though, isn't it? When that guy Christian took you into the bushes at school, that wasn't how you imagined things would turn out, was it?"

I shook my head. I went to say something, but he held up his finger. "And that Pete fella. Did you start to speak to him in the clubs and expect to be taken back to his house and gangbanged?"

"No."

"Exactly. So all you have been focused on is getting these people together and having their slimy little eyes opened to what they've done to you and Penny. If she's not interested, then so be it."

"She won't say anything, Charlie."

"Do you honestly believe that, Sash? You thought that she would be happy about this, didn't you? You thought that she would help out, but instead, she becomes a risk."

"Are you seriously thinking that she should go with them?"

"Are you not?" He was serious now. I could see something that I had not seen before: a flash of anger.

"I don't know," I said. "I just don't know."

And suddenly, I had to wonder: out of the two of us, which one of us was the puppeteer?

A Cold Retreat

Chapter 53

Travis - Friday

I sat down in the lounge area with a pint of cider just as another guy arrived. I was soaking up the place, but now glad that I wouldn't be the only other person here.

He looked like he worked outside. He had that weathered look. He was being slightly flirtatious with our host Sasha, but I suppose a few years ago I would've done the same.

We had been told that our order for dinner would be taken later, but for now, the bar was completely free. I certainly planned to take full advantage of that.

The guy nodded to me as he walked in.

"Free bar, I'm told," he said, and I noticed that there was a slightly rural accent to him. "I'm Chris."

"Hi, I'm Travis. What're you drinking?"

"Scotch."

The ice sounded loud as it hit the glass. I poured the drink, taking full advantage of being next to the bar already. He sat down near me and took a sip. He glanced around the room, looking at the paintings on the walls.

"You here on business?" he asked, probably noticing that I was looking at him.

"Yeah…that obvious?"

"You're wearing a suit, and you're on your own. It doesn't take a genius to work it out."

I looked down at myself, forgetting that I was suited and booted. "Good point. You?"

"No, not exactly." He looked a little uncomfortable. "I'm meeting someone."

"Really?" I said. "Mistress? Girlfriend?"

"It's complicated."

"If it's to do with women, then it usually is, mate!"

He swirled the liquid around the glass before taking another sip. "I met her online. We've not met yet."

"Ahh, right."

"You seem sceptical."

"Aren't *you?*" I said. "Have you spoken to her on the phone?"

"Once or twice."

"Face-timed?"

"Face-what?"

"Skype, you know, video-chat."

A Cold Retreat

He shook his head. "Nah. We're both busy."

"You realise she could be a fifteen-year-old boy? Or a thirty-stone hippo."

He looked suddenly hurt. I almost felt bad for him.

"Or not. I'm sure she is exactly who she says she is."

He nodded and stared into his glass once more. It was funny—just how many thousands, perhaps millions, of people had done that same thing, somehow expecting the answers to jump out of the glass? I suspected he was now weighing up the chances of what I had said, possibly contemplating whether or not this was worth it, and to save face, making himself scarce.

I smiled to myself but then had a sudden sinking feeling. Why was I getting so cocky? I was a fallen hero. Once commanding exactly what I wanted from people and females, I was now lucky if I was given the time of day by most people. When you thought about it, this Chris fellow was in a much better position. He at least had a dream that might come true today. It could also turn to shit, but that would be later. For the here and now, he held onto a hope and fantasy that I had not had in years.

I stared into my drink. I found no answers either.

We remained in silence for a while before a couple came into the room. They seemed somewhat lively, the girl extremely animated, swishing her long hair around, and the guy winking at her and tapping her on the backside.

"You two had a fight?" She giggled loudly at Chris and me.

"Maybe we were just waiting for you two," I said, glancing over at Chris, who smiled at this.

"Well, we've arrived!" she shouted. "To the bar I think!"

"Help yourself. It's all free!" I said.

"My kinda place," the guy said. "I'm Ben, by the way, and this hot-thing is Bronwyn."

"Hey, guys!" she squealed, pouring out a generous glass of red wine. "Usual, Benny-boy?"

"You know it."

"I'm Travis," I said, and we all automatically looked at Chris.

"My name is Christian. Or Chris."

"Christian or Chris?" Ben said. "Is that your full name or do you want us to choose?"

"Do what you like," Chris said, "but I think I'll have another one of these."

"Okay, Chris it is." Ben smiled.

"Hey, Chris!" Bronwyn said from behind the bar.

A Cold Retreat

Chris was hard to gauge. He was calm and quiet, but he also seemed the sort of person that took no shit.

I wasn't sure whether or not I could stay with these people for the whole of the weekend. On the other hand, we all might remain friends for life after this. You could just never tell.

Chapter 54

Christian - Friday

"Hi, I have a room booked. My named is Christian Raney."

The lady nodded her head as she tapped the keyboard and looked at the computer screen. She was attractive with dyed red hair cut quite short. There was something familiar about her, but sometimes an attractive woman can have that effect on a man.

"Ahh, yes," she said, looking at me closely again as if she had my picture and was checking my identity. "Mr Raney."

"You can call me Christian," I added.

"Can I now," she replied, slightly amused.

"Do you have a Penny Swaldon booked in here?"

The woman looked up and suddenly went serious. "I'm afraid I cannot give out details of the other guests."

I nodded, feeling disappointed. "I see."

A Cold Retreat

"Here are your keys," she said after I had filled in the registration form. This had mostly already been done for me, and it just needed my registration number, mobile number, and credit card details. I signed in hurriedly and took the keys.

"You are the first room on the first floor. Feel free to come down to the bar where the drinks are free all weekend. I'll be along later to take dinner orders."

"Brilliant," I said, again wanting to ask more questions about Penny, but I let it go. I didn't want to sound desperate.

I took my bag up to my room. It was spacious and looked out onto the gardens at the back. There was a pond and a couple of large outbuildings with woods in the background.

I liked the sound of free drinks, and being a man, wasting time unpacking my things was completely out of the question. I wanted to get some drinks inside me for when Penny arrived.

The stairs were old and wide with smaller steps than normal. I locked this detail away in my mind for when I was slightly more drunk later.

Within half an hour, I was sitting sipping scotch and feeling a little uncomfortable. There was a guy in a suit, who looked like the brother of Robert Downey Jr after an all-night bender, and then a couple that consisted of a guy with short, shaved hair, who looked like he took no shit, and his girlfriend, who looked like she could be a real live wire.

She reminded me of a girl from college who had been plain for the most part, but with a bit of warpaint and a few drinks had suddenly become quite slutty and ultimately desirable.

I sat looking up from my seat at everything around me, but then I was lost in thinking about Penny. She was hot in her pictures. I liked that she was not model hot, and she was middle-aged, but she still looked great. I knew that we had only been talking for a few weeks, but it was she that instigated this meeting. It wasn't like one of those TV shows that I'd heard about when people dated online for years without ever meeting up. We had both sent each other pictures. If nothing else, I had some great photos to remember her by!

We talked about music, and the woman, Bronwyn, needed no excuse to wiggle her hips to any song mentioned.

I even thought about some of the women from my past. This took me back to the girls at school whom we had taken into the bushes. There was a simple innocence from that time that I missed. To have girls besotted with you and wanting you so

A Cold Retreat

badly was something that, later on, I had taken for granted until suddenly it was an effort to even catch a woman's eye, let alone engage in a conversation—or God forbid something that resembled a lustful date!

And then another strange couple arrived.

"I see that the liquor is already flowing freely," a tall and skinny guy said in a posh accent. He was dressed in a pink polo shirt and steering in an incredibly skinny girl with him. She made Bronwyn look almost plump, and, with her pasty skin and stringy hair, looked like she had died and just been resurrected.

"Where are the drugs?" she asked in a loud whisper. Her eyes were half-closed.

"No drugs, baby. We are cleaning up," he said to her.

"Hi, what are you drinking?" Bronwyn asked, completely happy to be barmaid for the day.

"We'll both have a gin, right, Jas?"

She nodded. "I like gin."

If Ben and Bronwyn were strange, then these two were completely bonkers.

Chapter 55

Ben - Friday

I put the suitcases down on the bed. There was always that happy excitement of expectation when you first go into a hotel room. This was a B&B, but big enough that it was more like a small hotel.

"Come here," I said, pulling Bronwyn towards me. We kissed like we were on a first date, and my hands wandered.

She pulled away with a big smile on her face. "Hold on there, Romeo. We've got all weekend! Let's go and indulge in that free bar that she talked about."

She was right, and I knew Bronwyn. When she drank, she got even hornier that usual. The times that we had gotten the most explosive together had been the times that we had been completely inebriated or completely off our tits.

There was something that was bothering me slightly, but I couldn't quite put my finger on it.

It was something to do with the owner, Sasha. She looked familiar, although I couldn't quite get a good hard look at her. There was a chance that at some stage we had had sex, although she looked my age, so it could've been a long time ago. It might be amusing, but to be away on a weekend that was meant to be for Bronwyn and me and then have some ghost from my past crop up would do me no good. Experience told me that Bronwyn could get more than a little jealous, and there was no way that she would stay here under the same roof as a woman who I had fucked. That was for sure.

"Come on then," I said, grabbing her hand.

We skipped down the stairs, Bronwyn grinning at Sasha as we got to the bottom. "Free drinks in here, are they?" she said, to which Sasha nodded.

We walked into the lounge and spotted a couple of blokes sitting alone. They looked like they might have been talking, but were not close enough to be together.

Bronwyn was never one to be backwards in coming forward said, "You two been fighting?"

Both men grinned. Bronwyn had shimmied over to the bar and was proceeding in getting drinks for us and the two guys. One looked like he was some over-the-hill movie star dressed up in a suit, and the other guy looked like a gentle giant, a worker who was probably quite capable in a fist fight.

It was about half an hour later that a very peculiar couple appeared. At first, it looked like the guy was wrestling with the girl, but then it was obvious that she was being helped; whether this was a medical or psychological disorder was hard to conclude.

The guy was some toff who'd probably never done a hard day's work in his life, and the girl looked like some sort of crack whore. Perhaps that was being mean, but she really did not seem in a great way. Her clothes were new, but her body looked like she had just been released from hospital and it was giving out on her rapidly.

This point was underlined as she whispered loudly, "Where are the drugs?"

He replied with a posh, commanding voice. "There are no drugs, baby. We are cleaning up. This will make us feel better."

"Well, hello, one and all. A pleasure and all that." Considering he was carrying around a human rag doll, the posh twat seemed incredibly relaxed. "This is all rather nice and quaint."

But, of course, things were only getting started.

Chapter 56

Pete - Friday

This was a beautiful place, all decked out in oak panels and antiques. A grandfather clock stood prominently; its time seemed so official that you felt the need to check your own watch against it.

Jas was struggling. This was meant to be for me to get clean, but I felt the need to have someone else going through this with me. If I could concentrate on getting Jas clean, then by default, I would also straighten myself out too.

It was hard not to be conscious of what others might be thinking, and so I tried not to look too carefully at the receptionist—who turned out to be the owner. I filled out our details, all the while holding Jas up. My worry was what the owner would think, on individuals under the influence of narcotics.

When we heard of other people there, we hurried to our room and dropped off our bags. My theory was that, if we were to get clean, we needed to be around others who were not like us.

By rights, we should've knocked alcohol on the head too, but I had a theory that suggested that this was the lesser of two evils and so we should concentrate on one before the other.

There were a number of people in the lounge area, each already sipping away at drinks and beginning to get a little merry.

"Well, hello there!" an attractive—albeit a little rough-looking—woman said from behind the bar.

"Hello to you all," I said, holding up Jas. I needed to get her seated, although she would still be slouching for a while. It was funny, but once plied with liquor, she often came alive and certainly was then more in control of herself.

"So what are you both drinking?" the temporary barmaid asked. In truth, we would both drink anything. We were drug addicts, but we were alcoholics too. We both preferred to hit spirits first rather than beers, which seemed like you had to drink a lot of liquid in order to get the same buzz.

"Gin?" I mumbled to Jas, though this was for the benefit of everyone else. If I had said "alcoholic urine," then Jas would've gulped it down without question. Gin was currently popular as being somewhat fashionable, and the right stuff could still give you a big kick.

"Yeah, we'll both have Gordon's."

A Cold Retreat

"I like gin," Jas said loudly.

"Don't we all, love. Right you are. My name's Bronwyn, by the way, and that handsome fella over there is Ben."

"This is Jas," I said. "And I am Peter."

"That well-dressed guy is Travis," she then said, pointing to a guy who looked like he might've been handsome in his younger years, but possibly had been through a few hard years recently. "And that is Chris, or Christian, whichever you care to call him!"

"Hi," I said as we got our glasses.

"So, you two look like you rode hard on your horses. What's your story?" Travis said.

"Well, you might be right. Travis, isn't it?" I took a sip of gin, enjoying the way it slipped down my throat. I was itching for something else to take the edge off things.

"Jas and I have enjoyed our lives. We have partied now for way too long, and so it has been decided that a form of recuperation is required in order for us to level out and gain perspective on our lives."

"Rehab, you mean?" Ben added with a wink.

"If you like," I said. "We all battle our demons, right?"

There was a room full of nodding heads. Glancing looks around suggested that each had a story to tell, but whether or not this was the platform was undecided.

I pushed on. "So, Bronwyn, what about you? Any demons?"

She grinned and threw a glance at Ben. "Maybe."

"Let me guess," I said. "You and Ben are a couple, but sometimes you both want a little more?"

Ben threw me a glance that suggested I should be careful. "I mean no disrespect, mate. I don't know you, so I am only guessing."

"Come on, Ben. We both know he's right."

"It's a lucky guess. A parlour trick from a charlatan fortune teller. No offence." It was meant as a dig.

"None taken, as I do not proclaim to have any psychic powers, just the ability to make educated guesses."

"We can tell that you're educated," Christian said with a wink.

"Okay, let's leave, Ben, as I don't want to upset my new friends."

"What about Robert Downey Jr over there?" Christian said. "What do you think his story is?"

A Cold Retreat

I looked at him. Travis did indeed have a passing resemblance to the Hollywood actor, although, he looked like the paparazzi shots of him tumbling out of a club in the early hours, rather than the freshly clean-cut version.

"I'd say that at one stage you were Billy-Big-Balls. Women of all ages found you attractive, and you were having so much sex that you felt like a gigolo working pro bono. On more than one occasion, you even considered that very vocation, though dismissed it due to its clandestine nature, meaning you also crave the widespread recognition of success as much as sexual gratification. How am I doing?"

Travis grinned. The thing that I had learnt when doing these readings—or rather, guesswork—is that if you can guess with a theory that is positive and shows the subject in a good light, then even if the guess is inaccurate, they are less likely to admit to it; such can be the ego of the subject.

"Not bad," Travis replied. "Except that men found me attractive too!" This response told me everything that I needed to know. I left it there. I mentioned nothing of the obvious fall on hard times. This could be attributed to a poor decision somewhere along the line. The wrong gamble, the wrong woman, who knew. Maybe both.

"And Christian?" Bronwyn said, pointing.

I looked at him. He was not an easy one to read.

"Okay, I think I have it." I rubbed my hands together, more for effect than for anything else. "I think that as a youngster right into your later teens you were a tearaway, possibly cocky, and either you or your friends had some sort of brush with the law. However, in the last fifteen or so years, you have mellowed and calmed down. Whilst some people still fear you, you are more likely to break up an altercation than start one. How's that?" Again, this was simple psychology. I had suggested that he was both tough and strong, whilst also being seen as reformed and a peace-maker.

"There or thereabouts," he agreed.

Then suddenly Jas spoke up. "Has anyone got any drugs?"

There were shakes of heads, and I tried to look apologetic. I looked around. Not everyone here was telling the truth.

Chapter 57

Dex – A week ago

I sometimes wondered whether life could get any more strange. I had been roaming around for a while, and the minute I decided who I want to spend my life with, I found myself over three hours away. At first, I had been locked in the bathroom of a woman who had looked like she might want to kidnap me, and then I was met with this spectacle.

Apparently, Jez was unable to get through to his wife to tell her that he was bringing me back, as when we burst through the door she was blasting out Cher and singing along to "Turn Back Time." I was lost for words, as her short, cuddly figure was stuffed into the full, mainly-transparent cat-suit like Cher had worn in the video. Her eyes were closed as she came towards us, and she actually grabbed me thinking that I was her husband. As her eyes shot open, I was not too sure who was the most shocked.

"You're not Jez," she said, turning incredibly red and not being able to cover enough of herself with her arms.

"I'm not," I said, quickly turning my back and closing my eyes too. A visual double-bagging, if you like.

"This is awkward," Jez said.

If only I could turn back time, I thought, as I stood outside the door.

Then suddenly a voice called to me. "Hey, you! What are you doing skulking around there?" a stern-faced old woman said, walking purposefully towards me.

"You wouldn't believe me if I told you," I said.

"From that household, I would believe it. You know them, or are you some surfer-strip-o-gram?" I began to laugh until I realised that she was serious.

"Strip-o-gram? *What?* No. Jez's wife was dressed as Cher. You know, in that skimpy gear…"

"Alright, young man, I get the picture. My, that must've been quite an…interesting view. Mind you, if you are a friend of Jeremy's, then you must be used to all sorts of high-jinks."

Just then the door opened, and Jez jumped out of his skin as he saw the feisty old woman.

"Miss Chambers! Uh, what a…surprise!"

A Cold Retreat

"Indeed. And what tomfoolery have you got yourself into this time, Jeremy?"

He visibly hung his head before replying like a naughty schoolboy to a teacher. "Nothing, just a misunderstanding, that's all." He turned to me. "It's safe to come in now."

"Okay," I replied. "Nice to meet you," I said to the old lady and was ushered inside.

"Bloody old busy-body!" Jez sneered as we walked inside and then jumped as the doorbell rang loudly.

"I heard that!" Miss Chambers said accusingly.

"Sorry, just a joke. Good night." He closed the door and eye-rolled towards me.

A few minutes later, Jez's wife came in wearing a considerable amount more than she'd had on earlier. I had slept with women whose bodies I had seen less of than hers. This was a surreal day indeed.

After a brief hello, Jez's wife disappeared, presumably with embarrassment, as Jez pulled out some beers and we sat down to watch a couple of no-brainer comedies that Jez had on his SKY Planner.

We talked about the things that had happened to us, and he mentioned that he had come back from

Devon this morning, but then he became vague as to what it was all about.

I said that he sounded like my hitchhiker, who had also had an unbelievable story that she had failed to indulge me in. Jez just nodded, which was unlike him. I had to wonder whether Jez and Kim had perhaps ended up together in some compromising situation. With Jez, you just never could tell.

Mid-way through the second movie, Jez disappeared, and I found myself turning up the volume to drown out the sounds of Cher. Clearly, they didn't realise just how loud they were.

An hour later, the TV was off and I was laid out on the sofa with a cushion over my head. Jez was a strange one, but I couldn't help but wonder whether Jez was rather skilled at knowing his way around a woman's body!

I closed my eyes and tried to get rid of the picture tattooed into my brain of a shorter, younger, and chubbier Cher wobbling and writhing around the lounge…

Chapter 58

Sasha - Friday

So here I was, slap bang in the middle of this whole thing, and of course nothing was quite going to plan. It was not that it hadn't been a success, it was just that normal slightly flat feeling of things that you could not control. In my mind, I had imagined things differently. They weren't just obvious things that I could describe, but feelings and emotions. I had been convinced that I would be riding on a crest of a wave, on a high from how these people had all come together, but something was not quite right.

I was disappointed that Penny didn't share my vision. I guess, deep down, I did feel deflated knowing that I had begun this journey for her. Yes, I had hijacked it a little, adding in Christian and Pete, but this was meant to empower us against those who had treated us like shit.

But even before Penny, I had failed to feel completely elated. This was like a big party that I had been planning for months, and when the day finally arrived, instead of being overwhelmed with excitement, I just felt stressed and tired out with the rush of adrenaline.

I walked down the stairs and into the lounge; everyone was taking full advantage of the free bar. To be honest, that had been Charlie's idea. Yes, it had cost a bit to stock up on enough booze to keep them lubricated in the devil's water, but it would loosen them up, relax them, and lower any inhibitions. The last thing you wanted was somebody to be clear headed when you were looking to fool them…

"Good afternoon, everyone," I said in a loud voice, suddenly incredibly conscious of all of the eyes now on me. "Here are the menus. If you could pick what you would like, then I will get our chef to cook the meals for 7 p.m. tonight."

I walked around and handed them out.

"Ooh, this looks great!" Bronwyn said with a big smile, and I nodded as I gave Ben one too. I was worried about Pete, but thankfully he was fussing with the skank whom he had brought with him. He was definitely the most likely to recognise me, purely because I had seen him only a few months ago. Even with my change of hairstyle and my glasses, I was still the person whom he had seen regularly, and even though he was usually totally baked, he would be sure to recognise me. I had a realisation that perhaps with my clothes on I was just like everyone else, but then I also conceded that perhaps naked I was nothing more than sex organs to him anyway. So conversely, how disappointing would it be if he didn't recognise me? The months we spent together getting wasted, having sex, hanging out... Would he not recognise the laughter lines, the mole on my cheek, the size of my ears?

"Um, has anyone else arrived?" Christian said, and I felt something that might have been pity. The guy looked to be filled with hope that his date would be here looking exactly like her photographs and fuck him from here to next Tuesday. He would never know that she never existed. He would never know because it would be the last thing that he would soon care about...

"No, not yet."

"Don't worry, mate," Travis said. "I won't abandon you."

I took down the orders, making a special fuss to ask about allergies or specific requirements, before going out into the kitchen. Of course, there was no chef. There never would be a chef. These meals would never be cooked.

I supposed there should have been a part of me riddled with guilt. The hungry looks in their eyes picturing the delicious food that they would never taste and the fact that perhaps they wouldn't care later on…

I walked back upstairs to where Charlie had been hiding out. This was of course all part of the master plan. He could not be seen by any of them. We had talked this through at length. Originally, we had thought that keeping me away from them was the best idea, and that would have been the case if there would have been more than two of us. However, as the plan took shape, it was obvious that it didn't matter much if they did recognise me. The chances were that they would either keep it to themselves or mention it when we were alone, so if all went to plan, then they would only find out when we wanted them to: the great reveal, as it were.

"How are the guests?" he said as I walked into his room.

"Merry, cordial, and full of high spirits," I replied, walking over to where he was lying on the bed. I gently stroked my fingers up his leg.

"Are you ready for this?" he asked, watching the digits move higher.

"This is what I have always wanted," I purred.

"I wonder," he said, grabbing my hand with speed, "just who you are doing this for."

"What do you mean?" I said, pulling my hand free, grinning, and slapping him gently on the face.

A Cold Retreat

He half smiled. "You like to inflict pain... We both know that. This has nothing to do with Penny."

"It doesn't matter what you think, Charlie. It only matters that we follow the plan."

"The plan includes these," he said, handing me a couple of items.

Things were about to get very real indeed.

Chapter 59

Penny

There was a part of me that was touched by this grand gesture. Arguably this was the biggest thing that someone had ever done for me. At one stage, this would have been something that not only would have reduced me to tears, but in return, I would've done anything for them. This would include being quiet and accepting of her enticing a group of people from her past to come together in some bizarre trial, during which she would pass judgement and, ultimately, penalty.

The years had matured me. I had carved out a life that had overshadowed any dark times that I had been through. Again, I felt myself reliving them, but memories have an ability to change thoughts and perspective. We all know that nostalgia has a way of skewing reality. It is never a coincidence that our best memories don't always appear that way whilst we are living them. Time dissolves away the uncomfortable niggles of nerves, self-doubt, or

A Cold Retreat

general lows to leave remaining the excitement, laughter, and high times.

Kate walked in with a nervous look on her face. Things had turned dramatically. It was ironic that this whole charade had been put together supposedly for me. Kate had then slipped in another couple of people whom I was not aware of. One was somebody from school that I knew had hurt her badly. That now seemed belittling of the actual act, which again, had been so long ago that it was almost irrelevant. That was the real shame of it all; the fact that this was more than likely the catalyst to this whole thing suggested exactly the severity of it. I remembered though the time of the Starbucks Guy (which is what I always referred to him as). Kate had been adamant that I should seek revenge, when all I had really wanted to do was move on. I had always struggled to be able to fully evaluate what had happened that day. I had always tried to put the incident into some sort of perspective, which was that we had been strangers. I should never have gone back to his flat. Of course, he should never have invited me. The bottom line for me was that things happened slowly. I'd had many opportunities to stop, but part of me had wanted to do it. Not all of it, of course, but he was older, and I was younger. Had this happened to me when we were in a relationship, then I would've felt worse. I would've had the added distress of someone doing this to me who knew me—a person that I fully trusted, who understood my boundaries but still knowingly violated them. I had also heard that he had tried to contact me again. The truth was that I had still liked him, but I had felt it was all too much. He'd had a girlfriend for a start, and the fact that he had never mentioned this—albeit in the few hours that we had spent together—hurt me, but not as much as if I had been his girlfriend and found out that he had picked up a girl in a coffee shop and had sex with her the same day.

The other guy that had been invited here by her was the last person in her life to treat her badly. I didn't know all of the details, but it was obvious that where Christian had started the ball rolling, this guy had clearly completely tipped the balance, finally making her come to this decision.

"So, what do you think?" Kate said to me, and there was something in her eyes that looked like the beginning of tears as her voice quivered. She had a resignation about her that said she knew what I was going to say. It was like one of those awkward conversations between a couple that has broken up, the instigator being asked whether or not they want

A Cold Retreat

to give it a go again, whilst all the while knowing that it is in fact the end.

"I cannot tell you how much I appreciate the thought and effort you have gone to. You were always there for me when we were younger, and I really regret that we drifted apart when I went travelling."

Kate stood nodding and tried a smile.

"Okay..." She paused as she looked at the doll in the red dress. Then she smiled. "Hey, let me show you something. Come on."

"Okay," I replied, feeling slightly better that some excitement had suddenly appeared from nowhere.

We walked out of my room and towards another staircase.

"Where does this go?" I asked.

"The attic. I have some stuff up there that I'd like to show you."

I followed her and couldn't help but notice once again the amount of weight that she had lost. She'd always had a pretty face, and even carrying a little more weight she could attract the majority of the attention. She was always the loud, confident one, whereas I would blend into the background.

The attic was large, and there were a number of boxes around the outside. She walked over to one and pulled out a photo album. We both sat down against a board that ran between two of the roof beams.

The first picture showed two smiling girls in school uniforms. Both of us were wearing our ties the skinny way as per the style back then. I couldn't believe what I looked like. My hair was pulled back into a ponytail, but I was wearing a plastic hair band that I had pulled forward, giving my hair a little bump. Kate had natural blonde hair that, like others', would soon get darker with age. She had an armful of neon friendship bands and already a chest that was prominent.

"Look at us," I said, running a finger over the picture as if trying to feel for emotions.

"That was a week before Christian did what he did to me, Pen."

I felt the smile drop from my face. "You didn't tell me for a week," I said.

"I was ashamed… I thought I wanted to be the first one of us all to have sex…" She stopped, her voice breaking. "I never thought it would be like that."

"I wish…" I started, though I wasn't sure what I was about to say.

"What?" She then snapped. "That it was you? Of course you don't. You were always Little Miss

A Cold Retreat

Prissy. Scared to talk to boys. It would've never been you, because there is no way that it ever could've been."

"That's not what I—"

"Look, Penny. It wasn't you, was it? And before you get all sympathetic, without me you probably wouldn't have gone off with the coffee-guy, Travis, right? You said yourself that you were just trying to be like me…"

"Yeah, but I didn't—"

"Save it! It's what you said. And what about Ben? If it wasn't for me getting you to go out to the pub, then he would never've come over to us."

"You don't know that…"

"I know that you wouldn't have been sat there. You don't sit in pubs and bars on your own, but d'ya know what? I do. I've done it hundreds of times. I've chatted up men that I am not the slightest bit attracted to, because I just wanted someone to hold me and pretend that they loved me!"

"When?" I said, but realised too late what she was getting at.

"When my best friend decided to leave the country without me to explore far off places and shag exotic men. What did *I* have, *huh?* I had fat, middle-aged men cheating on fat, middle-aged wives fucking me in pub toilets or over the bonnet of their fucking Ford Mondeos!" Tears streamed down her face as my eyes welled up too. I had been so wrapped up in leaving Ben behind as I made a break for freedom that I hadn't thought about Kate. That was the honest truth. The opportunity to work and travel had come up, and I had taken it.

"I'm sorry, Kate... I never—"

"Thought about me, I know! I am happy for you that you got yourself sorted out, Pen. I am pleased that everything turned out fine. Things weren't so good for me, you see. I've been to the bottom where I was flat broke, drinking and taking drugs every day. One of those guys down there is called Pete, and he liked to bring me back to his large apartment and let his friends do whatever the fuck they wanted. This didn't happen once, but almost every few days on and off for months..."

"I didn't know..."

"No, you didn't, because you were no longer around..." She took a deep breath and slowly put her arms around me. "But you're here now, Pen. You're here now... Look, the only thing that motivated me to clean up my act was revenge. I had to do something; don't you see?"

I nodded slowly but really couldn't understand her point of view. This was extreme to say the least.

A Cold Retreat

It was a vigilante act that had no place in society anymore. The minute we took the law into our own hands, it became the first day of a lawless society where man killed man and the weak slowly died.

"Say you'll help me, Pen. Let's do this together, yeah?" she said, almost pleading. I felt the wetness dribble out from my own eyes. I couldn't believe what she was asking me to do.

"You don't have to do this, Kate. Just let them all go. We can work through this together."

"Don't say that, Pen... Please don't say that."

"I can't do it, Kate. It's not right."

Kate began to sob.

She moved her hand, and I felt something sharp poke into my chest.

The feelings of sudden pressure and pain were simultaneous. I made a sound like I had been punched in the stomach, and I felt tremendous pain as her hand plunged in and out a couple of times. Then everything went black.

I could not believe that she had stabbed me.

I found myself above my body, looking down and watching as Kate placed a mobile phone behind me and began to sob uncontrollably.

Chapter 60

Travis

I drained the last drop from my glass and got up. I was feeling a little tipsy and looking around at my new friends. I was certainly overdressed.

"Right," I said. "As you lot couldn't be bothered to dress up, I'll go and change and slum it too!"

"I think you look fine," Bronwyn said. She had stopped dancing around for a few minutes. At one point, she had had her phone out and was playing songs loudly on YouTube and dancing, most notably the Candi Staton dance track "You Got The Love." She had swayed her hips in a mesmerising dance whilst throwing her hands up in the air as the lyrics suggested. I knew that Ben was throwing me glances, but shit, she was something to look at!

"Yeah, we should pop upstairs too," Ben said. "Anyone else?"

Christian threw a glance out at the reception area again. "I'm gonna wait here for a while."

"Seriously, mate. I'm not sure she's coming."

A Cold Retreat

He looked like he now believed me, and I felt bad for him.

"She'll be here, babe," Bronwyn said, walking around grabbing Ben by the hand.

"We'll keep you company, mate," Peter said, though I thought him and his missus just wanted to drink more free drinks.

I walked out of the door and up the stairs. The other two were following, but at a much slower pace, and I could hear kissing, so I certainly didn't want to get caught up in that.

I got into my room and decided to take a quick shower. I'm not sure why. I think that it was something to do with being away in a place much cleaner than I was used to. At home, I would never shower before dinner unless I was going out on a date and looking to get lucky.

I pulled on a dress shirt. I still didn't feel that a t-shirt was the right look. Despite the others, I was still on business.

It was a good twenty minutes later when I came out of my room. I was just turning when I heard something from the staircase above.

A loud, piercing scream.

I ran towards the sound. It was what you would call blood-curdling. Until you hear a scream like that, you cannot know just how truthful that description is.

The staircase led to a large attic room, and there in front of me, slumped over, was a woman. She was leaking blood everywhere.

"Help!" I shouted down the stairs and, ducking slightly, ran over to her.

For some reason, I expected her to be cold, but her hands were far from it. I lifted up her head and saw the lifeless eyes staring back at me.

There near her hands was a knife—long and covered in blood. Without thinking, I picked it up just as more footsteps pounded up the stars. Ben appeared, followed closely by Bronwyn.

"What have you done?" Ben said.

"Me? It wasn't me…"

There were more sounds of feet on the staircase, and Christian appeared.

"Peter! Get help!" he shouted.

"She's dead," I said, paralysed by shock. Her blood was on me, and I was still holding the knife.

"Mate, why don't you put the knife down, yeah?"

I slowly placed it onto the floor and sat down, unsure what to do.

A Cold Retreat

Then the owner appeared. "What's hap... oh, my God! Okay, stay there. I'll ring the police." She headed off.

Peter and Jas then appeared. "What the fuck, Travis?"

"It wasn't me!" I said.

"What happened? Did she stab herself?" Ben asked, pulling Bronwyn into him. She was going decidedly pale, even more quickly than the body.

"I heard a scream, so I ran up here," I explained.

"Where were you?" Peter now asked.

"I was just coming out of my room."

"So you heard a scream and no one came down the stairs?"

"No," I said, shaking my head.

"Did she stab herself?" Ben said.

"It seems that way, mate," Peter agreed. One by one, we all sat down, conscious that a girl we didn't know was now dead. Here. In front of us.

"Is that even possible?" someone then said quietly.

Ben mumbled back, "I don't know."

Again, I was peppered with questions that sounded more like accusations. I couldn't blame them. This did appear like a fictional murder-mystery riddle, although as I looked around, all eyes were on me.

I tried for a pulse again. I even tried my phone, but couldn't get a signal.

Then there were footsteps on the stairs and a policeman appeared.

I don't know what it is about a policeman, but instantly I felt guilty. I knew that I was innocent, but those around me were not so sure.

He walked up to the body and made a show of checking the vital signs. A silence had fallen over us a long time ago, and it remained as we were transfixed by him.

He spoke into his radio, which hissed when he had finished. He nodded and touched his ear-piece, listening to instructions that we were not aware of.

"Right, listen here," he said in an authoritative voice. "I have a unit on their way to deal with the body. In the meantime, I need you all in one room. I will need to interview each of you separately and take some statements."

Everyone nodded.

He looked over to where the owner was. "Do you have somewhere everyone could go?"

She nodded, still looking shocked. "There is the function room out the back."

"Very good." He nodded to her and then turned to us. "Right, let's all go ahead and please try not to touch anything any more than you already have."

A Cold Retreat

We slowly walked out, but not before it clicked where I had seen the woman before. She either was or looked a lot like the girl from the coffee shop all those years ago.

If it wasn't bad enough that I had discovered the dead body of someone, it now appeared to be someone whom I'd had sex with.

Silently we walked down the three flights of stairs. The distance seemed longer than I'd remembered.

Instead of heading towards the front door or to the right into the bar/lounge, we turned and went back on ourselves.

Everything around me turned into a blur. Even though I knew I was innocent, there was something unnerving about this whole thing. A seed of doubt crept in even though I knew it was just my mind playing tricks.

We went out of the backdoor and along a path towards another building. I was not sure what I had been expecting, but inside the door were some toilets, and then it opened up into a large room with a bar at one end and a door at the other.

"Okay, if I could have your attention please." The policeman's voiced boomed out loudly, and he glanced around the room at us all. We all stood awkwardly, not knowing where to look or where to put our hands.

"If I can ask that you all remain in here until everyone has been interviewed, then we can try and get to the bottom of what has happened."

"Should we not all be split up?" Peter asked, a little more self-assured than the rest of us.

"D'you think you need to be split up?" the policeman asked, although the tone was a little accusing.

"No, but we might make alibis and collaborate with each other."

The policeman took a deep breath. "If it comes down to me arresting you all, then believe me, one or two of you will sing. Thank you for the advice; I'll be sure to come to you should I forget anything else in my role." He turned to the rest of us. "Any questions?" There were a few shakes of the head.

"How long will this take?" Ben asked. "Just wondering," he added quickly.

"As long as it takes," the policeman said, trying to hide the small smile that had escaped. He had enjoyed his own comment there.

Then he was gone. A lock of the door felt spooky and wrong, and we were left together. Again, all eyes fell on me.

A Cold Retreat

No one said a word, but I could tell that they were thinking how best to treat me.

Chapter 61

Sasha turned to the policeman and grinned widely. Charlie certainly looked the fucking part. She didn't even want to ask where he'd gotten the uniform from.

"What d'ya think?" he said. "D'ya reckon they believe I'm a policeman?"

"What d'*you* think? They followed us all the way down here and out there. I felt like the Pied Piper!"

They embraced and then kissed deeply.

Sasha pulled away. "Charlie?" He nodded. "Did we really have to kill Penny?"

"Of course we did, babe. We discussed this, didn't we? If she agreed with what we were doing, then she could've helped; but she didn't get it, did she? She would've just told the Old Bill on us."

Sasha seemed to accept this. "She thought I was being selfish. She said I was making it all about me."

"Come here." He pulled her close again. "Come on, cheer up. Look at this: we get to interview each of those fuckers, don't we?"

A Cold Retreat

Sasha nodded. She did feel better. She knew that there was no way Penny could have stayed alive. It had been a horrible inevitability and another of those things that you can't always have in life—a sacrifice for the bigger picture.

"I've dreamed about this for so long," she said, talking like she was describing a toy she was getting the night before Christmas. "I cannot believe that this is going to happen."

"Well, this is it now, babe… So, who's first?"

Sasha had given this some thought. The order in which they would be interviewed hadn't changed. As it turned out, it made even more sense. The first person was to be the one who had discovered the body, the one that, by some kind of luck, was on their own. Now suspicions from the rest of the group lay heavily at his door.

They would no longer trust him, which would mean for the next few hours he would be left to feel incredibly uncomfortable.

"Let's go and get Travis. He's the guy who discovered the body."

Charlie remembered him from the folder that Sasha had put together. He had all but groomed Penny for sex whilst getting coffee from her and eventually taking her back to his flat to fuck hard before shutting her in a wardrobe and having it away with his girlfriend. He sounded like a right piece of work!

A Cold Retreat

Chapter 62

Travis

The place was decked out to be some sort of entertainment venue, perhaps to be hired out for birthday parties and other celebrations. It looked newly refurbished, although the smell of paint and plaster was long gone. It was like they had piled money into this and then forgotten about it.

At first glance, it appeared quite bright considering the high walls; but like a prison gymnasium, there were larger barred windows nearer the ceiling that let the sunlight flood in.

I was of course looking around the place carefully to take my mind off the fact that everyone was wary of me, expecting me to unleash a knife at any stage and start stabbing people.

There were some mutterings going on within the group, specifically between Ben, Bronwyn, and Chris. The other two sat on some chairs and were talking a lot about getting high. I could just about hear them.

"Look, I thought this would be a nice place of relaxation where we could get massages and chill out in a Jacuzzi or hot tub," Pete was saying to Jas as she continued to scratch her arms.

"I just need something to…you know…level me out, Paul."

"Peter," he hissed in a quiet voice. "I cannot believe you can't even get my name right!"

"I'm just hurting, Peter. I need something to take the edge off."

He then took a breath. "Just hang in there, yeah?"

The other three sat on a separate table throwing me accusing glances, almost willing me to stand up, tap a bloody glass, and start a speech with, "I'm sorry that I killed her." But that wasn't going to happen.

I ran my hands through my thinning hair. I just couldn't believe it. So many years had passed since I had seen her, and yet when I finally did see her again, she'd been stabbed. Something just didn't sit right about this whole thing.

The door opened, and the officer walked in.

"Right, Travis Yew. Can I see you first?"

I nodded, got up, and followed him, aware that everyone was watching me closely. I'm sure they all expected me to have handcuffs slapped on and for me to then be bundled into the back of a van never to be seen again.

I followed him out and back into the house. We walked up the corridor, but instead of turning right to where the bar/lounge was, we turned left into another room.

It might've been a library at some point, although now whilst there was an impressive bookcase of leather-bound books, as well as a few contemporary novels, it was a little understated compared to the rest of the house.

"Please sit down." He motioned towards a chair next to a large table that could've worked as a second dining room table.

The owner was already standing there with a stern face that suggested I was guilty. It did seem odd that she would be present for a police interview, and I was sure that there should've been a second member of the police force, but I was nervous and didn't want to say anything. My experiences of police interviews went no further than the television shows I had watched, so who knew what the correct procedure was.

"She was already dead." The words toppled out of my mouth quite uncontrollably. I'd had no intention of saying this, so I felt a little surprised when they materialized.

"We'll get to that. Believe me, we'll get to that," he said.

He placed his mobile on the table in front of me. He said the date and time, named the three of us that were present, and got me to confirm my name and date of birth.

"How did you know the victim?" the policeman started.

I looked at both of them. "I really didn't think I knew her…but then I suddenly recognised her…"

"Go on," he said, encouraging me.

"I used to see her most days at the local Starbucks…"

"When was this?"

I shrugged and made a show of my palms. I had read somewhere that if you kept showing the palms of your hands, then this was a sub-conscious sign of innocence.

"2000. Something like that. A long time ago."

"So you just knew her as someone that worked in a coffee shop?"

"Sort of…"

"Please, can you elaborate on that?"

"We hooked up one time… Look, this was a long time ago. We would flirt as she made my coffee. I asked her out, and then one day we met after work."

A Cold Retreat

"Go on." This was his standard line of encouragement. I'd seen this done a hundred times on police TV shows. Sometimes the other technique of remaining quiet was used where the criminal filled in the awkward silences with babble that often tied their story up in knots, or got them to reveal more than they had initially intended.

"We spent some time shopping, and then she came back to my flat."

"And why did you go back to your flat?" he said to me through narrowed eyes. He knew. I didn't know how, but he knew. I noticed Sasha twitching like she had something to say.

"We've been through this," I said, knowing it wasn't enough.

He nodded, and when he spoke, the words dripped with sarcasm. "For coffee."

"That's right. We were having fun, and I didn't want the date to end."

"It was a *date?*" Sasha said, unable to hide her anger.

I nodded and then shrugged. "I don't know. I guess?"

"I get it," he said calmly to me. "You had fun around town, and you wanted more fun back at your flat, *right?* Look, we've been there. You came back and…"

Suddenly Sasha piped up. "You had sex with the victim, did you not?"

I nodded, but couldn't help but wonder how she knew and why she was speaking. Unless she was also a police officer too, I couldn't understand why she was still here. Even that would surely be a conflict of interest.

"Look, it's not a crime, is it?"

"I wonder," Sasha muttered just loud enough for me to hear. The policeman shot her a stare.

"Travis, the day you met her at the coffee shop, what was your intention?"

"Is she meant to be here?" I said, pointing to Sasha. It really didn't seem right.

"This is her place, so she has every right to understand what's gone on."

"Really? I would've thought that another police officer should be here."

The two of them shared a glance, but quickly dismissed it.

"If you have any complaints about how this interview has been conducted, then it can be addressed later."

"Isn't what I say inadmissible in court? Shouldn't I have a solicitor present?" I was speaking quickly.

A Cold Retreat

"We've not arrested you...yet. Therefore, unless you have something to hide, you do not need legal representation. You are free to leave at any stage, Mr Yew."

I nodded. I felt a little better, but not a lot. "Okay."

"If you are now satisfied with the situation, can you answer the question?"

"What was the question again?"

"Your intentions. That day when you met her?"

I was still slightly confused by the whole line of questioning. They had not mentioned today at all and seemed more focused on my previous relations with the victim. This might just be their way of establishing a motive, but it all seemed a little long-winded.

"What, when she made me coffee or later when I met her after her shift?"

The policeman was writing down things as I spoke. He stopped and looked at me. "Both, if you will."

I thought back long and hard. It had been many, many years. Could I really be expected to remember what I had been feeling back then? It was obvious that our memories were tainted with the life that we had led since or by our general feelings from that day.

"I stopped in for coffee. It was typically something that I did around the same time each day…"

"There are a number of coffee establishments around, so what made you choose that one?"

"Well, that's the thing. Back then there wasn't. The coffee culture was in its infancy, so there was still just the greasy-spoon cafes dotted around the place. Coffee, back then, meant a spoonful of instant into some hot milk…"

"Okay, okay, spare us the history lesson in coffee evolution."

I snapped at that. "I was just answering your question."

"Please continue," he said, unfazed by my little outburst.

"So, as I was saying, it was one of the only places for a decent coffee, so I went there. I got to know Penny, as she worked regular shifts and was most commonly the one to serve me."

"What did she think of you?"

I shrugged. Who really knew? "Look, officer, back then I was a little thinner and younger looking. I tried to always look my best, and I got the impression that she fancied me."

"And what specifically gave you that idea?"

A Cold Retreat

"Are these questions really relevant? Shouldn't we be talking about what happened tonight?" I was getting impatient. It felt like they were trying to build a case against me by feeding me lines.

"All in due course. We are trying to establish your relationship with the victim."

"There was no relationship!" I spat.

"You need to settle down. If there was no relationship, then how did you come to be having sexual relations with the victim? Please answer my original question. What made you think that the victim fancied you?"

"I'm good at reading people—or at least I was—she would smile warmly at me and fiddle with her hair. When she gave me change, her fingers would linger just a bit longer than normal, and she would often go red in the face, but specifically around her neck and chest... I know when a woman likes me, and you can take my word for it; she did."

The policeman and Sasha shared a look, and then the policeman carried on with the questioning. "So, your intention that day?"

"My intention that day was coffee. I enjoyed seeing her, but until I had spoken to her that day, I didn't know that later on I would be seeing her... Then we talked, and somehow it slipped out that I wondered whether she fancied meeting up some time, and she went red and agreed." I was trying really hard not to get angry, but when you have someone asking you these questions, it's hard to stay calm. They were making me remember a time when I was completely happy, but were doing their best to taint those memories. I felt so frustrated with the whole situation. Fuck the contract. Fuck my job. I just wanted to be out of here and back in my flat.

"So you didn't actually make a date?"

"No. It was later on when I had been working that I thought I would swing by and see if I could catch her after work."

"And your intention if you did meet her?"

"I don't know. I guess I wanted to speak to her more…"

"You guess? Travis, may I remind you that this is looking very much like a murder case, so guessing is not something that we can really work with now, is it?"

"Okay, I wanted to get to know her."

"And you had no intention of sleeping with her?"

"Of course it had crossed my mind. She was very attractive, and I'm a red-blooded male…but I didn't go looking to pick her up for sex, despite what you might think!"

A Cold Retreat

"Really? And what do you think that we think, Travis?"

I shook my head. They were getting me angry. Perhaps this was one of those techniques that they used in order to try and get the truth out.

"You want to make it look like I was stalking her, and then forced her to have sex with me and cast her aside!"

The policeman looked up, stopped his notes again, and smiled incredibly wide. "Interesting usage of words. Why would you say *forced*?"

"I say that because that is what you want to hear, but that was not the case."

"Okay, let's go back to when you met her after work. Tell us about that."

"I met her and we walked around the shops for a while. I then invited her back to my flat."

"So you could have sex."

"No, I was just going to invite her back for coffee."

"You picked her up from a coffee house and thought she might want a coffee back at your flat? Can you understand why we might not buy that story, Travis? Come on, you said it yourself…" He looked back over his notes. "What was it you said: *'She was very attractive, and I'm a red-blooded male,'* so you expect us to believe that you didn't take her back to your flat with the full intention of having sex with her, or forcing yourself onto her?"

"Look, she came back to my flat, we had some drinks, and slowly, one thing led to another. She wanted to be there…"

"She said that?"

"She didn't leave, nor did she ask to leave or at any stage insinuate that she was not having a good time."

"Were you single at that point in your life, Travis?"

"Sorry?" I said.

"Did you have a girlfriend or partner?"

I nodded, and a transparent blanket of guilt covered me. "Yes."

"And your girlfriend was okay with this?"

I couldn't believe how much they knew. "My girlfriend was not aware."

"And how was she not aware? Did she not come to your flat and let herself in?"

My stomach was doing flips. How did they know this?

"Yes, but—"

"But what?"

"She hid in the wardrobe."

A Cold Retreat

"How very romantic." I felt completely judged, and Sasha was looking like she wanted to stab me herself.

"And how long was she in the wardrobe for?"

I was gulping in air now. The room was stuffy, and the atmosphere was choking me. "Ten...fifteen minutes."

"And what were you and your girlfriend doing?"

I looked at them both. My eyes darting from one to the other. "We had sex."

My head was dropped down like more weight had been added around my neck. It was like everything that I had failed at was now rushing back at me. I felt like I was laid out on the floor and all of the negatives from my life were crashing down on me from above.

"Is it fair to say that when your girlfriend turned up, you wanted Penny gone quickly?" He didn't bother to even look up. There was disgust in his tone that suggested he fucking hated me and was pulling out all the stops to try and convict me.

"Yes, I didn't want my girlfriend to know."

"But she found out, did she not?" Again, I couldn't believe that he knew this. I also felt like this was less like a police interview and more like being questioned by a prosecutor in court.

"That was years later."

"But it affected your relationship, did it not?"

"It wasn't the only thing. Look, officer, I was popular with the ladies, and I enjoyed the attention. I am not proud of that now, but that is the fact. I didn't force myself on anyone for the simple reason that I didn't need to. If I was ever turned down—and back then that only happened if they were married or gay—then I would move on to the next one, as they were sure to say yes. So, to answer your question, that night didn't specifically end my relationship."

"And before tonight when was the last time you had seen Penny?"

"The night she came back to my flat... I went back to Starbucks, but she no longer worked there. I left a number for them to pass on to her, but she never called it."

"And what was it that you wanted exactly? To say that you were sorry? To ask for forgiveness? Maybe to stop her going to the police?"

"No, you've got it all wrong. Okay, maybe she did affect our relationship..." I couldn't believe I was about to say this. "It affected it because, for the first time, I found someone that I would do anything for. I became aware that my girlfriend was not what I wanted. I wanted Penny. I was in love with her..."

A Cold Retreat

The policeman stopped writing and looked at Sasha. She stood there with eyes watering.

The policeman took a breath and looked straight at me. "What about tonight? What happened?"

"I was just about to go downstairs. I had changed for dinner. I had come out of my room and was turning towards the stairs when I heard a scream from upstairs. I ran up them and, seeing no one else around, found Penny sat down with blood all around her."

"And you say you saw nobody else?"

"No, not until the other couple, Ben and whatsit, came up."

"And the victim's blood on you? How d'you explain that?"

"Okay, I picked up the knife. I don't know why, but I did it before I even realised what I was doing. I also tried to find out whether or not she was still alive."

"Okay. Lastly, what do you think happened to her?"

I wanted to tell them that he was the policeman and that was his job, but I shrugged again and showed my palms. "I have no idea. Could she've stabbed herself? Could someone have done it and stayed hidden up in the attic? I really don't know."

Again, the policeman and Sasha exchanged glances, which seemed to have hidden codes and messages, before he said, "Okay, Travis, we may have more questions after we've spoken to the others. I'll take you back to them now."

I nodded, unsure what else to do or say, and began to follow him, but not before noticing the picture on the wall. The one that I had been idly looking at without really taking it in. The pensive facial expressions on the people apart from one that suddenly looked familiar…

Chapter 63

Christian

I was royally pissed off. It was becoming all too apparent that I had been stood up, and now I was slap in the middle of a murder investigation. *How the fuck did that happen?*

There was something about that Travis guy. You could tell by the way he had sat there in his suit earlier that he had been up to something. He hadn't said much, although to be fair, that Bronwyn woman had talked enough for all of us. He had been transfixed by her, which made it all the more unbelievable that he would go off and kill a woman that we hadn't even met yet. And who the hell was that woman? I had heard that her name was Penny. Had she been a guest or something to do with the woman here? Ironically, I was here to meet a Penny, and now a woman called Penny was dead. Was this who I had been speaking with? She hadn't looked like the woman in the pictures, but Travis had told me that this would be the case. Why hadn't she found me before? I was saddened for a woman that I hadn't met, and I couldn't be sure whether or not it was *my* Penny.

There are some moments in your life that you snapshot and will be able to relive for the rest of your life, and for me it was as I looked up at Travis holding a bloody knife, whilst the woman was sitting bent over surrounded by blood. You never ever expect to see that much human blood. You just don't live when you lose blood like that.

Travis had looked shocked, but was that the shock of finding a dead woman? Or the shock of killing a woman? It was hard to tell.

When the policeman arrived and we were marched down and out into the function room, he just stared at the door. There was something about him that I was suddenly uncomfortable to be around.

"D'ya think he actually killed her?" Bronwyn said as soon as he was taken off for questioning. I shrugged, but this non-committal response was because I didn't really know what everyone else was thinking. Whilst we had all bonded a bit over alcohol, it was almost as if that bond had now been erased. I no longer trusted anyone. What if Travis was some sort of deranged killer? He went to these isolated places, booked in, and then slowly killed everyone…

A Cold Retreat

"There was something about him," Pete said and then looked at Bronwyn. "He kept staring at you."

"Maybe he's some sort of psycho," Ben added. "Or maybe he just fancied you, Bron."

"I need something, Pete," Jas then muttered, a little louder than she had intended. "Now... I'm freaking out!"

Pete pulled her close to him. "Let's just take a deep breath. As soon as we can leave, we'll go and score something, yeah?"

"You promise?" she said, suddenly full of hope and slightly more coherently.

"Is she okay?" I asked. I hadn't meant to say it, but it had sort of just slipped out.

"Yeah, she's fine. Thanks."

It was quiet for a while. We were all lost in our own thoughts, and then slowly we began to speculate what might be going on.

"I reckon they've arrested him," Ben suggested. "Banged him up in the back of the police car. They're probably attending to the body about now. Then they'll let us go."

"I'm hungry," Bronwyn said. "What d'ya reckon's happening with dinner?"

"I reckon we'll be let out, and then we'll have to leave the place," I said.

"They'll kick us out?" Ben said in disbelief.

"It's a crime scene, innit? They can't very well let us sleep here tonight."

Then, about twenty minutes later, Travis returned. He seemed to look less guilty, and that somehow seemed more worrying. If he wasn't guilty, then that meant that someone else was. Better the devil you know and all that.

"Okay, Christian Raney, you're next. Come with me please," the policeman said. My stomach dropped. I had almost resigned myself to the fact that, as Travis was the murderer, I would no longer be interviewed. I followed the policeman and tried to think that this would be purely to help the case against Travis. If that was the case, then why would he be allowed back with the others? Would the policeman not be worried that he would go psycho and kill everyone? Or top himself?

We walked into another room with some stuffed birds on the wall and a large fireplace. The owner was there, and I scanned the room, expecting another policeman.

"Please take a seat," the policeman said, offering a chair. He sat down adjacent to me whilst the woman, Sasha, I believe, looked at me accusingly.

We went through the formalities of confirming my name and date of birth before the policeman started with his questions.

A Cold Retreat

He said, "So tell me, why exactly are you here this weekend?" I suddenly thought, *If Penny was the person that I was communicating with, maybe they are now going to pin this on me?*

"I was here to meet someone," I said after a long pause. I knew it had been too long, as they both glanced at each other. I could hear their thoughts. *He did it*, they said to each other.

"Male or female?"

"I'm sorry?" I said.

"The person you were here to meet, were they male or female…or did you not know?" He looked at me with cold eyes.

"Of course I knew. Female."

"In our line of work, we cannot assume anything. So you have met before then?"

"Well no, not really… It's just that…"

"It's not a difficult question. It's one that requires either a yes or no answer, plain and simple."

"No, but we had talked on the phone, and I'd seen pictures."

"So is there a chance that the victim could've been the person that you were here to see?"

"She's not like her photos."

"Mr Raney, you seem like a clever fellow. Is there the possibility that she might've sent you pictures of someone else? Yes or no?"

"Yes, I suppose it's possible."

"Did you recognise her? The victim?"

It seemed like a leading question. "No…I don't think so… I mean, I didn't really get a good look at her…"

"Her name was Penny Teale."

I shook my head. There was something vaguely familiar about the name, but I really couldn't be sure.

"She had a friend called Kate Lyle." His stare was penetrating. Sasha took a step closer too.

"Vaguely," I said, although the name took me back a long way.

"I believe you went to school with them both."

I tried to make a gesture of thinking hard, and then nodded slightly. "Now I think back, yes, I do remember them."

"There were allegations against you with Kate," he said as a statement, not a question.

"I don't follow. *Allegations*?"

The policeman nodded. "You forced Kate to have sex with you, right?"

I stood up as a natural reaction. "Whoa, hold on a second now…"

A Cold Retreat

The policeman stood up, his face full of anger. "Now, you hold on a second! Sit down!"

Sasha then spoke quietly. "You forced her to have sex with you, and then you let your friends have sex with her too."

"No, that is not what happened…"

"Oh, I think that is exactly what happened!" The policeman said, raising his voice again.

"No, you don't know. You weren't there!"

That's when it dawned on me.

"Oh, but I was, Chris," she said, sneering at me. "I was laid there on my back whilst you had one hand on my throat and the other pulling down my underwear. I was telling you to stop, and you were forcing yourself on me…into me…and then…and then you let your fat friend do the same!"

"No!" I shouted. "That's not what happened!"

"You fucking liar!" she shouted. "You ruined me that day. You stole my innocence, and I could never get that back. I was tainted. I fucking hate you for that!"

"No, I—" I started to say, but suddenly she was on me, her hand clasped tightly around my windpipe. I swung a punch that caught her, but suddenly I felt an impact to the back of my head the same time as the bright light flashed and everything went black.

Jim Ody

My body collapsed to the floor, and like air from a balloon, my life escaped.

Chapter 64

Sasha

"Did you kill him?" I asked as Charlie put down the golf club. He bent over the body, searching for a pulse.

"I think so."

"Shit," I said. "Things kind've escalated a little quickly there."

"Is that not what you wanted? To reveal what he was too stupid to realise and make him feel bad before killing him?"

"No, that's not what I wanted. I wanted him to know how bad my life had been because of him. I wanted him to feel remorse… *Shit*, I wanted him to be begging for his life before I killed him! Shit, shit, shit!" I felt so angry. I hated the fact that I had put so much planning into this and it just wasn't going to plan. The way he had been so unaware of what had gone on and had been oblivious to my pain had just worked me up and I had seen red. Travis hadn't recognised Penny whatsoever, and Christian had died before I could make him properly suffer. It was just so infuriating!

"What about Dex? Where is he?" I asked, suddenly realising his absence.

"He said he was coming. We couldn't wait all night though, could we?"

I sighed. He could turn up at any minute and fuck the whole thing up. It just went to show that, despite all the planning, things could still go wrong.

"Sash, look, there are the others. Let's make sure we do it right with them, yeah? Try not to get so…*ya'know*…"

"What? Don't blame me!" I couldn't believe that he was saying this was my fault. I had put all the planning into this. He had pissed off to his little room outside doing God-knows-fuckin'-what.

"I'm just saying that you need to keep your calm, yeah?"

"You were the one that cracked him over the head!"

"Because you lost it!"

"Whatever. What are we going to do with him?" I pointed at Christian's lifeless body. Maybe I should've felt something. I didn't. The act of killing someone was beginning to get easier. Was this another by-product of how I had been treated?

A Cold Retreat

"Let's drag him outside and put him down the hole."

He was a big guy. We thought about trying to carry him, but dead bodies have a habit of being quite cumbersome and awkward to carry. We both grabbed an arm and dragged him, which appeared to work a lot better. *Who knew?*

As we left the room, I saw it on the floor: a key. And I knew exactly where it was for.

I felt strange. It was a mix of elation and excitement, but underneath was something else. Something that sat heavily in the pit of my stomach. At first, I thought it was because we were well in to the plan and I had yet to feel the highs that I had expected. I then considered that I might now be thinking about later, when this was all over. What was I going to do? I had spent so long planning this that I had not for a second contemplated what I might do afterwards.

But then I knew what the numb feeling was really all about.

It was Charlie. There was something about him. Our trust was based on circumstance and an inevitability to lean on each other, but we both must have been thinking exactly the same thing. The only way to get away with this was to remain together as a completely trusted pair—or we make sure that it was only one of us left alive.

I couldn't believe that these thoughts were now rushing through my head. I loved Charlie, but was that really enough?

"You're quiet. Are you alright?" he asked as we got past the pond and were headed towards the door in the ground. It was good to know that the rest of them were locked in the function room. It certainly wouldn't be good to be caught dragging a suspect outside and disposing of the body in full view of everyone.

"I'm fine. It's a lot to take in." He nodded at that and opened the door. We dragged and hefted the body into the space.

"Maybe we need to re-evaluate what you're looking to get out of this."

"What do you mean?"

He bent down with one hand on the door and was about to pull it back up when he said, "What are you getting out of this, Sash? Really?"

"What are *you* getting out of this?" I countered just as he closed the door.

"I'm doing this for you," he said, I was a little in shock, as before he had closed the door, I had seen movement and a pair of eyes…

A Cold Retreat

"Head on back and get yourself a tea. Have a think at how you want to play this now, yeah?"

"Why, what are you doing?" I was growing a little suspicious at what he was up to—how he disappeared for periods of time.

"I've got to check on something. Look, all will become clear soon. I promise." He kissed me on the forehead, winked, and wandered off.

I turned, headed back to the room, and snatched up the key.

The mythical trust tree was there swaying in the breeze, but neither myself nor Charlie were sitting in it. Instead, we stood below in cynical pastures wondering what the end game would be for us.

As I turned to leave the room, I glanced up at the painting that had been behind me. The one that I had seen when I was first here. Leonard was there, and then I saw the other person. The younger brother.

Of course. It was Charlie...

I probably should've realised that. I turned and quickly ran up the stairs towards the locked door.

I put the key in the lock. For a second, I almost wished that it didn't fit. But, of course, it did.

I turned the handle and opened it up. It was Leonard's room. Charlie had said that he didn't know where the key was, but I had always suspected he did.

I walked in and looked around.

It was pristine, which fitted with what you would expect from his twisted and scheming mind. A Bible taunted me from the side of his bed, and this produced its own set of feelings for me. I walked up to a picture of his family on the side.

More evidence that Leonard and Charlie were, of course, brothers.

"Well, well, well, and what do we have here?" he said, making me jump.

Chapter 65

Ben

My heart was pounding, and I could feel the adrenaline pumping through my veins. Something was not right here. Chris had been gone a long time, which didn't make sense, especially when suspect number one was sitting back behind us on his own.

I leant into Bronwyn. "Don't you think there is something a little weird going on here?"

"Someone died, so yeah, it is a little bit odd."

"No, I mean… I dunno. That woman that died, don't you think she looked familiar?"

"Ben, I tried not to look at her. She was bent over, so I only saw her body."

I turned to Pete. "Hey, Pete, you think something a bit strange is going on here?"

"I've now spent almost 24 hours clean, buddy. Everything is fucking weird to me!"

"You get that woman's name? The one that died?" He shook his head. Travis mumbled something.

"What was that?" I said, turning to him.

"Her name was Penny," he said without feeling.

"Penny? You sure?"

He nodded. "Yep, completely."

"Did you know her?" I'm not sure why I said it. I had no reason to suspect that he did. He shocked me again by nodding.

"I did. A long time ago."

"This might sound a bit weird, but did she have a pierced nipple? And a rose tattoo on her back?"

"She had her nipple pierced, but I don't remember a rose tattoo…" He paused. "She had a small black star on her ankle though.

"Fuck me," I said.

"It's not," Bronwyn added, her face screwing up.

Pete sat up. "You wanna tell me what's going on here?"

I looked at Bronwyn. "I have history with the victim…"

Bronwyn cut in. "What he means is that he was regularly fucking her whilst we were together!" She scowled at me.

I rolled my eyes. "It's complicated. We've spent a lifetime together, and in that time, we have split up how many times? What, five, six? In one of those times, I got together with Penny, and we were together for a few months, but in the end, things didn't work out and we got back together."

A Cold Retreat

Bronwyn shook her head. "He always has memory problems when he remembers with his dick. They got together when *we* were together! Sure, we split up, but we got back together a week later. He carried on with the two of us throughout that time…" I went to open my mouth. "Don't you dare deny it, Benjamin! She was a fucking interfering bitch!"

"Really," Pete said. "And, Travis, what about you? How come you ended up killing her?" He winked.

"I didn't kill her…" he said, and I could see that his eyes were red. "I met her in a coffee shop a long, long time ago. We hung out, we had sex, I never saw her again. End of it."

"What about you?" I said to Pete.

He shook his head. "Honestly, I have no idea. I don't recognise her, but then I've been fucking strung out for so long that I'm not sure that I'd recognise my own mum nowadays. I've been known to throw regular parties which end up with copious amounts of booze, drugs, and a bloody lot of sex."

"So you might've banged her too?" Bronwyn said.

He shrugged and looked almost proud. "There is a good chance…but you know what? Despite my talk of my defective memory recall, there is something about the owner of this place, Sasha…"

"What, you know her?"

"She reminds me of someone that I did know up until a few months back. Her hair is different, but I noticed that she hid her face from me a lot. I didn't think anything of it, as I was too busy wondering whether she looked the sort to get high, but now I think about it, she seems awfully similar to a girl…" He turned to Jas. "What do you think?"

"I want to get high," she offered.

"Don't we all… I think her name was Kate."

"You date her?" I asked.

"Not so much in regards to courting, more in the party-girl capacity."

"She was a regular at your parties who drank, got high, and had sex."

"That would be a fair description."

Bronwyn stood up. "You can't all think this is just some coincidence, right? We were offered this weekend free. Travis, you were here on business or something, right? How did that come about?"

"I was contacted as a lead for a business opportunity. This was a free weekend," he said, now engaging a little more.

"Pete? You were looking to get clean, right?'

A Cold Retreat

"Yep, I was offered a free weekend to help me get my shit together."

"And, Jas?"

"Yeah?" she said, looking up.

"Without being crude or crass, have you had sex with either Penny or Kate?" Bronwyn asked.

"More than likely, although I really couldn't say." She was a state, that was all that I could say. If I was to picture the definition of a crack addict—but one who had tried to quickly clean up a bit—then it would be Jas. I imagined that, as a teenager, she had been attractive and athletic, but now she was a bag of bones, a skin full of regrets and poor choices ghosting along and masquerading as a woman.

"Well, look at us. We are a fucking bunch. I also think that we're in a whole world of shit. Where is Chris?"

"Shit, yeah, he's been gone a long time," Pete said. "He was here to meet someone."

"Ah, the mystery lover," Bronwyn said.

"Not so much a lover. He'd never met her. She set this place up and paid for it."

"It sounds dodgy now."

"I told him it was a fix," Travis said. "He thought he was in love."

"We've all thought that and been wrong!" Pete smiled.

There was something slightly symbolic in the way we then all looked at the doorway that led out to the locked door.

"We need to find another way out," Jas mumbled, which seemed quite lucid for her.

"We're sitting ducks here." I looked around. There was a curtain at the opposite end behind where a band or DJ would be.

"What's behind there?" I asked, and I noticed that Bronwyn was on the same wavelength as me. She walked down there.

"Let's see," she said and pulled it back to reveal a door. She put her hand on the handle and tentatively pulled it open.

"Hold on," Travis said suddenly. "We don't know where that goes, do we? What if it's some sort of trap?"

"We're trapped already," Bronwyn pointed out. "And with all due respect, thanks to you, we're being framed."

"Listen to me!" Travis said loudly, getting the most animated that we had all seen him. "We've already established that there is some sort of connection between us, and suddenly one person that we have known ends up dead. Don't you think that this is a complete set-up?"

A Cold Retreat

I could understand what he was saying, and maybe he hadn't had anything to do with the woman's death, but I couldn't just sit here and wait. I was drawn into the proactive thoughts of my other half. I was certainly not going to let her go through that door without me.

"I'm with you, babe," I said, walking over.

"Yes," Pete nodded, standing and beckoning Jas to follow. "We can't stay here. Come on, Travis."

Travis shook his head. "I'm just not sure."

I followed Bronwyn through the door, down some stairs, and into a long corridor. Travis followed me, and Pete and Jas brought up the rear.

I heard the door shut, and then I heard the worried voice of Pete. "Jas?!"

"What happened?" someone asked.

Through the dim light I saw the shocked look on Pete's face. "I'm pretty sure she shut it deliberately." He tried the door, but the handle didn't turn.

We were locked down here, and now it seemed like Jas might've known exactly what she was doing.

Was she really as strung out as she appeared to be, or had it all been an act?

Chapter 66

Sasha

"You know, E.M. Forster once said *'Curiosity is one of the lowest of the human faculties.'* I wonder what possessed you to want to get inside this room, Sash?" Charlie stood at the door with a strange grin on his face. It reminded me of when you pull back a cat's top lip. The teeth appear to grin, but the sharp teeth remind you that caution is still required, and it then looks like a dangerous sneer.

"I just wondered what was in this room," I said. The air had now become thick with tension. It was like the first major argument in a relationship. I still had such strong feelings for Charlie—or had strong feelings. This was serious now.

Deadly serious.

"This is Leonard's room. I had already told you that," he said.

"You told me that you didn't know where the key was."

He wiggled a finger. "Incorrect. I said that only Leonard knew where the key was."

A Cold Retreat

I looked at the photograph that showed him smiling with his parents after his release—a small party thrown to celebrate his release from prison.

Welcome Home, Leonard.

"Were you ever going to tell me the truth...*Leonard*?"

He shook his head slowly. "And what would've been the point of that?"

I sat down on the bed, my legs suddenly weak and unable to hold me up. "So that was Charlie we killed?"

Leonard nodded. "He was a gardener of sorts. He contacted me in prison and told me to be strong. He said that God would protect me and that the Devil had manifested itself within the guise of temptresses looking to tease me. He was full of shit, but quite pliable and easy to manipulate."

I couldn't believe how easily the lies fell out of his mouth, his brain not even bothering to sense check anymore allowing every thought to be audible.

"Stop with the lies! He was your brother, right? I saw the painting!"

For a second he almost wavered. "Ahh, the painting. That awful day that we were made to stand there like some Edwardian lie, to portray some false class and act like a normal family!" He easily slipped into a memory, and even before more words were uttered, I knew what he was going say. It was a classic sociopathic trait deflecting the blame onto someone else. "*It's not my fault,*" and "*It was because X,*" or *"If Y hadn't..."* They were the centre of attention. They craved the limelight and didn't care what happened to anyone else.

"'*Stand still, Lenny, before I beat the shit out of you!*' my father said to me. He was a fuckin' joke. Parading around like he was the big man. Beating the shit out of us all. Well, not Charlie. No, that fucker was the apple of his eye!" He began to pace back and forth. "But little Lenny grew big and strong! He no longer took that shit. Big brother Charlie suddenly became scared of me."

"And prison? Were you both locked up?"

He smiled. "Oh, yeah. I was fucking sloppy, right? Okay, I admit it. I saw women, and I wanted them. My father and his poisoned seed had given me that gift. I got greedy. I didn't plan; I just reacted. I got caught, and I paid the price…the price of bad planning."

"Charlie too?" I kept glancing at the door. Could I make it past him?

"That useless twat couldn't do that. No, he tried, but was caught and failed a psych test! Can you believe that? The stupid fucker was crazy. Got locked up in some funny farm for a year. When he got out, his mind was even more fragile. He would do whatever I told him. I had full control of his meds. I knew how to make him react.

"Let me tell you, whatever he thought of me, when I let him fuck you, I became the best brother in the whole fucking world! You made quite an impression on him!"

"But it was you that had held me captive? Not, Leonard—I mean, Charlie?"

"Are you deaf? That is what I've been telling you." He paused and took a breath. He almost mellowed right in front of my eyes, switching gears, maybe changing personality.

"Does it matter now, Sash? You came here to get me, but you also came to get those others, *right*? You fell in love with me... Shit, *I fell in love with you*! I mean, I was always attracted to you. That's why you were kept captive here, but I actually felt something strong for you. Something that I have never felt before."

"So what now? You expect us to remain here and open up a B&B together? Maybe get married and live happily ever after? Or are you going to kill me too?" It felt like I would be lucky to get out of here alive. Part of me was trying to accept this. My fate was in the lap of the gods.

Jim Ody

"What d'you think I should do?" He made it sound like it was my choice, but we both knew that he had already made up his mind. The fact that he was dressed as a policeman was a sick joke. Of course, it had been his idea. He loved the fact that it was his Jekyll and Hyde act, another example of his sociopathic ways. *"See how clever I am?"* he was taunting.

"I don't get it though…" I said. It probably didn't matter that I was speaking out loud, but nevertheless, I carried on anyway. "So all the time you were outside in the garden, you were what, teasing me? Hoping that I would call for help?"

He raised his eyebrows like he was wondering if I was really asking him that. "You trusted me, because you naturally assumed that I must be the good guy. I made sure that you were knocked out every time I was alone with you. Charlie came in when you were conscious. I half expected you to attack him beforehand, but you didn't… Sash, for what it's worth, there was something about the way you looked when you were laid bare in front of me. I admit that normally for me a writhing woman, albeit one trying to get away, is a turn on. It fills me with such power, and I thought that was the epitome of sexual release for me. But then having you naked and stunned, fully submissive and unconscious…

A Cold Retreat

It...it took it to another level. I was in control and totally dominant, but I could also take my time, explore your body, and hold you. I found that caressing and taking my time far outweighed the fast and feverish acts that I had previously enjoyed. Holding down arms and legs whilst trying not to be kicked, punched, and bitten lost its appeal.

"And then when we were properly together as two conscious people, it finally clicked into place. The feeling of the person, who had previously been laid completely still underneath me, to now be accepting each thrust, grabbing me tightly, even making small noises with short breaths... It was something else."

"I was faking!" I shouted, tears beginning to well in my eyes, but we both knew that I was lying. "You disgusted me!"

"Just be honest, Sash." He was still there thinking about it. His eyes grew wide like a child reminiscing on a wonderful birthday party that he would forever hold dear to his heart.

"And then the time you rolled me over and held me down whilst you writhed on top of me. The sexual tables almost completely reversed as I lay still watching the way you nibbled your lips and the way your breasts swung. The curve of your soft neck as you arched your back and dug nails into my chest... Sash, that is not something that I ever want to lose."

I remembered it all: the noises I made as I felt the control I was unaccustomed to experiencing before. It was exhilarating and liberating at the same time. I had felt free enjoying doing exactly as I pleased with a guy that I had thought I held so much trust in.

I sat down on the bed with my head in my hands. I was suddenly broken, my fight all gone.

"I have lied to you, Sash. I know that. You are a wonderful woman. I have to ask myself: will you ever forgive me? I also have to question whether I will ever find anyone quite like you... The answer to both of these is more than likely *no*."

This shouldn't have been such a hard decision. I knew that from the outside looking in people would tell me to turn and run at whatever cost. I was a woman and he was a convicted rapist. It would be my word against his, and I would only have to retell my experiences here—of being held captive—to have him locked up for life.

I remembered our time together. My heart and my brain were in conflict. It was like surfing in shark-infested waters; you would look at the danger and say *why*? But speak to a surfer hitting those large waves and experiencing the exhilarating

A Cold Retreat

feeling of their own power against Mother Nature, and they don't see the danger, only the satisfaction and peace that such triumphs bring.

The weeks we had spent together in a relationship had been a magical time. I had a degree of guilt about that, but it was the truth. It had been an unorthodox meeting, and to stay here would be seen by most as a strange choice, but unless you have experienced what I had, then you really cannot understand my choices. I had spent years at the hands of abusers—some of it subtle and psychological, but most preyed on my needy existence—and I wanted of a romantic, happy ending. I had done some unspeakable acts, somehow assuming that I would get some sort of gratification in return. Instead, all I had received was guilt and self-loathing and was further away from an ivory tower and the dashing prince.

Leonard walked up to me. I saw a strong man with many problems looking deep inside me. I felt almost mesmerised and longed for those arms to wrap around me.

I stood up. As he leaned in for a kiss, I was sure that, whatever it took, we would get through this.

One of his arms slipped around me, and our lips touched. I relaxed as our hearts beat together.

And then he stabbed me once. And then twice.

I shot my eyes open, but found it hard to focus. I didn't so much feel pain as feel a numbness seeping out around my body.

I lost count of the number of times I was stabbed.

I felt tired and weary…

Chapter 69

Sasha

The sun shines through the gap in the curtains, sending a diagonal ray down to the floor. The drapes ripple with a fresh breeze as a new day has dawned.

I stretch my hands up above my head and towards the canopy of the four-poster bed. I idly run my fingers through my long blonde hair. I feel the excitement inside rise as I remember that today I will attend the prestigious Annual Ball. There has been much discussion between my friends and me about the eligible bachelors that will be present looking for women such as ourselves to take as their brides.

My spacious bedroom is spotless, the dressing table filled with all the things a princess would require.

I am about to ring the bell for Jasmine to come and get me my things, but decide that my pillow is too soft. I stretch out and then snuggle back under the covers. My doll, Sasha, sits smiling on the rocking chair beside me, her bright red dress standing out against the cream backdrop of the room.

There is a flash of darkness, then the room begins to blur. I close my eyes tightly. My stomach begins to hurt. Really hurt.

I feel a burning along my back, and my arms feel like they are being stretched out of their sockets.

After a flash of bright white light, I open my eyes to find that the comfy bed has disappeared. There are no curtains fluttering in the wind, just a large garden and a big house…

I looked down and saw that there was blood coming from my stomach, and I remembered that I had been stabbed multiple times.

We were heading for the hole in the floor—the bunker where the rest of the dead bodies had been thrown and abandoned.

In the distance I saw a figure, but I couldn't make out who it was.

He let go of my arms, and I was unable to stop them from banging onto the floor behind me. I no longer had any strength, and part of me wondered whether or not I had already died.

He picked me up. I looked at his face. Those eyes now held no feeling, where once I was sure

A Cold Retreat

that I saw a glimmer of what might have been love. Circumstance had not been a friend to me on a number of occasions, and now this was its final denial: a broken couple who had only ever loved each other had come to the end of the road. He was willing to murder his princess, and I was now held up in the loving arms of my prince, the way I had always desired. I would now die that way in my life's final act. It was almost poetic in the way this fairy-tale had come to pass. It was so far away from Disney that this would be the bastard child that was locked away and forgotten. Denied a dozen syrupy songs with clever lyrics and catchy melodies, this was scratched and broken, a horrific tale that would have no child wanting to play me.

As a final act, he actually kissed me gently on the lips. He bent down and mouthed, "*I love you*" before dropping me down the hole. I dropped and hit the floor hard. I no longer felt anything.

There was time just to see above me something swing at Leonard to send him toppling through the hole towards me.

He hit me in the chest, but I was already leaving this life.

I didn't see the door above slam shut.

I didn't see anything ever again.

Jim Ody

The Prince and Princess would now be together in death as they had been in life.

Chapter 70

Jas

I had spent a number of years with Pete. He liked to think that I was his Julia Roberts, but he was no Richard Gere. Not by a long shot. His wealth was able to smooth over a lot of the blemishes that his genetics had provided him, but underneath it all, he had an addictive personality.

Of course, I too had an inability to stop doing things that made me feel alive. So when things were offered to me and I enjoyed them, it didn't take long for me to be hooked. Drink and drugs had completely changed my perception of life, and once my inhibitions were lowered, then I was easily influenced. And like most things, when you have gotten over that hurdle of doing something once, then no matter what it is, a second time is never as bad.

Pete can say that he saved me. On some level, maybe he did, but Pete cut and pasted me from one level of depravity into another, the difference being that, whilst before I was offering blowjobs to old men in back alleys or being bent over the crusty sofa in the damp and dingy bed-sit, now I was living in a penthouse and being fucked regularly by strangers high and drunk.

I had met Kate there. Pete had loved her for the same reasons that he loved me. She would do anything, and the men loved her for it. I was skinny. I always had been, and then with a diet of coke and amphetamines, I was unable to take on board the calories that my hyper body was burning off. Kate had a nice body, but she always had these large breasts that hypnotised the men. I had had a guy pull out of me whilst we were having sex at a party, before he had finished, just to go and try it on with her. Do you have any idea what that feels like?

I liked Kate, but I was jealous of her.

We had gotten to talking about our situations, and she had confessed to having this fantasy where she would get all of these bastards together in a large hotel by the sea and, like some horror movie, would slowly kill them off one by one.

At first, I had been sure she was joking. We had both had similar upbringings, had been used as human sex dolls, and had been desensitised to the horrors of the world. Maybe I was a little more forgiving or pragmatic, but I wasn't sure how this would help.

A Cold Retreat

One night, we refused the advances of all of the men and got drunk and high together. We had kissed and even had sex, but it had been just the talking and the drugs that had led us there. Neither of us were into women, but somehow, when you were in a place where your senses were tingling for something and you were denying the men around, then it could go like that. And that's when we talked more about it, whilst lying naked together, cuddling by way of support more than anything else. The plan had evolved.

Kate became Sasha, but we had kept in touch, and when the B&B opportunity had come around, I had known that this was my way to get out too. It wasn't quite by the sea, but being surrounded by woods had its own appeal. And honestly, it didn't matter where it was situated. I would've done it in Timbuktu.

I had been clean for a while. When you'd been wasted for as many years as I had, then you got to know the world through junkie eyes. You begin to forget the normal perspective, so actually, pretending is quite simple.

Pete knew that I had gone missing for a few weeks. I knew that he hadn't even bothered to look for me as he had Kate. She had replaced me, plain and simple. What he didn't know was that I had gotten my life together. I had a sponsor (who thought I was away with my parents) and she had helped me to clean myself up. It had taken two weeks of complete hell, where she had literally had me imprisoned in her house. At the time, I had wanted to kill her. My body had craved the daily chemicals that it was used to, and the withdrawal had almost been too much for both my body and my mind. On my own, it had never been possible. People that judge us as junkies don't realise that when your body has become used to being that way, then total withdrawal is incredibly dangerous. Before the two weeks, I'd had to drastically reduce my consumption so as the shock wouldn't be too much.

Even though I was getting better, and my sponsor Lydia had helped me more than I could ever repay her, I was possessed. My irrational fears flared up as I lashed out at her, seeing her only as a blockade between me and normal euphoria. It was the epitome of tough love. But she had been through it, so she knew how I was feeling. She had come out the other side.

I was full of regrets from my past, but the way I treated her in those weeks was by far the thing that I was least proud of in my life—that and lying to her

A Cold Retreat

about this weekend, especially about being with Pete again.

Any ex-junkie will tell you that the worst thing that can happen to you is to be tempted, to have the thing that you were so dependent on being offered to you again. You know that it is bad for you. You know that you will hate yourself. Every single thing about it tells you to stay away, but deep down inside of you, growing within that self-doubt is that evil little voice that reminds you of the pleasure that you get for a short period. How you feel invincible and on top of the world. Nothing before in your life seems important, allowing you to be carrying on the path of self-destruction.

I knew from Kate that the other people were locked down underground now with no possibility of getting out. And even if they did, then what? I had done nothing wrong. In fact, no one would be able to prove that I was ever here. Pete was the only one that knew me who was still alive, and who was going to believe a junkie? My parents would cover for me as would Lydia.

I looked down at the door in the ground and at the trail of crimson from Kate's stab wound. If anything, I had some regret about Kate. This had been Kate's idea, and it had become her own death wish.

Jim Ody

Some people are forever victims no matter what they do. That would not be me. I refused to accept that.

I turned and walked away. I had no reason to stay here. I could take one of the cars, but I didn't know where any keys were. It would also tie me to this place, and I wanted to just get away from here and forget about it.

An eerie silence fell over the place. Everyone had been expecting a joyous free weekend, and somehow I was the only one to walk away from here.

The sun was beginning to lower in the sky. The only sound was a crow squawking in the trees, beckoning the others that now appeared. It seemed apt that they circled over the garden; that below the well-maintained surface was a tunnel of trapped people and dead bodies.

After a few weeks' time below the ground, they would all be dead. Again, I knew that I should feel something about this, but why should I, when they had all looked at me and dismissed me as a useless junkie? I couldn't blame them. That was exactly what I had been.

With a small urgency, I walked back to the house and removed my bag from our room. There would

A Cold Retreat

no longer be any trace of me. I felt the slight smile on my lips. This really had gone to plan.

I walked down the drive looking at the trees either side of the picturesque lane, glancing back for a last time, and wondered when this place might make the news. A week's time? A month? A year? The longer the better.

At the road, I ran over and into the field behind. I planned to cut across to the fields and join the back road into Marlborough, where I would hopefully catch the last bus back to Swindon.

I wondered what would happen when they realised that there was no escape. *How long before they turn into cannibals?* I smiled.

Chapter 71

Dex – A week later

I was still feeling pretty tired. I would never be able to look at Cher in quite the same way, and all I had was that bloody song running through my mind.

It was good to see Jez again, and we had made our usual promises to keep in touch and even to try and get some sort of band together again. In reality, we might meet up and jam, but the chances of us getting a band together was something short of impossible. We were no longer young and hungry for making music, now understanding that fame and fortune in anything was well beyond us, let alone in the music industry.

I sat myself in a Coffee#1 and tried to ring the B&B again. I suddenly didn't see the point in it. If the journey recently speaking to Kim, along with seeing Jez and Cher had taught me anything, it was that I needed to finally seize the moment. Moon and I belonged together. We both knew it.

A Cold Retreat

The clearing of my mum's house could wait. I would make a start, but love was not a thing put on hold. I knew this now.

Again, there was no answer from the B&B. I called Moon instead. On the third ring, she answered. "Hello?"

"Hey, it's me," I said, and I could hear the smile in her voice.

"Dex! Hey, you. How are you? Wow, I can't believe you're calling!"

"I'm good. I'm missing you, Moon… Look, I know it's not something that you believe in…and it's a silly thing, but…" This was a lot harder than I had expected.

"What is it?" she encouraged.

"Well, why don't we do some sort of marriage thing?"

She squealed so loudly that I had to pull my mobile away from my ears. I had been sitting on my own in the coffee shop away from others, but I was sure that even they could hear her!

"Really?!" she finally said. *"For real?"*

"Sure. I mean…of course."

"Yes! Yes! Yes! Let's do it… God, I'm crying… People are looking at me…and I don't care!"

My eyes began to well up. I was not normally like this, but love was a strong emotion. Absence does make the heart grow fonder, but it also allows you to re-evaluate things and give you a little perspective.

"I was going to stay here and sort out Mum's place, but I want to see you again," I said through hysteria. I then remembered the B&B. We could stay there together.

"I could come up and help?" she said. "I really should get to see your life and where you grew up, especially if I'm to be your wife!"

"That would be great. I think I know the very place that we could stay. Get some things together and look at train times. I'll ring you back in an hour."

"Great... and Dex?"

"Yeah?"

"I love you."

"I love you too."

I stared at the phone. Why had it taken the past few days to understand my feelings? *Why do our hearts work this way?*

I left the rest of my coffee and set off to the van. If I couldn't get through to them on the phone, then I might as well just pop in there and sort out the reservation face to face.

The whole journey was spent with me thinking about Moon. How could it not? It was like that

A Cold Retreat

telephone conversation had now opened up the door to another world and a future that would no longer be about me, but about us. I hadn't ever considered just how exciting this could be.

I turned into the drive, amazed at the spectacular view of the place in front of me. It was definitely the sort of place to come for a romantic retreat, and I remembered that it had even said something about a function room. I just wondered whether this might be worth checking out as a possible venue for our wedding.

There was an abundance of cars in the car park, so that showed just how popular the place was.

I walked in through the door and straight to the reception. I never liked to hit those bells that are sitting there on the counter, as it seemed rude. After a couple of minutes, I gave in and tapped it. A minute later, I hit it harder a couple of times and shouted, "Hello?"

I had been sure someone would be around. With all the cars outside and with it still being mid-morning, I would have thought that even the late risers would've had breakfast recently and so there would be someone around cleaning and tidying away.

I walked round to the kitchen. I pushed open the door and called, "Hello?" but the place was quiet.

I followed the hallway, calling all the time, but still got no answer. I walked out the back along a path and tried the function room, but it was locked. There was a key in the door, but there was little point in going in. I guess I would check it out another time with Moon.

If I ever found anyone!

I turned and walked out through the garden, noticing some buildings. There was a chance that someone might be out there and unable to hear what was going on in the house.

I opened the old door, which clicked as I turned the handle, and walked down a small corridor to a couple of rooms. The first one was locked, so I turned to the second one, noticing that the door was ajar.

I could hear the buzz of electrical equipment as soon as I walked in, and I was surprised and slightly shocked to see a wall of monitors.

As I looked closer, I noticed that these showed bedrooms and bathrooms throughout the building.

But it was the last bank of monitors that took my breath away. There was movement of people in a dark area that couldn't have been within the house. The people looked dishevelled and unkempt like they had been there for a while.

A Cold Retreat

On other monitors, I saw lifeless bodies laid out with limbs missing. Bars, sticks, and other seemingly homemade weapons were left telling their own story.

A handful of people were walking almost purposefully in one direction, like a pack of wild animals looking to attack, and when I scanned to another monitor, I saw four people huddled behind a door in a room looking incredibly fearful.

And then I saw the door almost disintegrate as the pack charged it, and as the two groups came together, I turned my back to the horror that was happening somewhere nearby.

I backed out of the room, and suddenly I was turning and running round the side of the house towards the van.

When you see something like that, what can you do? I didn't even know where it was or how to get there. And even if I did, I couldn't rush in there like some 80s action hero. It imprints itself into your mind. I was only thankful that the monitors were old and grainy. Sometimes HD isn't always better…

I wheel-spun the van out of there, not caring two shits if Cher's song was in my head. That would be extremely welcome after what I had just witnessed.

I pulled over next to the green in Marlborough and left an anonymous call to the police.

I'm not sure why, but I headed back to Jez's house to call Moon.

"Mate," I said. "You really won't believe what I've just seen."

He looked at me and said, "Whatever it is, I bet I can beat it!"

"That is highly unlikely."

"You'd better come in then," he said, and after I called Moon, we sat down and told each other two separate stories that neither of us would ever believe…

A Cold Retreat

Chapter 72

Ben lay on the floor, a sharp object sticking out of his stomach. His throat was filling up with blood, and breathing became almost impossible.

He blinked again. Each time seemed more of an effort to open his eyes. He looked around at the room that they had made almost their home and tried to make sense of it all.

At first, they had thought there was another way out. They had walked around searching for another exit.

Travis had been the one to find the heap of bodies. The body of Christian was lying there on top. Bronwyn had lost it and had blamed Ben for bringing her there.

But then they had found that they were not alone. There were other people alive, and these people were hungry.

They had run back the way they had come, finding a room and barricading themselves in. The people outside howled like primitives and banged deep into the night.

Pete had tried to take charge, but he was struggling with the lack of drugs in his body. Travis and Ben had fought each other as tempers flared through frustration.

And the people outside the room just waited...

When the attack finally happened, it was almost a relief. For days they had felt that they were being taunted. Travis had tried to make a run for it, but had been pounced on. The sound of limbs being ripped out of sockets whilst a man screamed in pain had been too much for Bronwyn, who had sat silently shaking in the corner.

But then they had burst through the door, and it was a bloody fight until the end. Pete was swamped, and whilst Ben was able to do his best and kill the rest, Pete bled out.

And now, with Bronwyn's mangled body still warm, there was a macabre scene of undernourished dead bodies missing body parts.

We nearly made it, Ben thought, taking his last breath, unaware that the bodies of Penny, Kate, and the policeman were now only a few hundred metres away on the first pile of bodies that Travis had found a week ago.

***

A Cold Retreat

Later that day, it was all over the news. A mystery tip-off had sent the police to a B&B in Wiltshire, and at first it had been thought to be abandoned. However, they had soon discovered an underground tunnel with rooms, thought to be secret tunnels used for defence in the First World War, but now set up with cameras as some sort of gruesome makeshift prison.

A total of fifteen dead bodies were found, which included the proprietor, convicted rapist Leonard Horton, and his brother Charlie. Police were going through footage to gain more understanding of what had gone on there. Leonard would almost certainly be the number one suspect, but it was unclear whether something had gone wrong with his master plan. Several rooms had traces of blood in them, which only added to the puzzles left to solve.

Later, a barn full of cars was found, which helped identify the victims. Most of them were single women with no family to have reported them missing.

***

Dex and Jez both agreed that each other's stories were just as unbelievable—but not quite as bad as when Dex burst into the lounge unannounced to find Jez's wife naked on an exercise ball doing an impression of Miley Cyrus singing "Wrecking Ball"…

The End

A Cold Retreat

Acknowledgements

There have been a lot of people who have helped me to get where I am today. Too many to mention in but a few paragraphs, but I'll have a go!

A big thank you to Kara and the kids for just being them.

A huge thanks to the members of my street team Jim Ody's Spooky Circus, who listen to all my crazy ideas and advise me whether they are worth pursuing!

Thanks to all of the members of: UK Crime Book Club (especially David and Caroline), Crime Book Club (especially Shell and Llainy), Crime Fiction Addict, One Stop Fiction Book Club, Book Connectors, and all of the wonderful spooky people in Beyond The Veil.

A huge thanks to Erin George. Not just because you are a wonderful publisher, but a great friend. You guide me through everything that you expect of me and fill me with the desire to write more! An extended thanks to everyone attached and associated with Crazy Ink including all the Crazy Inklings around the world!

A special thank you to photographer and friend Andy Netter and model Kelly Sumal. I apologise that the cover changed but this was purely for continuity and nothing to do with the original photograph. The time you took out of your busy schedule to do this for me will always be appreciated.

I would like to thank all the authors who have helped me by answering my inane questions. You know who you are, and the list is ever growing!

A big thank you to my friends and colleagues at Arval UK, especially to Jeff for selling my books in the shop. I understand reading my book is now in all employee objectives – and rightly so I might add.

As ever a huge thank you to all the editors working tirelessly to make my meanderings be able to be enjoyed by the masses. Especially to Shelagh who is also my personal advisor on all the choices I make. I don't always listen, but she is still there shaking her head at me, ready for my next maverick idea.

And finally thank you to you, the readers. For reading, for enjoying, and for getting behind me. Without you there would really be no point!

About the Author

Jim was first published in an English School Textbook in 1987. He won a competition to draw a dog-walking machine. Having won an art competition the year before, he felt that at the age of eleven he had peaked and consequently retired from the world of art.

For 10 years Jim wrote for a number of websites reviewing and interviewing bands in his own unique way, as well as contributing dark poems and comedic features.

Jim Ody

He writes dark psychological/thrillers that have endings that you won't see coming, and favours stories packed with wit. He has written three novels and a novella all released by Crazy Ink. He has also contributed to around a dozen anthologies.

Jim has a very strange sense of humour and is often considered a little odd. When not writing he will be found playing the drums, watching football, and eating chocolate. He lives with his long-suffering wife and three beautiful children in Swindon, Wiltshire UK.

40017665R00265

Made in the USA
Middletown, DE
23 March 2019